# FLYOVER STATES

# Grace Grant
# & P.J. MacAllister

# FLYOVER STATES

**RED DRESS INK**™

First edition May 2005

FLYOVER STATES

A Red Dress Ink novel

ISBN 0-373-89521-6

www.RedDressInk.com

**Printed in U.S.A.**

Grace Grant dedicates this book to the memory of
Robette Washington, teacher of English
at Wakefield High School, and to teachers everywhere.

# ACKNOWLEDGMENTS

Grace Grant would like to thank her parents,
Bruce and Judy, and her sister, April. The author gives
thanks, especially, to her friends for their ongoing support,
help with edits and the occasional half-priced martini:
Bernadette Murphy, Leonore Dluhy, Alexandra Cordero,
Elaine McSorley Gerard, Erica Kan Dodd, Michelle Ross,
Amanda Hong, Christina Cordero, Heather Angney
Edelman, Megan Briggs, Steve Lookner, Larry Tanz,
Dave Mandel, Dan Periera, Mike Mattison,
Bill Wu, Vanessa Ward, Tyler Chapman, Jeff Galbraith,
Karen Smith, Joseph Morrisey, Heidi Dollinger
and David Prestidge.

P.J. MacAllister would like to thank her family,
Brian Ingram, Sabrina Williams, Mimi Lind
and Cathy Bowman.

Both authors especially thank their agents,
Neeti Madan and Rosalie Siegel, for their dedication
and support, as well as Ms. Madan's assistants,
Kate Prentice and Sarah Walsh; much thanks to
Susan Gubar and Linda Charnes, for inspiration,
for being invaluable mentors and friends; Kathryn Lye,
our editor and advocate; Margaret Marbury for her vision;
and, finally, neither author would have survived graduate
school without Romayne Rubinas Dorsey, Damon Dorsey,
Thomas Jones, Bob Bledsoe, Laura Yow, Len Nalencz,
Scott Maisano and Melissa Jones.

# Doris

I, Doris Weatherall, am in the process of becoming a hateful person, or a snob, or just flat-out bitter. Largely it's because I have done-that-which-I-ought-not-to-have-done (begun relationship with pretentious, sexually ambiguous, any-fool-would-know-better poet-worse-yet-poetry professor), and not-done-that-which-I-ought-to-have-done (left town years ago, with or without my advanced degree, begun the process of falling for the standard married professionals and computer-dating last-ditch efforts like my citified sisters). Being in your early thirties and single is a challenge no matter where you are. Being in your early thirties and single in a college town in the Midwest is sort of like an extended episode of *Sex and the City* but minus the sex and minus the city. It is, of course, possible to have sex in the Midwest, just as it's possible to drive two hours to Louisville or Indianapolis—

both prospects having the same discouraging effort-to-payoff ratio.

Qualification of the "snob" thing: the aforementioned is not to say that there are not highly datable, corn-fed, socially conscious examples of Midwestern hetero-male fabulosity. There are. They just generally get married at twenty-five, and probably don't hit that first round of divorces until they've given it the real God's-honest, Pat-Robertson-would-surely-approve, college try. Ages twenty-five to forty, menwise, might as well be the dead zone. Thus, the problem with my poetry professor, Luis Gonzales, who is famous in that other-poets-have-heard-of-him kind of way. He writes passionate odes about Latin American revolutions, but lives in a split-level with a satellite dish. Some students find this disappointing, but it doesn't really bother me all that much. What's he supposed to do anyhow—organize the skate-rat hippies who clutter the sidewalks over the summer with their "Anarchy" backpacks? I don't think so.

This afternoon, I'm meeting Luis at his office to go over my poetry portfolio from last semester. Second semester ended two weeks ago, and when classes aren't in session, I avoid the English department like the plague. Valentine Hall, which houses the English department and most of the other humanities, is a grotesque architectural monstrosity at the heart of Langsdale University's otherwise idyllic, colonial-style campus. Valentine was erected in the early 1970s, when hideous concrete towers were au courant, and it now stands out from the other buildings like some poor soul sentenced to wear parachute pants and shoulder pads for the rest of eternity.

I would never have agreed to meet Luis at school, ex-

cept for the fact that casual settings haven't been working to my writerly advantage. The last time Luis and I
"went over" my poetry was the weekend before last,
when I met him at his house, and his critique of my vil-
lanelle somehow segued into a protracted make-out session on his brown leather couch. Then we tried *again* the
following week over margaritas, to the same shameful
end. I say shameful because Luis is technically still my professor, and professors carrying on with graduate students
is about as classy and original as some 1950s boss schtup-
ping his secretary. Shameful, too, because for all the
naughtiness, it never gets very hot and heavy. I've been
blaming it on bad timing, but it might be one of those
square peg–round hole situations (or, as my friend Paolo
insists, the problem is that I have a hole when Luis is really
a "peg" man). Luis's office is on the sixth floor, and I have
my hair swept underneath a wide-brimmed straw hat,
with dark sunglasses so as to be as incognito as humanly
possible. No luck.

"Doris," I hear from behind me. "You have *got* to get a
load of this. It's Ripley's believe it or not un-be-leeeevable."

Ronnie Williams, my very best friend in the whole of
Indiana, is moving from the stairwell in my direction at
twice her usual walking speed, fist clenched in workers-
of-the-world-unite manner with a pamphlet of some
sort that she's waving in my direction.

"Look," she says, unfolding what I now see is a
brochure for the university and holding it up like the
menu board at some fancy restaurant.

The brochure reads Work, Play, Learn: Langsdale
University, and beneath it are four pictures of classroom
scenes and sports events displayed like an overlapping

checkerboard with a larger photo in the middle of an African-American woman playing tennis.

"God," I say. "That almost looks like you."

Ronnie pushes the brochure closer to my face. The tennis player has long dreadlocks pulled away from her face, and is wearing a pink-and-white-striped polo shirt that I associate with being a hip kid in the eighth grade. She's smiling as if she just won Powerball.

"Doris," Ronnie says. "It *is* me."

"But you don't play tennis."

"Not only do I not play tennis," she says, "I have never, not once, held a racket in my life. I went to the English department, to listen to J. J. Jones lie to my face about why I didn't get teaching this summer—it was the one thing I was looking forward to. Some nonsense about my 'lack of experience.' Anyhow, on my way out of her office, as though my head was not just filled to the brim with bullshit, I see a stack of these, bound up and waiting for delivery."

I take the brochure from Ronnie and look at it more closely. On further inspection, the picture looks more like a paper-doll version of Ronnie, where someone has superimposed two white terry-cloth wristbands and pasted a tennis racket on to her outstretched hand.

"So what is this exactly?"

Ronnie's hair is pinned artfully up from her face, with a few stray dreads framing her high cheekbones. Her blue-green sundress is low-cut and breezy, and her full upper arms belie a lack of tennis or any other extreme physical activity. "Part of the university's 'diversity initiative.'" She looks angrily from one end of the deserted hallway to the next. "I got the runaround from three different officials, and finally someone fessed up to the fact that they digitally altered a picture that they'd taken of me shaking Professor Lind's hand after some reading last year. They just cut me out, dressed me up, and figured that 'for the sake of diversity,' and I'm quoting Dean Stone on that one, I wouldn't mind."

I hand the picture back to Ronnie carefully, as if it might self-destruct at any second. "This is insanity," I say. "Aren't they worried you'll sue?"

"Evidently not," Ronnie says. "Not worried enough to make sure I get summer teaching. And now I have to get to the temp agency before they close, since my tennis-playing skills aren't going to keep me fed this summer. And they wonder why black folks run like hell from Langsdale University. I could write three dissertations on the subject."

"Are we still meeting later?" I ask. "Paolo called. He's expecting us at the Wing Shack at six."

"Fine," Ronnie says. "Fine." She keeps turning over the brochure in her hands, as if the picture might be different when she sees the front again. She shakes her head and sighs. "What are you doing here anyhow?"

"Meeting Luis," I say. "We're going over my portfolio."

Ronnie puts the brochure into an overstuffed black book bag. "Really. Is that what they're calling it these days? 'Going over the portfolio'? You'll have to fill Paolo in on the details. He's still convinced Luis doesn't have the proper…motivation?"

"Paolo is jealous," I say. "I'll call you later this afternoon."

"Cool." Ronnie shifts the book bag on her shoulder and heads out the door. I push the elevator button and wait. Our friend, Paolo, has been driving me crazy about Luis for the past month. While I may have been blessed with God-given taste in shoes and poetics, I am cursed with $3.99, blue-light-special gaydar. Luis is a tough case. He has had two wives (both now exes) and two affairs of the committedly heterosexual variety that I, personally, know about. Last wife: Barbie-esque styling babe that he picked up at an art colony three summers ago and lost two summers later. She was a stick-thin blonde who wore dominatrix heels and never bothered learning anyone's name. I met her three times and I'm quite sure she couldn't pick me out of a lineup.

Anyhow, rumor had it that one of two things precipitated the end of CityBlondBarbie's stay in Langsdale. Rumor (A): Luis was caught making out with an ex-student of his, Carla (or "Southern Bell," as Ronnie called her), in the back of his very own house while City-BlondBarbie got plastered in their living room. Rumor (B): Luis was caught pants-below-his-knees with a "visitor" of the gender-not-named variety while City-BlondBarbie defaced his office door. What is known for sure: first, Carla and Luis did have some form of "encounter." Second, Luis's door, which was once cluttered with pictures of half-naked men, *poets,* of course, was stripped bare the day CityBlondBarbie left town.

When I get to Luis's office, the door is still bare, except for a note taped to the frosted-glass window: *D, Back in five, L.* I take the note off the door and remove my hat, smoothing my recently dyed hair down into a low ponytail. I was going for a rich, brown shade, but instead the color looks jet-black and severe. The hallway is deserted, and I slump down onto the floor outside Luis's office, wondering if Paolo isn't right about Luis.

Things that I know to be true but am ignoring: First,

an unspecified human of the hot-and-male variety has recently moved into Luis's split-level love nest. "My cousin," Luis told me. "In from Chile." And second, male poets are, categorically and regardless of sexual preference, just below serial killers for undatability. They should come with little warning signs tattooed below their belly buttons—BEWARE: SUCKING PIT OF NEED.

Luis finally is ambling down the hallway, apologizing and waving a bag of onion rings. His sandals make a hollow, slapping noise as he walks my way.

"Low blood sugar," he says, unlocking the door. I follow him into his office, which has his Harvard degree mounted prominently behind his desk. To the right of it is a framed copy of Luis's first book of poems, a slim volume titled *Claro* that won him a National Poetry Series award. Luis looks tired to me, with big rings under his hangdog eyes. He's gained a little weight. He's five foot six in loafers (tasseled ones, but I'm not saying anything) and puts on the pounds easily. But Luis's appeal has never really been predominantly physical: it's more about how he reads a poem and the poems he writes—the attention he pays to the world around him. He does have nice hands, though, clean and well manicured.

"My cousin," he tells me, "he's driving me crazy. So *very* Catholic. He still considers me married, in the eyes of God, you know, Catholic shit. I don't want to upset him. Thinks anything but a first wife is *desaseado*."

"Diseased?" I asked, shifting my gaze to the framed portrait of Jack Kerouac and William Burroughs, bare-chested with arms entwined. Note to self: under "cousin" see "peg, not hole."

Luis sits down across from me. He tugs nervously at his

left eyebrow, twisting the hair one way and then twisting it in the other direction.

"That, too. He'll be gone soon enough, no reason to rock the boat."

"Better be soon," I say. "Or this here ship just might sail."

Luis passes me an onion ring.

"It's just a cousin. He wanted to look at Langsdale, see if he'd like to come."

"What kind of cousin?" I ask. "Kissing cousin?"

Luis smiles, but it's one of those fake smiles that uses just the mouth and not the rest of his face. When Luis really smiles, his eyes squint and the skin underneath looks thin and crepey. "You're funny, Doris. That's one of the things I wanted to talk about in your poems. I think you're hiding behind humor, or just going for 'cute' in the endings. It's not that they're bad. They're great. I want you to push yourself more. Your bird poem, it's nice, but tidy."

He pushes one of my early poems across the table:

## Against Birds

There is no wind that whistles in my soul,
and my sympathies have never lain with birds
above the earth and choked with song.

When volunteers were needed (as a child)
to feed three starlings to a snake, I raised my hand
disdainful of those six- and seven-year-olds

pleading clemency for starlings (as they might
for rats, had they been winged). And when nothing
remained but three small lumps, stretching

and tightening the ebony plates, I wondered only
when it ate again. And still if asked at parties
by voices confident and shrill, "What animal

would you like to be?" I cannot say for sure.
But certainly a creature undersea, silent and gliding,
able to withstand the pressure of something heavier

than air.

"The line break at the end," he says. "I think maybe
you should rethink it."

"Okay," I say as Luis rifles through the packet of my
work in front of him to hand over a second poem, chas-
tising me for always resorting to form. I like that Luis
gives a solid critique, that he's actively engaged in my
growth as a writer. It's exactly the reason that I came
to graduate school in the first place: to be challenged.
Before I came to Langsdale, my only feedback on work
was from my sister and a couple of disembodied edi-
tors at literary magazines scattered across the country.
Here, I get immediate feedback and am pressured to
improve. There's not much room for complacency in
a program where poetry is considered a vocation, not
a hobby.

Luis is almost finished with his onion rings, and I
reach across the desk to wipe a bit of grease from beneath his chin.

"No playing, Doris," he says. "I have to pick Armando
up from soccer, and I said I'd be there five minutes ago.
Later this week?"

"Armando," I repeat. "Your cousin has a very Chilean porn-star name."

"Why would you say something like that?" he asks.

Never mind, I think, but I'm looking at the picture of Kerouac.

Luis walks me down the hall to the elevators. We ride the six flights down together, making heavy eye contact, and before the elevator doors can open, Luis pushes the "close doors" button and kisses me, long and sweet.

"I thought you said no playing," I say.

"I'm the professor," he says, fingering the fringe around my blouse. "I make the rules, I change the rules."

"But school's out," I say, pushing his hand away playfully. "And aren't you always telling us to break the rules?"

"Just be fluid," he says. "Open." And then he switches back into full professor mode. "Especially in your work, Doris." I roll my eyes *yeah, yeah* and Luis leaves me to pick up Armando. His gait is cocky, self-assured, and as he disappears from view, I see him high-five the supertattooed, latter-day Beat-poet from our workshop last semester. Openness and fluidity: good for the poetry, not so hot for relationships.

I should qualify that I am not spending *all* of my time waiting for Luis to become more closed or rigid (no pun intended). With attraction, it's all about fractions and proportion. My life, then, breaks down as follows. Luis counts for, maybe, three-fifths of a relationship, since Ronnie claims that "sometimes a cousin *isn't* just a cousin," and Luis *has* asked me to keep our relationship on the down-low. Option B is Chris, who constitutes two-fifths of a legitimate crush, since he services my computer and has the decency to look at me, on occasion, in a sexual manner.

Chris works in the computer lab at the library, and is the only noncondescending member of the geek-patrol staffing the campus computers. Chris helps me when my sister gluts my mailbox with updates and instructions about her midsummer nuptials, and retrieves poems otherwise lost to the ages when I can't get my floppy to open. With the rest of the staff, I come in with my malfunctioning disks and they look at me as if I'm still rubbing sticks together for fire.

I have the rest of the afternoon to kill before meeting up with Ronnie and Paolo, so I decide to make a trip to the lab to check my e-mail. Chris is hard at work at one with his keyboard, hair back in a hippie-blond tangle, the faint scent of patchouli wafting off his sunburned skin. The lower half of his Tweety Bird tattoo peeks out on the exposed half of his upper arm.

"Got a zip drive yet?" he asks without looking up from the keyboard.

"No," I say, adjusting my straw hat. "You mind helping me with my e-mail? I can't get it to open. I think my sister's crashed my system again."

"You entered your password and everything, Lula Mae?"

Chris slaps his thigh. He really cracks himself up commenting on my wardrobe.

"I love this hat," I say. "It's fetching. I got it discount off the Web."

"Farmer-surf," he says. "Did the flip-flops come with?"

"Don't make fun of me," I say. "I have limited resources. You try looking cute with what passes for a mall in this town. They haven't cycled the department-store racks since 1985, at the *latest,* and I may well be the *only* person who even *notices."*

The devil may wear Prada, but it's safe to say that the rest of the country is making due with Old Navy. This is not to rag on Old Navy. I like both very much, and shop at Old Navy, but with an eye toward the fascist/fashionista New York–style goddesses. Which is not to imply that I respect and/or actively emulate their way of life, only to say that I acknowledge their existence by working for a funky knockoff version. Cheaper, less offensively classist and wasteful, but cute.

"We can't all look good in tie-dye," I say, doing my half-assed flirt routine.

"You can come over one day. I'll dress you up regular."

Chris works at the computer keyboard like some latter-day mechanic, putting me to shame at the fact that I can merely write creatively, yet do nothing of any real value—even to myself. One of my ex-boyfriends visited me last year and told me that he'd never seen so many smart people who couldn't figure out how to make any money for themselves. I could tell he was thinking "stoopid." Such is the nature of graduate school.

There's nothing really wrong with graduate school, except that it's one of those Brigadoon-like time-sucks wherein you enter as a fresh-faced twentysomething, and KA-BOOM the mist clears and a decade has passed. Amazingly, life has gone on around you, and you just have a stack of student loans plus in-depth knowledge of something no one else in the world cares about. In my case, it's Latin American poetry, which I study, and Chatty American poetry, which I write.

"Done," Chris says. "Try signing in."

I type my username: DMWEATHE and password: writergal.

Miraculously, my e-mail opens. There are seven new e-mails from my sister, Lisa, and her fiancé, Marvin. Seven. IDEAS FOR DRESSES. DON'T FORGET TO RE-SERVE NOW. TENTATIVE SCHEDULE FOR RE-HEARSAL DINNER. SHOWER IDEAS. To say that Lisa and Marvin have lost their collective mind is an understatement. You couldn't even get my sister into a dress when she was a kid. Now you can't get her out of one so long as the label reads Calvin Klein or Marc Jacobs. I'm supposed to be planning her shower, but it's low, low, low on my list of priorities.

"Two thousand sixty-eight e-mails in your in-box," Chris says. "Do you delete anything?"

"Shut up," I say. "I haven't read all of them yet."

I quickly open the "IDEAS FOR DRESSES" before Chris can get a good look at anything else in my in-box. I don't want him seeing my shameful trail of sordid flirtations; it undermines my vixen-in-control vibe.

Chris meanders back to the consultant's station, and I'm left to my own devices. My feet are starting to itch, another problem with being reduced to fashionista-style knockoffs—lots of nonleather causing allergic-type reactions. I don't know how the vegans do it. Until they make a nice hemp Mary Jane pump, I'm all about the leather. It's funny, but in New York, I never cared that much about fashion. In fact, I was often a bit disdainful of the whole enterprise: anorexic tweens hocking ridiculously expensive fabrics and reveling in frivolity as if Isaac Mizrahi had discovered the cure for cancer, rather than simply making a decent pair of shoes or two. But in Indiana, I miss fashion the way I imagine Ronnie misses it being summer all year long. She says that in L.A. fifty degrees is freezing, and a simple rainstorm stops traffic. Yet here we are—coastal refugees—in the land of tornados and Keds.

I forward the last e-mail from Luis to Ronnie with an attached note:

```
Ronnie—Perhaps after wings we can scare up
alcoholic-flavored beverages at the Office
Saloon? You can traumatize ye olde bar-
tender. I hear he got a haircut (whatever
will you hold on to?). Must see evil in-
terloper Zach. Will send voodoo curses at
him and J.J. xo Doris
```

After sending the message, I do my best to saunter by Chris's station.

"Later," he says. His eyes don't even move from the computer screen. Alas.

Outside, the light is practically blinding. I fumble for my sunglasses, only to look up and realize that my e-mail has conjured Zach Patterson himself, fifty yards away, playing ultimate Frisbee with a group of graduate students who look vaguely familiar. He waves in my direction, and I pretend not to notice, opting instead for the "I can't see anything behind these sunglasses" facade.

Zach Patterson is an endless source of embarrassment and shame—the living embodiment of everything I do not want to become as a graduate student. He's been here even longer than I have, TEN YEARS, just took his qualifying exams, and has been known to cut his toenails in public, at parties. Disgusting. More disgusting, the first semester I was here, I got very, very drunk on some pink wine and made out with him. I decided, in a Zinfandel haze, that he looked like Harvey Keitel in *Mean Streets,* which is sexual whiskey for the Irish in me. So, in the early months of my twenty-fifth year, I had a PG–13 encounter with Zach Patterson because I did not know that he had a veritable triumvirate of dating red-flags: a girlfriend, no direction and reprehensible grooming habits. I still think he looks a *little* like Mr. Keitel, with the squinty-brown-eyes thing, but in the absence of extreme youth and pink wine, have never even been tempted since. And now he is my TROOPS tutor: my right-hand man and coteacher for the next six weeks. And he's the incarnation of a waking nightmare. Double the nightmare because Ronnie applied for that job, was turned down for "lack of experience," so that the departmental über-slacker could be employed.

Zach's one genius move was to get in tight with J.J.— J. J. Jones is the faux-hippie controller of all teaching assignments. She is the closest thing that graduate students have to an actual "God" figure—the true arbiter of our destinies. J.J. has the leathery-skin, hair-past-her-ass look of some aged surfer-queen, but with a complete lack of Zen. If you don't know her well, you'd think she could potentially be Zen, cool, what-not. That's sure the vibe she's after. She'll use words like *bitchen* and *dude* and has the usual lefty rhetoric plastered all over the back bumper of her 1983 Volvo: "I'D RATHER BE SMASHING IMPERIALISM," and "THE MORAL MAJORITY IS NEITHER." But she's careful, careful, careful only to pick summer teachers she doesn't think will give her any trouble. I realize that this doesn't say much for me since I was, in fact, selected by J.J. for this job, but it remains disgraceful that she didn't pick Ronnie. She had precisely one actual, qualified African-American apply for the job, and she picked Zach—the white-boy toe-picker. Welcome to *actual* race in the academy.

TROOPS is a series of classes run by the university each summer for first-generation, low-income college students from bigger cities like Gary and Indianapolis, or small farms from all over the state. It's a how-to-write-and-study composition boot camp, and the one truly diverse classroom you'll find on this campus. So much for Ronnie's poster-girl status for Diversity, Inc.

The program is called TROOPS because they put the students into these little "legions" in which they Work, Play and Learn for the summer. It also means that as a class, they are largely won or lost as a whole, since they will run you up and down the flagpole if they sense any sign of weakness. Plus, they're straight out of high school, which means that they're always at least partially confusing TROOPS for a kegger/orgy, and my classroom for some 1980s *Hot for Teacher* video. During the regular year, undergrads generally confine their crushes to pseudo-stalker e-mails and stick with inventing distant-but-dear uncles and aunts who drop like fruit flies when the hangovers start piling on. Nor, might I add, is it to imply that I am some sexed-up librarian-by-day, pole-dancer-by-night kind of teacher. I am not. All that I am is "not butt ugly" and in teacher terms, that might as well be a pole dancer. I have a theory that some students would be attracted to a space alien if it showed up with a grade-book and functional sex organs. This theory is partially based on my own experience, as Luis, in all honesty, is not someone I would have picked off the street. Classroom erotics—a dicey business, indeed.

Aside from being one of the rare instances where I feel even vaguely sexualized in my daily life, TROOPS is also a different experience because it's the time that I feel most self-consciously white. I grew up in Brooklyn, and not once in my life did I feel so racially implicated as I do in Langsdale. When I was driving through Indiana to get to Langsdale, I spent the night in some tiny town where the local news was reporting on the KKK marching in honor of "white pride." I thought they were *kidding,* but no, it was for real. My sense of the KKK was that they were as antiquated and—frankly—as out of use as phonographs and the rhythm method, but there they were. Not a civil-rights protestor in sight. It was like watching pink elephants on parade.

This is not to say that I romanticize the East Coast as the land of peace and racial harmony, but in Brooklyn, one need not use a digitally enhanced photograph to create a black woman who plays tennis. It's a wonder Ronnie doesn't go postal on the whole lot of them.

By the time I get to the Wing Shack, Ronnie and Paolo are already hunkered down over a plate of wings, and Ronnie has filled Paolo in on my visit to Luis's office. Paolo is Ronnie's and my newest friend, another West Coast transplant who refers to Luis as "Way Gay Faux Che," thus condensing every rude, but possibly true, rumor about Luis into one neat moniker. This is Paolo's gift, or his second gift, since his first gift is as a balletic demigod. He was once a principal dancer in the San Francisco Ballet, but now he wants to do arts administration. *Run my own show,* he'll say. Paolo is canonically gorgeous, quite tall for a dancer with olive skin and enormous brown eyes. Even though he moved to Langsdale for the dance program, which is world renowned, he doesn't like hanging with other dancers. *Always with the upchuck,* he'll say, motioning a finger down his throat. *I've had my career. Now I want to drink in peace, not watch a bunch of pubescent girls count the bones they can see through their leotards.*

I think Paolo over gay-ifies Luis, but the rumor has always been that Luis doesn't *actually* know Spanish. Supposedly, one of his grad students of ages past (with whom he was probably sleeping, but that's beside the point), brought him some untranslated Neruda and he completely flailed. Luis is always talking about his Chilean roots, and while he was, indeed, born in Chile, he was also raised in suburban New Jersey. The Spanish I get from him is largely the kind I imagine coming from a book to get frat boys laid internationally on their spring breaks. I'm not sure it's a testament to anything.

"Doris," Paolo asks me as I sit down on the wooden bench next to him and pick out a chicken wing and some celery for myself, "ask Luis if it's getting stuffy in the old *gabinete, el amario.*"

With one semester of "reading" Spanish, I can't even pretend to understand.

"*El closet,*" Paolo proudly translates. "And that 'cousin' of his? *Not* in there with him. *Cómo se dice* 'flaming'?"

"Paolo," I say, "*Cómo se dice* 'mind thine own business'?"

"Fine," he says. "But don't make me remind you that *you* once upon a time had a crush on *me*."

Ronnie has been fully engrossed in a plate of the red-hot special until that moment, but even she puts down a chicken wing to further the hard time Paolo is giving me.

"Doris," she says. "That is just *sad*."

"He could have been straight," I say defensively. "Think about it, if Paolo were your ballet teacher, and you had to normalize ballet wear, and factor in the profession, there was like a thirty-three percent chance he was straight, or kind of bi, and I'm an *optimist*."

Ronnie can barely keep her chicken down.

"There are so many things wrong with that sentence, I can't even begin to count."

As many things as Ronnie can count, up that by a factor of ten and you have what's wrong with being single in Langsdale. Which keeps Luis in the running, if only for the short term.

"Not as many as are wrong with this," Paolo says, procuring the brochure of Ronnie in her tennis gear. Ronnie closes her eyes and shakes her head. "Maybe it's because your last name is Williams. Maybe they thought that you could be the lost Williams sister. Venus, Serena and Veronica. You'd be like the eighth wonder of the Midwest."

Ronnie snatches the brochure from Paolo's hands.

"Wonder if they can airbrush me into a Valtek office," she says. "Because that's where I'm going to be spending the rest of my nights."

"You mean days," Paolo says cheerfully, arranging his chicken bones neatly across his plate.

"No," Ronnie says. "I mean nights."

"What kind of office works nights?" I ask.

"Hooker!" Paolo says. "You're a temporary hooker! It's so Julia Roberts."

"More like Norma Rae," Ronnie says. "It's a factory. Maybe they have some documents that need editing. They weren't too clear on the details. Next week I have to meet some dude named Ray."

"Ray," I say. "Maybe he's a 'Billy Ray'?"

"Probably a Bubba Ray, with the way my luck's going. Probably has some confederate flag and David Duke for President sticker shined up on the back of his made-in-America pickup."

"Cynical," Paolo says, pushing his plate across the table.

Ronnie picks up the brochure and dangles it from between her index finger and thumb.

"Okay," Paolo says. "If you're not back by morning, we'll call someone."


The next day, I sleep later than usual and wind up rushing to make it to campus on time. The back seat of my Toyota is a disaster area, cluttered with poetry drafts and student evaluations from last semester. I push the papers into a lopsided stack to give some semblance of order; then I drive by Starbucks and pick up a double-latte to make sure I'm alert for the meeting.

Some days, driving down the streets, it's still hard for me to believe this is where I live. Langsdale, Indiana, land of Walnut Bowls, "Liquor, Guns and Ammo" ads, Libertarians who meet in coffee shops to politely discuss overthrowing the government and *pharmacies* where you can buy vodka in the aisle next to the tampons because you can't buy vodka in the *grocery stores.*

If it took me a while to get used to Indiana, it was worse for Ronnie. As I mentioned, she came from L.A. where she'd lived her entire life. The first time we went for a walk on one of the trails near campus she pointed to a robin and asked, "What's with the pigeons with the red chests?" We bonded over lost shopping opportunities, a love of writing and an absolute belief that people evolved so as to keep nature at bay. No hippie degeneration for us. I expect her to slap me and call for an airlift to a designer shoe warehouse if I so much as look at a pair of Birkenstocks. Not even for the hippie-love of Chris.

Once on campus, I head directly for the meeting and seat myself next to Mandy, one of the less militant lesbians in the department and a very fine teacher. She and I are sharing Zach as a tutor. Lucky us. Mandy isn't a hippie proper, but she definitely prioritizes comfort over fashion, she's wearing cargo pants and Tevas with a white T-shirt. It's her standard summer uniform. She has small, precise features and bobbed brown hair. If I took her to the MAC counter, she'd be capable of a showstopping makeover. Never going to happen. In Langsdale, the "natural" look is always in.

Mandy is actually friends with Zach, who is, of course, guaranteed to be at least fifteen minutes late.

"Why Zach?" I whine, pulling my feet out of my shoes and rubbing the sweaty upper part against the back of my calf.

"He's the best tutor," Mandy says. "Look around."

I do look around. It's like being on the magic mountain—everyone's pasty-faced and looks vaguely ill, bespectacled, hunch-shouldered, tight-lipped with the requisite underfed-yet-flabby body type.

"They should have picked Ronnie."

"She applied?" Mandy asks, eyebrows raised like little daggers.

I nod conspiratorially. Mandy actually likes J.J., a fact that I superficially chalk up to lesbian solidarity, but she looks appropriately and legitimately disgusted by the news.

"J.J. didn't pick her? Any reason?"

I shake my head.

"Damn," Mandy says. "You're never safe."

It's true. Sometimes it feels as if we're on some crazy game show where contestants get picked off one by one for no apparent reason. And for less than minimum wage. My ex-boyfriend was right. We are stooooo-pid.

"So what's she going to do for money?"

"Temp," I say. "I guess. It's slim pickings around here over the summer. I don't think loans are an option anymore, since she's just taking the one course."

"What's she taking?" Mandy asks.

"Professor Lind's class," I say. "Something about Shakespeare and the sublime. I just know that since it's Professor Lind and a serious workload, she didn't want to take a second class, and that leaves her financially up a creek."

J.J. walks into the room with a stack of purple folders. I will be thirty-one in August, yet this feels like the first day of elementary school. We all turn to face J.J. obediently while she passes around the teaching materials. And like clockwork, Zach slides in at 3:18 p.m., late even by slacker standards.

"Sorry, girls," he whispers at Mandy and me. I try not be a fascist politic-a, but I loathe being called a "girl." "Honey," by an oldster—fine, but "girl" by Zach, absolutely unacceptable. I give him my slimmest, faintest smile in acknowledgment. He's cut his hair close to his head, and I feel like telling him that he's rid himself of one of his two good features, the brown curls. He looks like a serial killer. He's dressed exactly like Mandy— their attraction must be narcissistic; a stunning, twin-like display of apathy toward one's appearance. I close my eyes and try to imagine men walking down the streets of New York City, men in three-piece suits, with expensive haircuts and faint traces of cologne. Shoes that cover the entire foot. My sister doesn't know how good she has it, living in the city, even if she is getting married.

"Nice haircut," I say.

"Nice beret."

I hope that I'm not turning red and just open my folder. J.J. is breaking down the incoming-student demographic. *Ages range from seventeen to one student who's twenty-five. As usual, it's sixty-two percent women and thirty-eight percent men. Forty percent of the students identify themselves as white or Caucasian. Forty-one percent African-American. Nineteen percent Other. Some are international students. We have one Iraqi, two students from the Sudan and a pair of identical twins.* How she goes from Iraqi to twins is beyond me, but I'm barely listening. Instead, I'm dreaming of a short glass of bourbon with three big ice cubes. I'm sitting outside some trendy hole-in-the-wall Chelsea bar where everyone loves my beret and a large man with a dull-but-respectable white-collar job is making moon eyes at me. I can taste the bourbon burning the back of my throat, like a match being slowly dragged across the back of its cover.

"Quit it," I hear Mandy say, and look over to see Zach picking at a callus on the side of his foot.

Six weeks of this, I think, and make the imaginary bourbon a double.

# Ronnie

It's 10:25 at night. I'm too early to walk up to the back door of the factory, so I sit in my car and wait for five minutes to pass. I roll my window down on the passenger side because the window on my side doesn't work. It's summer steamy even if it is nighttime. I've driven fifteen minutes out of town, to Clarkstown, wherever this is. I'm supposed to meet someone named Ray, the shift manager, and he's supposed to train me and give me the rundown on how things work at Valtek. How I ended up working in a car-part factory this summer, when I left a perfectly good copyediting job—with an office—to go to grad school is a story of such vast levels of fuck-upedness that I don't even want to think about it. Not even if I've still got three minutes left now. Except to acknowledge that I'm good for absolutely nothing. My whole life I've been a nerdy bookworm, nevertheless incapable of parlaying that bookishness into anything practical or moneymaking. When I got the shaft from J.J. and the English department and realized I wasn't going to be teaching this summer, I tested at the temp agency, thinking it meant something that I was in grad school.

I scored low on nearly everything except the stuff that required alphabetizing, so low that no one with any sense would let me near their office or computer. I walked into the agency thinking I was the shit, and left with the understanding that I was full of shit. Two totally different things.

When I told my family and friends I was leaving L.A.—for the Midwest—they thought I'd get over it, and when they realized I was serious, they shook their heads, saying I'd be back. Even if grad school doesn't come close to what I thought it was going to be, is in fact, often the opposite of what I thought it'd be, the crappiness of it is still not enough to send me packing. It's going to take a lot more than J. J. Jones and a whole lot of *other* crazy white folks to do that.

"Dude, I hate to say I told you so," my ex-boyfriend, and now dear friend, Sammy, said to me after I called and told him about the brochure incident and not getting a teaching assignment. He is supposedly my number-one supporter back home, an intelligent brother and the most mellow person I know. Indiana, though, worried him. Challenged the mellow. "But don't let them chase you away," he said. "Fight the power," he said, which made me smile on the other end of the line. We always used to argue over which was better, the Isley Brothers'"Fight the Power," or Public Enemy's, neither of which would ever be played on the radio in Langsdale. So I'm not letting them chase me away. Not yet, anyway. And I will fight the power. As my mama always says, I've got a hard head, a big mouth and a stubborn behind.

Now, I've got one minute before I start work. I get a crazy lurch in my stomach and talk it away as I climb out of my beat-up Volvo from the passenger side, because I haven't been able to open the driver's side for months— rust or something. It's a '74 but runs like an 1874. I bought it years before my academic tendencies, not realizing it was part of academic packaging—a raggedy package, but still. I walk up to the back door of Valtek. I'd called the temp agency to figure out what I'd be doing exactly, because I couldn't figure out what kind of office work happened at night. Doris and Paolo got me to thinking. That was when I found out there ain't no office work happening at night, and if there was, I was too hopeless to do it. After talking to Sammy, I called my brother, too, and told him I'd be working in a factory— just for the summer until the fall semester started. He thought it was hilarious. Someone who's worked in a factory since graduating high school, whose sister went to UCLA and then managed to get to Europe every other summer since then, but now finds herself punching the clock for five dollars an hour after the agency gets its share, would have to find my situation hilarious. He's been leaving me messages, *Hey, Factory Girl. How's that* real *job going? Sucks, don't it? Heh heh heh.* I tell him I haven't started yet, and I tell him that I've always had a "real" job, but he says that sitting on your ass all day reading articles and marking them up is hardly work. And forget about trying to explain the "work" of grad school. But now, waiting to start what can't be a leisurely job, even I have to say to myself, there's *work,* and then there's work. Both are hard, but one is preferable.

A stream of people who look like sleepwalkers are coming out of the factory now that their shift has ended, and I hang around by the door waiting for Ray. When a baby-faced kid pokes his head out the door and peers at me from underneath his baseball cap, I stare back at him and try to look relaxed. A pair of goggles hangs from his neck.

"You Veronica Williams?"

"Yes," I say. "Yeah," when I hear how I sound. Like a goddamn prissy secretary.

"Well, let me show you what we do around here," Ray says. He holds the door open for me to pass through and I follow him into a building with the worst lighting I've ever seen. Everybody looks green, and nearly everybody's wearing goggles. It's loud, too, like cymbals going off, a hundred wrenches hitting a hundred pipes, and a thousand cars with their engines running. The first thing that Ray does is hand me a time card and my own goggles when we get to where everyone punches in.

"You got to wear these at *all* times," he says, keeping his voice loud so I can hear him. "'Cept on your breaks. There's lots of stuff flying around here liable to get you in the eye, and you don't want that."

"No," I said, shaking my head.

"You get three ten-minute breaks, and one half-hour lunch break."

"Can I take them anytime I want?" Three ten-minute breaks don't sound like a whole hell of a lot, but if I can spread them out, it won't be so bad.

"Anytime you want?" Ray looks at me with his clear

brown eyes like I'm simple. "Oh, no, sweetheart. Somebody'll come round and tell you when. Now, let me show you where your station's at." I let the "sweetheart" pass, because even though he looks younger than me, he walks and talks like an old man, so it sounds natural coming out of his mouth. That, and the Midwestern twang that sounds slightly Southern, like folks in my family, which actually makes me appreciate the sound of it.

I follow two steps behind him, careful not to run up on him when he stops. We're standing in front of a conveyor belt with what looks like a giant robot arm hovering over it.

"This is station eight," Ray says. "You gone be working here, and on station nine." He points. Station nine is a good ways away from eight.

"At once?"

"At once?" When Ray says it, it sounds like "wonts." He's giving me that simple look again. "You mean at the same time?"

I nod.

"Two for starters," he said. He adjusts his cap. It's got Dale Earnhardt Jr. stitched across it with the number eight. I've been living in Indiana long enough to know Earnhardt's a race-car driver. "We'll get you worked up to two and three in no time. Let me tell you how to work it."

Ray's explaining the machines to me, what they do, how to handle them and I'm already lost. I have to ask a lot of questions and concentrate really hard to make sure I get everything he's telling me. Machine eight makes the plastic covers for car-stereo speakers, and machine nine makes the vents that go on car dashboards. It never even occurred to me that these little pieces had to be made by

somebody or some thing. I'm going to have to run between both machines while the robot arm drops parts
onto the conveyor belt, and pack boxes full of speakers
and vents. In the middle of Ray explaining something
really crucial, something that's going to keep me from losing an arm or burning myself with hot plastic pieces
shooting all over the place, I realize I have to take notes.

"Excuse me. Ray?" He pauses with his mouth open in
midsentence. "I'm going to take little notes on this, to
make sure I get it all right."

Ray works his jaw at that request. "Notes."

"Yes. Yeah. I can't remember all you're telling me
otherwise."

Ray coughs out a laugh. "Well damn, that's a new one.
Notes." He goes to his station and comes back with a
nubby, chewed-up pencil and a scrap piece of paper.
"This ought to do you," he says. "You can use this to mark
with." He talks slowly, pausing every now and then to turn
my way and look me in the eye like he's dealing with
someone elderly. When he's done, he asks if I have any
questions.

I notice my station is missing its chair. "Where's my
chair?"

"Chair? For what?"

Now I look at him like *he's* simple. "To sit. I need a
chair to sit."

"Oh…" His voice trails off and then a grin spreads
across his face. "Well, there ain't no sitting down, now. You
cain't run the machines sitting down." He pokes his
tongue on the inside of his cheek, trying not to be tick-
led, as my mother would say.

"Oh." I let the weight of what he's telling me settle.

I'm going to be working graveyard shift from eleven to seven, and I'm only going to be able to rest my legs for a total of sixty minutes.

Ray gets tired of me standing around looking dazed like someone's slapped me and vanished into thin air. "You good? 'Cause if you are, I got work to do."

"I'm good," I say, and take a deep breath. Before he leaves me, Ray lifts his goggles and raises an eyebrow to remind me to put mine on before I work.

Ain't this a bitch. I shake my head and mutter to myself like I'm crazy. I don't even have to mutter, I can speak out loud in my normal voice and nobody would hear me anyway, it's so loud. I could be teaching TROOPS with Doris, but no, J.J. and her little ego-tripping hippie ass, for reasons that are still way unclear to me, passed me over for another, hemp-wearing fool. I can't stand these people sometimes.

By "these people," I mean academics, whom I really hadn't paid attention to—at all—didn't even think about their existence, until I came to grad school. My idea of grad school was that it was a place where people sat around and talked about ideas, a place where I'd get some good writing done, and a place where I'd brush up against enlightened, generous people who "got it." I was wasting away at my copyediting job, being harassed by a Napoleonic boss who picked his underwear out of his ass all day. I'd sneak chapters of Faulkner while I should have been editing articles on entertainment law, so grad school seemed like my dream, my destiny. It wasn't my dream, but my tragedy is this: it probably *is* my destiny. What else can someone with zero skills, who likes books and teaching, do?

I drove *through* Langsdale the first time I visited, expecting the town to open up into highways and traffic. It didn't. Worse, the folks I was looking for, the ones who "got it," were scarce. Most folks in the department "got it"—something I don't want to catch. I had a bummer epiphany when I realized that knowledge in the academy was often treated as something to be preserved and doled out in stingy little portions, rather than shared in a come-one, come-all generosity. The more hoops to jump through, the better. And hearing folks talk about their exams, the flip outs, the antidepressants and the suicidal thoughts after what amounted to academic hazing makes me feel like a visitor in a psych ward. How long before I become contaminated and flip out?

It's not quite the same for me, being an MFA in an English department, being black in a mostly white department. It sort of goes without saying that I'm not really a member of what I've been calling the Country Club. Around the hallways and in class, faculty and students seemed to have not met, talked to, or even *seen* an actual Negro in a good thirty years. Oh, there are Negroes in our department, but you have to use that term loosely here at Langsdale University. They're sort of watered down, myself included, though they may not have arrived that way. But still, with my dreadlocks, dashiki, skirt barely covering my ass, black boots *and* fishnets, I looked like an escapee from some black-militant prostitution ring. Definitely not Midwest. Now that I live here, though, I understand that the fishnets, for starters, were over the top. It's taken a while, though. Doris and I actually used to wear them around like normal clothing, which is okay in the Midwest if you're twenty and going for the whole punk thing, or even thirtysomething, trying to go for the sleek, elegant, 1940s thing. But if you're thirty, and trying to teach undergrads, and taking a while to figure out why half the faculty and students are looking at you as if they want to ask how much you're charging, that's a problem. I know that now. A bigger problem is that Doris and I *think* we're normal mixed in a pot of crazy, but the longer I'm here, I think maybe I'm the crazy mixed in a pot of normal. There's the university, and then there's the world, and it's tough figuring out how to be where, who's normal, with quotes around it, and who's not. But "wah, wah," as my brother would say. "You don't know a damn thing about tough."

The robot hand is dropping the plastic speaker pieces down faster than I can pick them up, stack them and box them. I realize that the vents at the other station are being dropped down on the belt fast, too. I feel like Lucy and Ethel trying to keep up with the candy coming down the line at the factory, except ain't no hilarity ensuing. My legs are already tired but I've only been standing for forty-five minutes, tops. I try not to look at the clock because I know that only makes time go slower, but I can't help it. I walk over to the other station and start stacking the vents. I'm supposed to *inspect* them, too, for irregularities, but that's not happening, not exactly, and then I run over to the other station, and stack and pack the speakers. I do this over and over again until I find some sort of rhythm that works for me, even if I do mess up here and there. A few times I put two left speakers together when I pack them, instead of one right and one left. I worry about the speakers I may have missed, imagine them going off to some car dealership or something, and someone open-

ing up the box, seeing two left speakers and saying, "Goddamn. See? This is why I hate American shit, it's always
half-assed." And they might imagine some factory worker
who's undereducated, and therefore, in their minds, "less
than," who's overworked and just dropped the ball, but
it'd really be me: the screwup at stations eight and nine,
overeducated to the point of stupidity.

After a while, I even get used to the noise. I even find
the rhythm, and realize I can empty out my brain enough
to really get to thinking about that crazy-ass J.J. I can even
find some humor in this shit. I love it: part of the reason
I'm here in Langsdale, as opposed to another grad school
in an actual city, is that they're trying hard as hell to im-
port black folks from other parts of the country in the
interest of "diversity." I never would have come here if
the package wasn't so seductive. A stipend, teaching undergrads, that was hard to say no to, so I finally said, what
the hell. It's only a few years of my life. How bad can it
be? Doris clued me in to "how bad," because she'd already
been here for three years. We bonded over clothes and
men and alcohol at the first English department party of
the year, and by "party" I mean strange, library-like gath-
erings without music, with harsh lighting and not a meat
product in sight. I learned a lot about hummus and pita
bread my first year in academia, I can tell you that much.

Doris was sitting at a table talking to a dowdy woman
named Iris, who looked ten years older than she was, and
who looked as if she hadn't seen the sun in a long time,
and now I know she hadn't. She was always in the library,
all day, every day, hunched over a desk or wandering
through stacks. But Doris caught my eye because she was
wearing *makeup*. Lipstick, even. I clomped over in my

black platform shoes. That night I left the fishnets at home, but I was wearing a sarong with about twelve different colors happening. Loud as hell. "Oooh, that's so beautiful! Very ethnic," one of the older faculty members said to me earlier. When I reached Doris, she was telling a story about the last guy she dated, who had arthritis in his ass. He had to carry a cushion with him everywhere he went and so her friends started calling him Cushion Boy. But he broke up with *her* because she'd merely pointed out some history, after he showed her his framed Thomas Jefferson poster highlighting his five greatest accomplishments.

Doris ranted and picked at her nail polish. "He kept going on and on about the Declaration of Independence. Fabulous, of course. But then he had to talk about Jefferson's vision for all humanity. And so he got mad at *me* because *he* didn't know history. I said, 'The sixth thing that Jefferson stood for was thinking that slavery was apparently *necessary,* especially if your name was Sally Hemings. The guy never freed any of his own slaves!' Cushion Boy got mad and had the nerve to call the Hemings story hearsay, to which I responded, 'Not hearsay, DNA.' Since when did speaking the truth become evil? It doesn't make the Declaration of Independence any less fabulous! He called me a ball buster, when ten minutes before I was the prettiest thing in stilettos. It was a good riddance, anyway. Am I right?" She raised an eyebrow at me.

Doris knew what she was talking about. I thought about the first time I read Jefferson's *Notes on the State of Virginia.* A few lines were etched in my brain because they were so stunning. *Being an inferior race it would be futile and harmful to attempt to make them equal… In imag-*

*ination they are dull, tasteless and anomalous… I think one can scarcely be found capable of tracing and comprehending the investigations of Euclid. Blacks are inferior to whites in the endowment of both body and mind.* If that was his "vision" for humanity, he had some major blind spots. I smiled and pulled up a chair next to Iris. I've since had Iris in my British lit course, and now she's in my Shakespeare course. She's a pain in the ass, that one. Knows everything, she thinks, and should share it all, she thinks.

Iris clasped her hands together in what I'm sure was supposed to be an intelligent way. "That's quite an interesting cultural phenomenon, the sort of primacy placed on masculine expectations of femininity." Doris looked at her. "I mean, particularly in this day and age, with post-feminism and cultural studies doing a kind of reexamination of gender and sexuality."

I nodded. I didn't know what language she was speaking. Doris chugged her wine, turned the glass upside down and tapped the last drop against her lips. She looked at me. "God, why don't they serve hard liquor at these things? And it's Sunday. We can't even go get some Stoli."

I frowned. "Why can't we get Stoli if we want it?"

"You don't know? No liquor on Sunday. Or on voting days."

"What? For real?"

"Oh, yes. But for real," Doris said. She patted me on the shoulder and turned down the corners of her mouth sympathetically. "Welcome to hell. And your name is?"

"Ronnie," I said.

"Kick-ass skirt."

"Yes," Iris chimed in. "I was admiring it when I saw

you earlier. It reminds me of one of my trips to Africa. Senegal," she said. She looked at me knowingly, and Doris crossed her eyes to try to make me laugh.

"Well, I ain't never been to no Africa," I said. I could tell that Iris couldn't tell that I was just putting some flavor into my conversation, having some fun with words like I always do. Oh, that affirmative action and the lowered standards. "But Italy's nice. Lot's of hot men in Italy. They love me, and I love them."

"Good," Doris said. "You understand that it's normal and healthy and fun for women to actually *lust*."

Iris peered into her glass and pursed her lips. "Sure," she said. "But let's not forget the exoticizing and othering that inevitably happens when a woman of color travels to Europe. They're probably attracted to your difference, more than they're attracted to who you are."

Doris narrowed her eyes and raised her eyebrows at the same time, like she'd just tasted something tart, or like she was waiting for my fist to fly toward Iris. What burned me is that Iris was telling me something she *thought* I didn't know, like she was the official spokesperson for black people. I didn't even have to read about it in no book, either. It took me a while to figure out that the problem with race in the academy is that there are black people in books, and actual black folks with whom most of these people have had exactly one actual *conversation* in their lives.

"*Let's* not forget? Maybe *you* can forget," I said. "And anyway, it's not my brain I was looking to reveal."

Doris laughed. "That's funny. Wine," she said. "Must. Get. More. Wine. Yeah?" She motioned toward the table full of half-empty wine bottles across the room. We stood up and weaved through people to get to the table. She took my cup and poured me some. "Okay, I just have to say this, like, officially—all the white people here are not totally insane."

"But she is."

"Okay, yes, and also, confession: if not *all* of them are insane, then *most*. I do have to clarify. Plus, I'm not even talking about myself. I may be slowly driven insane. I'm just saying, not *all*." She poured herself some more wine and clinked my cup with hers. "And I'm only telling you this because I'm on my way to drunk, and you're, like, the only normal person, I can tell, that I've talked to in like, three years, and you *can't* leave. So, cheers."

I smiled and shook my head. "Wow. Man."

"Exactly," Doris said.

Since then, some people in the department have turned out to be nice, interesting, pretty normal people. Most have landed on the opposite side. I'm not sure that J.J.'s clinically insane, I think she's just "paternalistic," if I may speak the lingua franca around the department. In any other lingua franca, I could just say that bitch is crazy, and folks would know what I was talking about. After a year of living in Langsdale and teaching exactly two black students, I salivated at the thought of the TROOPS program. A room full of students with backgrounds like mine, who would probably be uneasy about going to such a big university. It sounded like a dream job to me. I told J.J. that. I also sorta kinda said that it would be nice if the students had a black instructor who knew what it felt like to be intimidated by a roomful of white people. It fucks with your head sometimes. You end up not doing the work you should be doing because you want to be invisible. Well, now, I know that was not the answer J.J. was looking for during our little interview. "You don't think a white instructor would be effective?" she asked me.

"Sure," I said, thinking I'd been educated by only white teachers my whole life. I'd turned out fine. But it would have been nice to have had one or two black teachers. The bottom line is that it's cool that kids, no matter what color, who hadn't had everything handed to them, were brought together to be educated. "A good teacher, period, is effective. But I do think I understand certain things that other teachers might not."

"I see," J.J. said, twisting her long ponytail.

Like a fool I waited for a phone call that never came. Now I know. You can't get too uppity around here. Your ass'll end up in a factory over the summertime instead of teaching.

And now, I can't *believe* how my legs hurt. Tomorrow, I'll have to wear two pair of socks and looser shoes, but tonight I just have to make it through. Two hours into my shift, Ray comes to relieve me so I can take my first ten-minute break.

"How you holding up, uh, uh…"

"Ronnie?" I sound like I'm asking my own name.

"Sure is, right. Ronnie," he says. "Sorry, sweetheart. We get so many people coming through here, what with the temps and all."

"No problem," I say. I stand there for a moment, because I realize I never asked where I'm supposed to take my break.

"What?" Ray asks. He pushes me to the side and starts stacking the speakers that are pilling up. "What?"

Everything I say and do in this factory makes me feel stupid, but how should I know where the break room is if nobody's told me? "Where do I take my break?"

"Oh. Follow that white stripe down there on the floor? Follow it around the corner, then go up the stairs when you get to 'em. But better hurry up, because you already used up two of your ten minutes."

I grab my backpack and follow the line like Ray tells me, and when I finally get up the stairs and see a chair, I'm so happy to see that chair, I barely know how to act. I don't even care that it's the most depressing room I could have possibly imagined, with all kinds of bullshit plaques up on the walls about producing the most this or the most that in this year or the other. I'm still so happy to see the weird plastic orange chairs. But when I sit down, my legs feel like they're still moving. They're vibrating. Where's that goddamn tennis racket now? There's another woman in the room, with long black hair and green eyes. Tiny, like a little girl, but wise-looking, like a woman. She's pulling her pink T-shirt away from her chest and then blowing down into the opening. She watches me jiggle and massage my leg for a minute.

"It's gone get better, but they gone hurt till you get used to standing."

"Hmm, I don't know if I can get used to standing."

She stood and crumpled her coffee cup before she chucked it into the trash can. "If you need a job, you gone to have to get used to it." She stretches. "Have a good one…" she says before pausing. I think she's waiting for help with my name.

"Ronnie," I say, but she's just yawning after stretching, and then she's out the door.

Somebody calls out "Howdy-do, Mona," before the door slams shut, so at least I know her name.

I get a Mountain Dew from the machine and take out one of the books I've brought with me. *The Sublime Object of Ideology* by Slavoj Žižek. I have to read it for my Shakespeare class. I open it up to the first chapter called, "How Did Marx Invent the Symptom?" and start to read:

*According to Lacan, it was none other than Karl Marx who invented the notion of the symptom. Is this Lacanian thesis just a sally of wit, a vague analogy, or does it possess a pertinent theoretical foundation? If Marx really articulated the notion of the symptom as it is also at work in the Freudian field, then we must ask ourselves the Kantian question concerning the epistemological "conditions of possibility" of such an encounter: how was it possible for Marx, in his analysis of the world of commodities, to produce a notion which applies also to the analysis of dreams, hysterical phenomena, and so on?*

Uh-huh. I squint at the page and then squeeze both eyes shut. I imagine I can hear my brain making a loud screeching sound, like a fast-moving train coming to a rail-grinding halt. I open my eyes. No, I'm in a loud-ass car factory in the middle of nowhere, in the middle of America, in a workers' lounge that is lit like a fluorescent hell. Was this what I moved from L.A. for? Left my family for? Dumped a good man for? *Hell* no. As Otis Redding says, a change is gonna come. I think about all those brochures out in the world, me, with a tennis racket in my hand, and I literally crack open the Žižek. I break the book's spine, I'm so pissed.

I take out a highlighter and underline what I think are interesting parts. I get to thinking about the epistemological conditions of possibility until I realize I have two minutes left before I have to go back downstairs, and I'm just goddamn too tired to give a shit about Žižek and that motherfucker Freud.

# Doris

*Teaching, Week One: Establish Dominance.*

Being a teacher is a bit like being a parent—you may very well want to be liked by those in your charge, but you are absolutely doomed if you (A) let them know it or (B) make it your first priority. The first semester that I taught I was twenty-five years old and fresh out of a fascist, corporate, button-down-blouse-and-bad-shoe desk job. I wanted everyone in my class to feel as good as I did. I did the fruit-loopy teacher routine day one of "Beginning Poetry" with a stack of ratty old books, and a poem with dirty words that I read out loud ("Your mom and dad, they fuck you up"), and a big stupid smile, and a pair of jeans and strappy little sandals. I was all "Call me Doris. We're all here because we love poetry," just vomiting peace and love. A veritable hippie myself. They took one look at me and it was as if the voices of angels were echoing from on high: *Come late to class! Turn in un-spellchecked poetry! Run all over this silly, simpy dimwit with the fruity prose! Run. Her. Down.*

While a classroom is not, nor should it be, a totalitarian state, neither is it a democracy. All packs need an alpha dog. Even packs of poets. Especially packs of just-away-from-home high-school grads. 'Tis better to err on the side of big, bad, bitchy-Mc-bitch-bitch and let them slowly earn their freedom.

"Hate me now, thank me later," is what Ronnie always says. Of course, her students *love* her.

'Tis also better to err on the side of not getting ever so slightly trashed the evening before teaching, but Ronnie had such a bad night at the factory that Paolo and I had to meet her and have just a wee tiny bit of alcohol. Then a wee tiny bit more. Once in the bluest of moons I think, *gee, maybe this is how alcoholism starts,* but I've given myself this parachute clause that I only have to worry about that if I'm still a lush when I have my actual Ph.D. in hand. By then I'll probably be letting myself off the hook for getting drunk because I'm bored and alone.

I felt bad for Ronnie last night. Bad-bad. She's not the type to let things get her down, but I'm ninety percent sure that she was seriously considering killing herself or J.J. after three nights of factory labor. It was just the three of us at the Office Saloon, plus a local playing a video game that allows you to put a naked woman together for points. I could tell by the rapidly materializing boob job that he was no stranger to the game.

"It was *insane,*" Ronnie said. "If I see that goddamn

J.J. I'm gonna stand her on her bony hippie ass for seven hours straight. See how she likes it."

"Tell me you didn't wear those platforms," Paolo said, downing his gin and tonic in three languid sips. "Tell me, tell me you didn't."

Ronnie leaned forward and raised an eyebrow. I know for a fact that Ronnie has not purchased a pair of non-platform shoes in at least a decade. She wears tennis shoes for nature walks (i.e., the track), otherwise, standard summer footwear is a flip-flop with a three-inch heel.

"I wore sneakers. Platform. Shut up," she said before she saw Paolo's face. "I didn't know *that* was where the temp agency would send me. It's so *Dickensian*. Truly. I cannot even *pee* without clocking out."

"Eww," Paolo said. "And that's without even knowing what 'Dickensian' *means.*"

I swirled the last, watered-down bit of my drink around in the glass and debated getting another.

"Do you have to do that all summer?" I asked.

"Only the weeks I want to eat and have a roof over my head."

"That sucks," I said, which is all I could say, because I was and remain the one who does not scare J.J. and consequently has a decent job.

"I saw your maaaan today," Paolo finally mustered, and God Bless America, Ronnie did perk up a bit. Only a good cut of *actual* meat makes Ronnie happier than a pretty man.

"Where?"

"Elevator."

"Outfit?"

"Oh, God," I said, remembering that I, too, had seen

Ronnie's latest diversion. "Neon-green tank top. Nice, normal pants, but I mean it was neon, Day-Glo, green-green."

Paolo mouthed *gay* from across the table.

"Uh-uh," Ronnie said. "I say *not* gay."

"I say not gay, too," I added. "I say bad dresser, but not gay."

Paolo pointed at me, circling his finger at my face.

"And we should trust *you* about not gay?"

"Give the brotha a break," Ronnie said. "I hear he's from California. Maybe I'll show him the town, *if* ya know what I mean."

Two large drinks and the promise of a live, heterosexual black man coaxed Ronnie off the metaphorical ledge.

"I say you make him your summer project," I said.

None of this, might I add, is any good for my working relationship with Zach. I sat there, looking at Ronnie, looking at video-porn guy, and thinking what whiners we are when we even dare to complain about the work we do. Neon-green tank-top man is a visiting scholar, working on some post-doc. Good, since that means he's way smart, maybe even smart enough to hold his own with Ronnie. I think, sometimes, that's why Ronnie has this thing about Italian guys—they generally don't have the language skills to be properly intimidated. It's just crazy that Ronnie, whom they practically promised the moon to, to get her to come here, is working temp jobs for the summer. And not even city-temp jobs where you can read a book and just pretend to work like everyone else in the office. Then I thought about Zach, and how he should have been the one standing in the factory in his ugly, eco-friendly shoes. So I had another Manhattan, which leaves me where I am today, trying not to look like the boozehound teacher these kids all probably remember from high school, while I double-check my notes for the first day of class: INTRODUCE SELF, GO OVER SYLLABUS, DO NOT SHOW WEAKNESS, DO NOT CURSE—EVEN ACCIDENTALLY.

Zach and I decided to meet an hour early to go over the day's lesson plan. Since the program is TROOPS, Zach and I are supposed to go in as a united front, talk about how it's a TEAM effort and whatnot. Be firm but kind. Trick them into thinking that they're going to *like* writing when they're fresh out of twelve years' conditioning to hate, loathe, fear and dread it. Build confidence. Gaslight them into thinking that Zach and I enjoy each other's company.

I'm running early, so I buy a veggie-wrap sandwich from the sub shop near the library and sit on one of the park benches in the Center Campus. Langsdale University is divided, illogically, into North, West, South and Center Campus. Center Campus is the showpiece spread, the foldout, drool-drool piece of property that seduces the unknowing into thinking the whole campus is this beautiful, colonial-style academic Mecca. Not featured in any brochure are the dorms on West and North Campus where most of the students live, cinder-block structures that make prison look cozy. I lived in one for exactly three months my first year here. I had a tiny sink in my room and had to bring my bathroom supplies to the shared showers down the hall. The couple above me had sex like clockwork every evening at 11:00 p.m. I used to fear that they were going to fall through the ceiling. What had been acceptable to me at twenty was institutionalized madness, having just moved from my own apartment in

Brooklyn. I didn't want to spend my morning looking for the shower curtain with no feet beneath it and hoping for the occasional moment when I could floss my teeth in private. I didn't last the semester—yet there are graduate students who manage to live there for eight- or nine-year stretches.

Center Campus, though, is truly beautiful, and allergies aside, May is almost reason enough for moving to the Midwest. Beneath the rows of dogwoods, students who've stayed on during summer lounge on blankets, reading for pleasure or just chatting and holding hands in G-rated displays of puppy love. Indiana is utterly different from the East Coast in that the land is flat and the sky is large. I'd never seen landscapes that made me feel so tiny. Skyscrapers have the opposite effect on me. While I might feel small standing next to the Empire State Building, it's very human and mechanized. Driving through Indiana, certain parts, it's like people might never have even existed. I like that.

Fifteen minutes later than we'd arranged, Zach arrives. If I didn't already know Zach, I might almost say that he looks debonair. He has on a nice pair of khaki pants and a crisp, white button-down shirt with a pair of snazzy loafers to pull it all together. I have on a conservative sundress, white with bright red flowers: breezy but with knees and arms securely covered, a frightening match for my clammy white skin and bloodshot eyes.

"You look like someone's mom," Zach says.

He sits down beside me on the bench outside the building we're teaching in, a little too close but I'm not in the mood to make a federal case about it.

"Right," I say. "That mom who was screwing the lawn-boy and getting tanked enough to smile at her husband when he came home from work."

Zach shakes his head. "The good kind of mom. MILF."

"MILF?"

"Don't you even listen to the kids you teach? Mom I'd like to foooornicate with, as is the common parlance."

"Believe it or not," I say, "I avoid the frat parties that might make one fluent in drunken-date-rapist, but glad to hear that you're keeping up. I'll be sure to call if I ever need a translator."

"Doris," Zach says intently. "Lighten up."

"Zach," I say. "Could you please speak *softly.*"

He opens a sack from McDonald's and pulls out a hamburger and at least twelve packets of ketchup, which he opens in record speed, dousing the burger beyond recognition.

"Rough night?"

"You've noooo idea."

"Dunno," he says. "I've seen you around a box of wine. You get that glazed euphoric look in your eyes."

He's trudging straight onto a minefield of things I don't want to talk about.

"I thought maybe you could do the introduction part," I say, cleverly changing the subject. "Maybe lead the class in a getting-to-know-you activity after I've gone over the syllabus."

Zach nods his head. I wait for him to finish the bite he's working on, but he opens his mouth and squirts one of the last remaining ketchup pouches directly down his throat.

"Oh, God," I say. "That is so completely disgusting. How can you even taste the burger? You might as well just order a bag full of ketchup. You could lick it off a napkin for as much of the food as you're getting."

Zach shakes his head. "I've tried. No ketchup without an actual order."

"Vile. Just vile."

Zach leans in closer.

"And to think, once upon a time, you let this very same…"

"Do not *even* go there before I have to teach. I do not need my students thinking that I've got some weird sexual vibe with their tutor, or that I have some weird sexual vibe with any human being walking this planet, for that matter."

"Not even Luis?"

At that moment, I cannot say for sure, but I am ninety percent positive that my face goes utterly red. I feel a flush of heat rise and wash over my chest and throat.

"What do you mean?" I ask, measuring every word.

"I just heard that things were getting hot and heavy in the poetry workshop. I mean, everyone knows about the blow-job-in-his-backyard thing, some townie from ages past. I thought he'd crossed over for good, for sure. But word on the street is that he's got his eye on our little Donna Reed."

"I do not like Luis," I lie. "And even if I did, that blow job is strictly hearsay. And I do not look like Donna Reed."

Zach raises an eyebrow.

"Okay, maybe a little bit—if she had jet-black hair and carried around Kant instead of cookbooks."

"She's the original MILF."

"And you're the original PIMA—Pain in My Arse."

Again with the head-shaking.

"C'mon, Doris," he says. "You're a poet. You can do better than that."

Before I can launch into a self-righteous, self-defensive rant that would probably, ultimately, get me absolutely nowhere, Mandy shows up in (again) all but the same outfit that Zach is wearing. She has her hair back in barrettes and looks young enough to be an undergraduate herself.

"Hey, babe," Zach says. "You ready for me to come by later this afternoon? Doris and I are just hashing out the next two hours for her class. I'll have a half hour between to get to yours. We could get coffee."

And I'm thinking that it's odd for Zach to be calling Mandy "babe," and that he's being awfully nice in an awfully non-Zach kind of way, when he stands up and gives Mandy a light kiss on the lips. A sweet but decidedly heterosexual kiss, and then he smoothes his hand down the back of her hair.

"Okay," Mandy says.

I am speechless.

"C'mon," Zach says to me. "Duty calls."

I cannot tell him how totally depressing it feels to know that even the lesbians now have boyfriends.

Bowling and lonely, misguided women do not mix. Thursday night, Ronnie and I meet up at Winchester Lanes, an alley about a mile north of Langsdale that sponsors "midnight bowling" on Tuesdays and Thursdays. I have on white socks and a white shirt, all of which glow an eerie iridescent green beneath the fake moon and stars plastered across the walls of the bowling alley. Blue jeans cuffed at the ankles for a 1950s date-night vibe, minus the date. Paolo is meeting us later, since he refuses to wear bowling shoes and refers to Winchester Lanes as one of the many "townie" places that Ronnie and I have "normalized" since moving to Langsdale. There are a lot of pickups in the parking lot, and a statistically high number of mullets per male, but Ronnie and I have never been bothered. We bowl under fake names, "Ruby" for me and "Magnolia" for Ronnie. Since I learned bowling from watching *The Flintstones* and Ronnie played at maybe two birthday parties when she was a kid, we nurse our Mountain Dews and consider ourselves regular aces when we break a hundred on our scores.

"How's teaching?" Ronnie asks. She's poised to pick up a spare, holding a marbled-purple bowling ball in front of her face and concentrating on the two remaining pins.

"Good," I say. "For the first week."

Week one of teaching went fair-to-well. In terms of exotic subjects, I have a farm boy named Will who has yet to say a word, just glares at the rest of the classroom like he's waiting to get assigned to his *real* classroom. I also have our one Iraqi student, Ali, who after a mere three years in the United States already has a better command of English grammar than most of the kids who went through Indiana public schools. There are three young women, Linda, Tina and Sharelle, who come to class dressed so well they make us all feel ashamed. Tina is my current favorite, as she's this sweet, sweet girl whose family is originally from Peru who looks as if she'd never say a bad word about anyone: all dimples and big smiles, yet she wears shirts that say things like "Fallen Angel," and "I want your BOYFRIEND." And then there's Claus, a large black kid who looks like a M-A-N, wants to be a pediatrician, and is of the disposition that if I say the sky is blue, he'll look out the window and say, "That's your opinion."

Ronnie's beating me by seven, and our scores are an abysmal twenty-five to thirty-two going into the fifth frame. I cross my right leg behind my left, wind up the ball and launch it gracefully into the gutter.

"Nice," I hear from behind me. "Good form. You look like you're getting ready to do a cartwheel, not hit some pins."

I turn to face Chris, grinning a Day-Glo smile, dressed in a baby-blue bowling shirt that reads "Herman's Hampsters" and cutoff jeans. His right sock glows brighter than his left, and he's trying not to laugh at Ronnie's and my scores.

"'Ruby' and 'Magnolia'?" he says. "I hope they're in the bathroom, because if those are your scores, you ladies need help. Which of you is next?"

"Me," Ronnie says. Chris moves up beside her, and I watch him take Ronnie's arm and move it back into a perfect arc. When he moves, his shirt unbuttons, and I see a hint of his stomach. His skin is lightly tanned and there's a trail of blond hairs leading to his belly button. It's all I can do not to reach out and touch it.

"Damn," Ronnie says, watching the bowling ball clear out every one of her pins. "Strike."

Chris looks around, glancing in the direction of four other computer geeks (his team, I'm guessing) in baby-blue bowling shirts, then pulls up a chair beside us.

"So what are you ladies doing here? Doesn't seem like your style."

"What's that supposed to mean?" I ask.

Chris points at Ronnie and then at me, making the sort

of face I associate with watching really bad television in groups.

"I see you ladies sitting outside the ice-cream shop. You watch everyone walk by and tear 'em to shreds. *This isn't even real ice cream. The ice cream in New York City is made by Gucci cows. The cows in L.A. are tough enough to milk themselves.*"

"What's the matter with the cows out here anyhow?" Ronnie asks.

Chris laughs.

"Yet here we are," I say, attempting to assure Chris of my commitment to non-regionally-biased sexual activity. "Having a great time with you, at this fabulous recreational activity in Langsdale, Indiana. And it's a beautiful evening, and bowling is bowling wherever you go."

"Truly," Ronnie says. "We'd play just as bad in L.A. or New York."

"You've got us completely wrong. All of Ronnie's boyfriends hang out here."

Ronnie gives Chris a big smile and playful series of nods.

"Bring me my Billy Ray," Ronnie says. The great thing is, she's serious. In addition to black men and Italians, the move to Langsdale revealed Ronnie's true penchant for homegrown made-in-Indiana menfolk. We call all of Ronnie's potential Langsdale boyfriends Billy Ray after she admitted to thinking Billy Ray Cyrus was cute: tight jeans, mullet and all. There are always locals aplenty at Winchester Lanes, making sure that John Cougar Mellencamp loops an infinite repeat on the jukebox, with the occasional Lynyrd Skynyrd or Tom Petty interlude. Ronnie says the Billy Rays can look country, but can't look mean—like they long for the days when the States were Confederate.

"Speaking of Billy Rays," I say, picking up my bowling ball and concentrating hard on hitting at least six pins. "I have an actual student named Claus this summer, and it's not even some Teutonic homage to white supremacy. He's this huge black kid who, I am positive for sure, does not think that I have the sense God gave an ant."

"And why would he think that?" Ronnie asks, holding her Mountain Dew like it's some chichi martini. "Did you make the mistake of telling them about your shoe collection?"

"Not even," I say, backing up and positioning myself for an effortless strike. "It burns me to no end. If I give an answer to some kind of question, he'll literally turn around, just crane his head in the direction of Zach to see what he thinks. I loathe it. Zach. A manifest moron in at least half his daily life."

"Damn," Chris says. "Wouldn't want to be Zach. Man can't catch a break with you two."

"You don't know Zach."

Chris moves in beside me, takes my arm and holds my wrist in his one hand, the bowling ball in his other. His hands are warm, and his breath smells faintly of alcohol.

"Doris," he says. "Tell me this is not how you hold the bowling ball."

"What do you mean?"

I have my thumb in the big hole, and my index and middle fingers in the two smaller holes, with my remaining two fingers curled underneath the edge of my fist.

"You'll kill yourself like that," he says, removing my index finger, moving my middle finger down, and placing the finger next to my pinkie into the last hole instead. "Feel better?"

I hold the ball close. It feels lighter, more secure. I'm not even going to tell Chris how many nails I've broken bowling in my usual style. Something tells me he wouldn't sympathize. When I finally let the ball roll, all but one pin goes down.

"Brilliant," I say. "This is genius."

"Not genius," Chris says. "Normal. That's how normal folks bowl."

"You two can figure out what's normal at Winchester Lanes," Ronnie says. "Time for me to move on over and see what's playing at the jukebox, *if* you know what I mean."

Although I cannot see his face, there's a promising Billy Ray in tight jeans with curly brown hair hanging over the back of his collar and a torso thick as a tree trunk, leaning hard against the jukebox and puzzling over the song selection like it's page one of *Finnegan's Wake*.

"I do indeed," I say.

Chris rolls his eyes as Ronnie stands up, adjusts her shirt and jingles her coins at us like they're dice, before heading over.

"You ladies are trouble."

"Uh-uh. We're just angels in disguise."

Unfortunately, Paolo arrives at exactly this moment. He's highlighted the tips of his hair a golden-blond, and looks fabulous, as always, in a tight black T-shirt and perfectly fitting jeans. I give him a kiss, exaggerating my happy-happy at seeing him, to prove to Chris that I am, indeed, a fabulous and generous babe with loads of friends of every kind who looooove to hang out with me.

"What's with you," Paolo asks. "They discount the Prozac?"

Chris laughs. Paolo gives him the once-over, up-down-back-again—face utterly neutral.

"This is Chris," I say to Paolo. "He translates computer wizardry into dumb-English-major."

"Great," Paolo says. "Maybe next you can help her stop translating gay Chilean into straight boyfriend."

I smack him, harder than I should.

"Easy," Paolo says. "Kidding."

"Doris is all right," Chris offers. He stands up and taps playfully on my back. "We're hard on the gal, but only because she needs a little breaking in."

"That tickles."

"Habit," he says. "I used to do that to my brother every night. He had cystic fibrosis."

Paolo's eyes widen sympathetically.

"I'm so sorry," I say.

Chris shrugs.

"Sometimes I do the tap-tap thing without even thinking about it. It's like muscle memory. Like I'll sometimes play scales or 'Mary Had a Little Lamb' on the computer keyboard. Won't even notice."

Paolo looks as if he wants to say something, but Chris makes a noise like "aaahck," to signify it's *game over, don't want to talk about it with you, silly Gucci-cow lady and your silly gay boyfriend.* His friends in the baby-blue shirts are motioning him down to their lane.

"Nice to meet ya," he says to Paolo, and to me: "Later."

HOWEVER—I distinctly felt the deft, computer-callused palm of his right hand grace the underexercised, overfed back of my derriere.

"He touched my ass," I whisper.

"Maybe he confused it for a hard drive."

"Oh, come on," I say. "Don't even try to homosexual-ize my last chance at a real boyfriend. And why on God's green and beautiful earth did you bring up Luis? I don't need my computer-lovah thinking I have some gay boyfriend. Which would be giving your suspicious mind too much credit, since I just got an e-mail from Luis about how he wants to have dinner tomorrow night."

Paolo cringes.

"I cannot believe that you and Ronnie come here on *purpose*. Look at that, what is it, a moon? It's *peeling* at the edges, and I'm not saying anything about anyone, but it smells a bit like pee in here, don't you think?"

"Fine," I say. "Don't respond about Luis. But do you realize that there are lesbians in this town who are now getting recommended daily allowances of testosterone-based activity?"

"You mean Zach?" Paolo asks. "Sorry, doesn't count."

He crosses his arms defensively, like he might catch something from just sitting here.

"Billy Ray wants to take me to his cha-let in Ten-nessee," Ronnie says, returning from the jukebox.

"And mail you back in pieces," I warn.

"Cynical," Paolo says. "And *totally* true." He wags a no-no-no finger at Ronnie. "But maybe that's your problem, Doris, the lesbians are keeping an open mind."

That night, home, watching Letterman and plotting alternative lives that do not involve Freud, bowling, nor any form of sexually ambiguous human being, I realize that something terrible has happened with Chris. I have started to like him for real. Not just the performative "Hey, Paolo and Ronnie, isn't it wacky that I like the computer guy," nonsense, but a real live legitimate crush. Maybe it's even more than I feel for Luis?

Women love to bitch about men. How there aren't any good ones, or they're all stupid, or some form of married/homosexual/cannibalistic-latent-serial-abuser-of-small-animals. While I plead guilty-as-charged to engaging in such ranting, I must also say that when men claim women are crazy, they may have a point I could be proof positive of that. Let's face it. No truly, deeply, committedly normal woman would even give Luis a second look. Gay or not gay, I'm convinced that he does face masks because every once in a while he'd come to class with little flecks of blue clay ground into the edges of his eyebrows. A serial abuser of women's beauty products is not exactly my girlish dreams come to life. Add to that my "brief encounter" with Cushion Boy, the latter-day Jeffersonian, whom I tried to excuse to myself every second we dated. He'd talk about his neighborhood back home in Connecticut being "good," when I knew in my heart he meant "white," but convinced myself that he just meant "safe." I tried to be polite about his jingoism and white shoes after Labor Day, but by the end of it, I was just fooling myself for the sake of having someone to believe in. And I wonder why I walk around confused, manwise, at any rate.

I believe that in order to get some kind of answer, one must go back to the beginning. I can't speak on behalf of all women, but I can say quite honestly that I never intended to become this crazy. I know for a fact that I never, ever intended to even look twice at some human compost heap of marriages and extramarital dalliances with men, women and whatever else isn't nailed down. At twenty, I was clear about things. I was in love with my then boyfriend, a cooler-than-thou painter type, who had more than a passing acquaintance with paint thinner, and wound up in rehab where he came clean and fell in love with some hyperactive recovering alcoholic who let him paint her naked. What I wanted was not good, but I knew that was what I wanted. And it wasn't so deeply vested in compromise.

But this Chris thing. The Chris thing could prove to be totally different. First off, I have started to refer to him as "Chris," not just in my own head, but to others as well. He is no longer "hot hippie computer guy," but Chris, who makes fun of me, and who had a brother whose back he used to tap, and who can do just about anything one might ever need with any sort of computer. Luis has yet to become that much of a person to me. That's the problem. Thinking of the men I date as fully formed, wholly evolved sentient human beings is no longer my de facto position. If a guy did that, I'd call him a jerk. An objectifying, depersonalizing "WARNING—Do Not Enter" kind of jerk. But when I catch myself doing it, I just think it's sad.

I write myself a quick note before falling asleep: GOAL FOR WEEK—THINK OF ALL MEN AS PEOPLE (EVEN ZACH, EVEN LUIS).

From across the room I can see that my message light is blinking—joy incarnate, since I was out with the only two people who usually leave me messages. The number reads 2 in digital red. The first voice is my sister's: *Did you get my last e-mail? I need to have the dresses re-sized, since*

*Theresa says that hers doesn't fit, and it's a size six, and she just KNOWS that she doesn't wear a size EIGHT. Drama, drama…* I press the Skip button, unwilling to deal, at the moment, with Lisa's documentation of Theresa's fluctuating and reportedly bulimic ass. Next voice is less familiar, thickly accented and decidedly male: *Dor-ees? This is Dor-ees, right? Dor-ees, I know about you and Luis. You know, Luis, mi Luis. Maybe you think,* mujerzuela, *you can just dooooo… I know, you writers… And I think…that you owe me an apology.* BEEP.

I have that deep down sickening feeling that Luis is going to need a *lot* more than a little humanizing.

# Ronnie

The Luis thing that Doris has going on was trouble from jump, but it gets so demoralizing in grad school, in the good old heartland, I thought, well, at least it's something. If you're not a sorority girl gone wild among countless frat boys—or somebody's wife—you start to feel weird. It's like someone's snatched your brain and replaced it with a gray mess of bad judgment. Because flirting doesn't exist in academia, you feel like a chair or a table, for all the sexual vibes coming your way. It's not even a question of dating, but a task of trying to stay a well-rounded, therefore sexual, human being. Between getting evil eyes for showing cleavage, or being called a ball breaker for not automatically deferring to every James Joyce wannabe in seminar, times is tough if you're a broad in academia who happens to like both her brains and her breasts.

So that's how Doris got caught up with Way Gay Faux

Che, and that's how I started to unironically lust after some of the good ol' boys around town. They don't know from Hélène Cixous and the phallocentric order of language or the male symbolic. They just tell you you're purty and want to buy you a drink. To be honest, I'd never actually date one of them; I sometimes imagine the faint pickings of "Dueling Banjos" when I'm stared at a little too long. But, to continue being honest, most of the local guys I've exchanged words with have been plain old nice people, "down-home," as my mother says, unlike most of the Lit people who are so "awkward," as I've learned to say, that they can't even speak when they pass you in the hallways.

An example of down-home is Earl. From the first time I walked into the Office Saloon full of, I have to admit, L.A. condescension and general black-person fear of a whole lot of white people in a group looking at you, he treated me nothing but nice. When I yelled my order of double Jack and Coke so that he could hear me over "Free Bird" playing on the juke box, he gave me a wink and said, "Now that's what I like. A lady who can handle her own." Of course, if he were in the classroom, eyes would have rolled over the "lady" part, but he made all the difference between me grabbing Doris and telling her that we were getting the hell out of that bar, and not. He's always polite to me and always gives me that extra top-off of Stoli or Jack. He used to look more mountain man—long blond hair and a beard that took up a lot of his face—but now he's cut off his hair and cut down that beard because he's trying to look more respectable, he says. "I cain't ride a Harley and bartend for all the rest of my days, Ronnie," he told me. "You're smart to be in school."

"I don't know about that," I said. "There's such a thing as being so smart, you're stupid."

He winked at me again. He's a great winker. "I'm not gone hold it against you," he said, and dried his big hands on a bar towel.

I thought, just for a second, about the kind of women those big hands had handled. We'd heard talk around the bar that Earl was careful and particular about not mixing business with pleasure. And business, the Office Saloon, seemed to be his whole life. I heard that Earl had at least gone to college for a bit. But I imagine he got out while he could, because he wasn't a smarty-pants dum-dum like me.

So good ol' boys—except for Earl—and Italians, it is. The Italian thing is a little easier to explain: for better or worse, they seem to really like women. Okay, so they take the macho thing too goddamn far sometimes. But it's better than dealing with guys who've traded in their masculinity and eros for the desire to always be the smart kid in class, who somehow keep reminding you that if you're a girl, you couldn't possibly be that kid.

I have about ten minutes to kill, so I'm in the graduate-student lounge, the Langsdale Workroom, eavesdropping on all kinds of asexual one-upmanship. I usually avoid the room because it's depressing. Lots of beat-up, hodgepodge seventies office furniture. A small microwave in which someone's always microwaving a pitiful, single-portion frozen entrée. No one remembers to turn off the coffee machine, so it always smells like burnt coffee. An oil portrait done in, it says, 1946, of the biggest donor and town mogul looms over the line of computers, so you can't avoid the cold gray eyes of Mr. Langsdale, dead for fifty years now, but always watching. His eyes do that thing where they follow you, like you're in some spooky movie. I've been everywhere in the workroom—on the couch, by the windows, at the coffee machine—and Mr. Langsdale's eyes are always on me, as if he's saying, like good old Thomas Jefferson, "Where'd you come from? When I donated a fuckload of money to this place, I wasn't thinking about *you*."

I flip through my Shakespeare and watch the clock. I try to ignore the guy snoring on the couch across from me but he sounds like a low-powered lawn mower. A young woman doing research on one of the computers turns when the guy snorts three times in a row. She adjusts her glasses, glares at him, and then she looks at me. I shrug.

"He's freaking me out," she whispers. "I can't think."

"What are you researching?" I ask, just to be friendly.

"I'm studying multilimbed erotica, exploring the phenomenon of people who eroticize someone who might have an extra foot, or two arms. I'm trying to argue that the extra limbs, sexualizing the extra limbs, is actually a substitution for the phallus."

Sleeping guy mumbles something. *He's* freaking *her* out?

"Oh," I say, and look down at my Shakespeare.

Two guys at the worktable chime in. "I heard of that," one with tie-dye and long hair says. "Who's that professor at Duke? Campbell? He's been doing multilimbed research for a while now. I know, because when I was at Dartmouth, I took a class and came across an essay."

"Duke?" the other one asks. He's dressed like a wannabe professor, complete with satchel and tie. "Yale is doing a much better job in that area, and I'm not just saying that because I went there."

"Well *I* went to Brown," the scary girl says. I wonder if they're all going to whip out their degrees and measure them.

Their eyes turn to me, waiting, but I just flip through the pages of my book. I stop and decide to pack up and head to class when Nigel Rutherford walks into the room.

Last semester, I'd gotten it into my mind that I had a crush on Nigel, this British Ph.D. I realize now, it was all about the accent. "If you date Nigel Rutherford," Doris had protested, "I will kill myself." Dramatic, that Doris, but now I see her point. I'd been giving him the eyes for a long time, because I *thought* he was vibing *me*—as much as a British academic can vibe anyone. That is to say he looked me in the eye *and* said hello whenever we passed in the hallways. At Langsdale, that's practically pervy. Our first conversation was just that. We both were waiting for pages to come out of the printer in the copy room. I'd just finished a story for a workshop, and he was printing out an essay for a conference on "Film and Ethnicity in the 21st Century." We'd asked each other the obligatory question of "How's it going?," when he paused dramatically. He hugged himself after checking the machine to make sure his pages were still coming out, and then leaned up against the supply table with all the staplers and paper clips.

"So," he started, "will you be going home over break?"

I smiled, "Just for a little while. Why?"

He stroked his goatee. He'd been trying to coax it into growing for half the semester. He's got jet-black hair and it suited his angular face, I thought. "Oh, I don't know. I thought we might catch a film. Have you seen *Imitation of Life?* I quite liked it and thought of you."

*Imitation of Life* is that film that had been done twice about a self-loathing black girl trying to pass for white. The second time with Sandra Dee. So when he said he thought of me, I didn't know where he was going. Was he trying to tell me something? Or did he think I'd be interested in it just because it was a movie about black folks? Either way it was a funky invitation, so I said, "Because it's about black people?" It sounded bad once I heard it come out of my mouth, because for once I didn't take the time to make sure my words were comfortable enough for whom I was talking to. I've gotten pretty good at the whole assimilation and language thing, so much so that my voice is pretty damn schizophrenic. But right then, I wasn't thinking about Nigel and his goddamn feelings. It went from bad to worse. I was watching Nigel's color turn back from deep red to pasty.

"Oh, God, no. Of course not. I'm just interested in the film, and one of my dissertation chapters is about it…." he stammered. "I just thought it would be a nice opportunity for us to… Oh, forget it. I know how I must sound right now. I just thought it would be lovely for us to meet, and I was thinking, too, if you wouldn't mind, that I might like to show you my chapter on that particular film."

Doris was no longer in danger of committing suicide. If Nigel had just come out and said, like that rare breed of creature called a man, that he wanted to go out on a *date,* then maybe I would have. But no, he wanted to show me his *chapter.* Since then it's become part of our group's repertoire of shit that makes us laugh, no matter how old it is. "Hey, baby," Paolo's always saying. "Come up to my apartment. I got some Barry White playing, candles burning. Come on up and let me show you my chapter. You have *no* idea how long my chapter is, baby. It's the thickest chapter you have *ever* seen." After that bit of verbal fumbling around, or academic heavy petting, Nigel stopped looking me in the eye, though he sometimes still says hello. The hot-and-heavy flirtation is over.

"Hullo, Veronica," Nigel says, and immediately turns red. He puts his backpack down and takes a seat at a nearby computer and turns his back to me.

Jesus. Why turn red at hello? What is so traumatic about "hello" around here?

But I'm not thinking of Nigel anymore. That ship has sailed. I hear a voice just outside the doorway, low, rich and velvety. I know it must be the black man we all keep seeing. I tuck my book under my arm, grab my bag and try not to look as if I'm hurrying. He and Iris are waiting at the elevator and I take him in. We lock eyes, exchange a flicker of recognition and tentative smiles before he steps into the elevator. He's lanky tall and strikingly dark. Carries himself with an air of "I'm not intimidated by you." True, the clothes are problematic. Day-Glo muscle tees are a bit odd this day and age, that whole Wham, CHOOSE LIFE look is sort of old, unless, of course, you're on George Michael's team. Paolo says it's so, but I'm not willing to give up on this one just yet. It's kind of like being lost in the desert and you swear you see some water just in the distance. It might be a mirage, but hell, only a fool would stop walking toward it.

I'm taking a Shakespeare class first-summer session because I'm trying to shave off some of my time at Langsdale, just in case I can't take it anymore and have to leave before I crack up. The master's of fine arts I'm working on is a three-year degree, and after wrapping up my first two years, the remaining year all of a sudden seems like a tough row to hoe. Yes, I'm grateful for my deferred tuition and my stipend, but if I can knock out the classes and go back to L.A. for my third year, why in the world wouldn't I? Why stay here? I'll never be able to complain about grad school being hard, especially not after punching the clock at Valtek. The thing is *place,* the feeling of being out of place, that's crazy-making. On the other hand, I like school, I like teaching, and I'm just trying to figure it out: How much of choosing to be a part of academia just comes with the territory, which has nothing to do with Midwestern states or any other geography, but could be just as much a part of any landscape?

To get my MFA, the English department requires us to take at least four lit classes as proof, I guess, that we didn't earn our degrees by sitting around talking about our feelings, or as insurance that we can talk about literature in ways other than writing "This is neato" on each other's manuscripts. The ironic thing, though, is that writers think and write about literature one way, and scholars think and write about literature in another. It should be complementary, not competitive. So, half the time in Professor Lind's class, "out of place" doesn't even begin to describe how I feel, but the other half of the time, I'm actually happy to be talking about stuff that makes me think I can understand the world a little bit better.

Now we're going over the Žižek stuff we should have read. Professor Lind is asking about Žižek in terms of *Hamlet.* I'm still stuck on Žižek, in terms of Žižek.

"What," Professor Lind asks, "does Žižek mean by the term *'Che vuoi?'* when we consider Hamlet's father's deathbed mandate?"

Silence. And a lot of eyes looking down at desks. Professor Lind is patient as hell, though. She'll wait until Jesus rises again if she has to. That's why she's scary—that, and she's for real brilliant, without posing, without having to make sure you know it. If you're going to give her shit because she's a woman and doesn't suffer any fools, or a Jew, or has a tattoo that says *This is not flesh*—in French—like a band on her arm, or has a really loud laugh, or whatever the hell, that's your problem, not hers. She's a fifty-year-old academic assassin. She also happens to be the only professor who openly smiled at me, stuck out her hand and introduced herself when I was wandering the hallways trying to get to my first class in graduate school. I thought she was the secretary and later found out she's as famous as academics come. She leans forward in her chair and scratches her scalp. "Let's back up some. Let's make sure we all know the term *'Che vuoi?'*. Anybody," she says, and leans back in her chair.

John Casey, one of those who wants so badly to be the smart kid, even though he's a haggard-looking thirty-five and wearing a pair of glasses that look as old as he is, raises his hand. Professor Lind nods at him. He sits up straight and clears his throat. "*'Che vuoi?'* represents that which exists between the planes of what a certain vernacular posits, and what the speaker of the vernacular nevertheless intends upon attempting to communicate."

He clasps his hand on top of his desk. This, I've learned, is body language for pompous.

"Good," Professor Lind says. "Now." She locks eyes

with me until I look away. "In English. John's right. But
he's actually illustrating *'Che vuoi?'* right now. There's an
even more definitive, common way to explain this term."

Because this may be the only one out of a hundred
fifty assigned convoluted pages that I understand, I raise
my hand.

"Ronnie. Yes." Professor Lind leans forward in her
seat again.

"I, uh…" I take a deep breath. "I think one thing Žižek
means by that term is that sometimes there's a difference
between what someone's saying and what they mean to
say—or do—by speaking in the first place. There's some
implicit desire behind what they're saying."

"Excellent. Go on."

"Uh, that's it."

Professor Lind stares at me and waits and waits. But I'm
not so afraid of her that I'm going to look like an idiot.
I've always played it close to the vest in class. When the
only black person—in anything—screws up, you never
live it down. Lucky the first black guy who shined shoes
didn't fuck that up. I guarantee all these years only white
folks would have been "qualified" to shine shoes.

She sighs and gives me a look as if to say, *I'm going to
let your ass off the hook for now, but just wait until next
time.* "What John and Ronnie are getting at is good.
We're talking about the question of, 'You're telling me
something, but what do you want with what you're telling
me? What is your aim?' We're talking about speech acts
theory here. For example, I said that John's statement was
*'Che vuoi?'* because he made a statement but in fact ex-
pressed another desire with that statement, the desire to
appear intelligent." She says this matter-of-factly while

everyone looks around, glad she's not serving us our asses on a platter. She doesn't seem phased. She points at John. "Look. I'm not trying to pick on you all. I'm trying to make Žižek as plain and ordinary as I can. This *'Che vuoi?'*, this gap between what's articulated, and what's actually desired, is as real and common as any crap that's on MTV. And don't mistake it for hypocrisy. It's something else. Think of Hamlet and how this applies for next time." She stands up and looks at us, waiting and waiting. She reaches into her black jacket, pulls out a stick of gum, unwraps it, shoves it in her mouth and chews while she stares at us for a lifetime. Then she gathers her books and is out the door.

The rest of us, there are only nine, are slow to get up. Iris, who's, of course, in the class because that's my funky karma, walks out with John. I hear her say how "inappropriate" Professor Lind's "attack" on him was. But to me, this class was the most appropriate thing I've come across in a long time; how, exactly, I don't know, but something feels like the truth.

"This is all happening to me because of my feng shui," Doris says, pacing around her apartment, ripping things off the walls. P. J. Harvey's singing about how some dude is not rid of her. See this *angel,* and the little cherub? The little bastard, he's coming *down.* I read in this book that you can totally fuck up your love life if you have too many girlie things in one place, facing the wrong directions, and this is why, now, after that psycho message, I have to look out the peephole every time I hear a knock on the door. We're in the Midwest! Who needs to look through a peephole in the Midwest?"

I shrug and look around Doris's apartment, which *is* sort of girlie, lots of nail polishes and shoes lined up on shelves as decor, but since when is this a bad thing? And the unnecessary peephole: this is a new philosophy for both of us since, being women born and raised in big cities, we were practically born with eyes in the back of our heads and gaits that say, "I will cut off your balls if you *even*." But two years here, and I've stopped worrying about getting robbed or mugged. It's creepy stuff like squirrels and deer you have to watch out for. "Luis's 'cousin' isn't so crazy that he'd come to your house and try to off you or something, would he?"

"Cousin. Isn't that *rich*. Who knows? I mean, never mind that he's a pansexual, pathological liar, he's totally jeopardized my health. Mental *and* physical. Just listen to this thing. *Listen* to it." Doris dumps a mermaid sculpture into the box of bad girlie things and disappears into her bedroom, which you can see from the living room, to play her answering machine. "Are you listening? I'm playing it right now."

I listen to the message. Doris stops the machine and then comes back into the living room. She holds her hands out, palms up, and looks at me with her eyebrows raised.

"Scary," I say. "He's definitely scary," I repeat, nodding.

"Oh, God, no! I needed you to say it wasn't that bad!"

"Well, for what it's worth, he sounds pissed off but not violent."

"Great. That's the bright side."

"Have a drink," I say, refilling her glass.

She sighs and drops down beside me on her couch. "I wonder what Luis told him. I can't get Luis on the phone to *save my life.* Probably thinks that I'm some stalker. Or his *other* cousin. He's a sick man. This is sick, sick, sick."

"Luis's probably got somebody else besides who probably tipped the cuz off to throw him off *his* trail."

"Not. Funny."

"It kinda is."

P. J. Harvey is screaming now, and Doris gets up to change the CD. "This is so not the kind of music to be listening to when being stalked. I'm going to put on some Johnny Cash, some old-fashioned matter-of-fact badass to toughen me up."

"Sounds good."

See, I knew this would happen with Way Gay. From the moment I met him, he was slick and phony and just plain "performative," to use grad-school language. Being a poet, and male, and therefore thinking you're God's gift is strike one, but he was always milking the Chilean thing a bit too much and then giving me knowing looks like, *Hey, we two minorities, we know the score around here.* I know there's no getting around the whole double-consciousness thing, especially in academia. It ain't no joke. But I think even Du Bois would say, Dang, tone that shit down unless you're planning on joining the Screen Actors Guild.

I try to make Doris laugh. "Now you won't ever be able to outfit your baby in little revolutionary outfits, with little matching berets for the three of you."

"You're totally demented," she says, singing along with Johnny Cash.

"Oh, wait. I forgot about the double consciousness, so some days would be beret days, and other days would be… Wait, what are considered white hats?"

"You mean hats that only white people wear?"

"Yeah."

"Okay, you're officially out of your mind. But thanks for making me more concerned for *you* than I am for myself right now." Doris gives me a side glance. "What's *not* funny is that I could be fooling around with somebody who has four, count 'em *four,* consciousnesses." She holds up four fingers.

I wrinkle my nose. "Wha?"

"Chilean conscious, Anglo conscious, straight conscious, gay conscious. That's four. No, five. He has jackass consciousness, special bonus and *fully* utilized."

"Wow," I say. "That's a whole lot of stuff going on."

Doris slaps her hand to her forehead and keeps it there. "This is the opposite of normal."

And this could be one of those nights where I get way too deep into the bottle, but it's only six, and I have to work tonight. I can't afford to be here, and I think of Mona with her two jobs and something like four hours of sleep. "D.," I say, "I have to go try to take a nap before work. But call me if you need anything."

"It sucks that you have to."

"Yep," I say. But it's an old conversation at this point.

I'm having time-management issues. I'm trying to socialize in between the factory and the classroom. Something's got to give, but I don't know what. I certainly can't fake it in Professor Lind's class, and when I'm at Valtek, I'm *at* Valtek. Ain't no goofing around at the watercooler and taking a stroll around the block when I get bored, like at my old copyediting job. Punching the time clock is like bars slamming closed once you enter the cell. It's final and ongoing until you punch out. Giving up the Office Saloon is out of the question, too, because it's the only place I tend to see what I've taken to calling "normal" people—folks who aren't university related. Some do sneak in from time to time, but I can't get too snobby and purist about it. After all, Doris, Paolo, Chris and I are university related.

I'm on my last break before I clock out for the day. It's 5:13 a.m. and I can see the sun coming up through the lounge window. The sky's a pretty lavender-and-wine color, and the sun brightens the room and takes the edge off the fluorescent lights. I started my shift at eleven, after taking a two-hour nap and after having too much at happy hour the evening before. I'm paying the piper, and no amount of Mountain Dew can help me out right now.

I put my head down on the desk, after checking the clock on the wall. I have seven minutes to rest, so I listen to the hum of the vending machines, which lull me into a half nap. I can't take a real nap because I'll fall into a deep sleep. I've slept through two earthquakes in my life and the last thing I need is Ray coming up here looking for me. Five minutes. I hear the door open so I lift my head up. It's Mona. She's not what I'd call a talker, but since my two weeks here I've found out that sometimes when you've only got a half hour or ten minutes of peace before you go back downstairs, you don't want to talk, you don't want to do anything. The first few nights I'd bring my schoolbooks in, like I was going to read something, but since then I've finally understood the concept of leisure. If you read at work at all, you read something that goes down easy, something you don't have to think about. You read for pleasure, and if you read, you read because there's nothing else more important, like massaging the pain out of your legs, or trying to keep your eyes open in the middle of the night so stacks of plastic speakers don't bunch up and go crashing to the floor.

Mona sits down across from me and flips her long black hair behind her shoulders. She picks through a newspaper that somebody left and concentrates on the coupon sections. She's got sharp green eyes that would be pretty if she didn't always look so tired.

"I'm a have to get down to Winn-Dixie when I get off work. They got chuck roast, two pounds a buck fifty." She's holding the paper up in front of her, so it looks like she's talking to it.

"Wow," I try, not knowing what else to say. I'm still not used to people speaking to me, and when they do, I don't know how to act. Much like at the university, I've not seen any other black people on my shift, so I used to think that they were just being chilly to the black girl. But, not much like at the university, I know it has nothing to do with race or being "awkward." Folks are just too damn tired to walk around all chipper and conversational and tap-dancing and shit.

Mona puts the paper back on the table and looks at me. "My kids eat so much. My boy, all he likes is meat. I try to give him a vegetable and he can barely get it down." She smiles. It's the first time I've seen her smile. "He's only eight and as big as a fifteen-year-old."

"Hmm," I manage. I'm trying to think of something to say, and I can't. Am I "awkward"?

Mona rests her forehead on her hand that's propped up on the table. She rubs her temples and sighs. "How old are your kids?"

"Me?"

She gives me the look Ray's always giving me, the look that establishes me as simple.

"Yeah. How old are they?"

For some reason I feel like I've been caught. I'm startled that she assumes I have kids, and startled, all of sudden, that I don't have any. "Oh, I don't have any kids," I reply. It sounds like an apology.

"And you're how old?" She squints at me and looks my face up and down.

"Twenty-nine."

She's still peering at me, like she's looking for something she recognizes. "Well, you're smart, I guess," she says, and she stretches her legs and arms, and yawns. "When I get off at seven, I got to go wake up my boy and my girl, get 'em washed up and dressed for school, and then I got to walk them over to the bus stop. Then I go to my second job over to Winslow gas station."

"Well," I manage. "We've only got about an hour and a half to go." But what I'm really thinking is, When does she sleep? No wonder she always looks tired. I'm just about to ask her how she does it when she's already getting up and leaving. I'm right behind her though, because my ten minutes is up.

It's the factory bell ringing and ringing and ringing. Why won't it stop? I keep wondering why it won't stop when I realize I'm dreaming and it's my phone. I keep it right by my bed, an old habit from my L.A. days, in case anyone comes into my apartment and tries to ax me while I'm sleeping. I fumble a bit before I find the thing.

"Hello?" I sound extra alert and awake, like I've been up for hours, but I have no idea what I'm saying.

"I *saw* him," Doris says on the other end. "He walked *up* to me."

"No. *Way.*" I sit up in bed and turn on my lamp so I can wake up proper.

"I was in Winn-Dixie, and this skinny man in ill-fitting soccer-wear tapped me on the shoulder."

I'm quiet until I figure out Doris isn't going to speak. "Well, what the hell *happened?*"

"It was a complete *Days of Our Lives,* daytime-television moment. God, I'm not even sure *what* he said, it was this angry, angry Spanglish hybrid-talk, but no one missed the 'Dor-ees. *Prostituta.*' And lots of hand-waving. I believe I might have been pushed."

"Damn."

"You said he wouldn't make a scene," Doris says. Her voice is shaking. "That was definitely a scene."

"God, I'm sorry. Are you okay?"

"And then he just gives me this cold-ass stare with these crazy eyes and says, real low, 'Stop it,' before he turns and walks away from me."

"Man. That's some crazy Clint Eastwood shit right there."

"Exactly."

"See, I hate this, I'm willing to go with his whole calling-you-a-whore thing—"

"Thanks a lot."

"No, but seriously, women always go after other women when they need to start knocking heads at home, and now gay men are doing it, too?" I look at my clock: 10:30 a.m.

Doris sighs. "I didn't sign on for a head-knocking. Why isn't Luis's head the one getting knocked? He's so phony. He'd probably just go and write a poem about it."

"Cain't do wrong and get by with it."

"In theory," Doris says. "In theory."

# Doris

Teaching, Weeks Two and Three: Accept Defeat.

"Accepting Defeat" seems more of a cosmic thing these days than a strictly teaching thing. Getting attacked at Winn-Dixie: deeply not my fantasy. It *sucked*. And you know if there'd have been a $3.99 can of dumb-ass in aisle ten, I would have handed it over and said, "Okay, go 'head." But whoop-ass? That's what the "cousin" was laying on, and that I refuse to accept. Unfortunately, the only Spanish I could think of in the moment was *"me llamo Doris,"* which he obviously already knew, and "Luis is a LIAR," which didn't seem to be translating. I *knew* better than to listen to Luis. He told me, when he first started with, "Doris, you know how people in this department love to label things, make drama where there isn't any. What you've heard, forget it. My feelings for you are strong, real, *physical*. I think sexuality is more like a

river, you let it wash over you and take you where it may."
River? More like a cesspool. New dating math for Doris:
sexual fluidity=confused-ass bullshit. I almost felt sorry
for the "cousin." His eyes looked weepy, and his voice kept
cracking. Dor-eeees. The "whore" thing was way too
much since there ain't a local in Langsdale who can't
translate *prostituta*.

"I loathe him," I said to Ronnie on the phone. "And
to think, I was so *blinded* by the fact that he liked my poetry, like he helped me rediscover my voice, like he's the
original Jesus Christ of iambic pentameter, and I'm just
some dumb-ass waiting at the bus stop for any asshole to
pick me up, show me the way, fly me to Jonestown and
pass me the Kool-Aid."

"He's one prize ass," Ronnie said, "But do *not* self-
flagellate over that man. Do not do it."

"He's a liar and a coward. And he doesn't even have
the balls, yeah, the one tiny ball it would take to pick up
the phone when I call to ask what on God's green and
beautiful earth might have been going through his mind."

"But you knew that about him," Ronnie points out.
"I'm not excusing him, no way, but you shoulda known
that 'way gay' mighta had a little glimmer of truth to it.
You don't see us nicknaming Earl 'way gay,' do ya?"

"I thought he was a sensitive man," I said. "A tender
human being. A human being who believed in beauty
and poetry."

It's probably a blessing I haven't seen Luis. Someone
said that he packed up and left town. This morning,
though, before I have to teach TROOPS (and might I
say, that was my worst nightmare, standing in Winn-
Dixie, accepting Biblical retribution for a nonexistent

wrongdoing, the idea that one of my students might have been in aisle eleven, listening close and buying construction paper to handcraft my very own scarlet "A"), I check my e-mail and—like chickenshit clockwork—Luis has written. He has the *nerve* to send me an e-mail. Not even call like a half-decent half-gay Chilean jackassito.

Doris, I am so sorry that Armando found you
like that. Please know that I never meant
to hurt you or him. I'm trying to know where
I stand myself these days, what I want and
how to get it, how to live. I am trying to
be true to who I am, true to Armando, and
true to you. Sometimes life gets in the way
of who we want to be. Believe that your
beautiful voice has meant the world to me.
Please keep a door open for us until things
settle down.

I'm so angry I can barely see straight, and I have to teach in twenty minutes. No time to respond properly, but I feel the need to respond *promptly,* so I type: All doors
closed. Have been called a "whore" in front
of respectable shoppers. Over it. Locked
door and threw away key. Please. Go Away.

I was trying to think of something more clever, or mean, but at a certain point the only thing left to be said is, "No. No. Thanks, but No." Oprahism: "No is a complete answer." Move on to nonmarried Chris, teach the kids how to write, don't ruin self over incredible, nigh-on-unbelievable lack of judgment, don't overdo the shopping therapy. Don't keep door open for Way Gay Faux Che.

"You okay?" I hear from over my shoulder, so I send the e-mail without rereading it, and close out the window as quickly as possible. Chris pulls up a chair beside me and looks at me like I'm some charity case. "You don't look so hot."

It's all I can do not to burst into tears, because if I cry now, I'll look like Armando in the Winn-Dixie when I go to teach. That's blood-in-the-water, classroomwise.

"Rough week," I say. I have on the same outfit that I was wearing the last time he saw me, and I don't even have the energy to care. My one wish at this exact moment is that I don't literally smell. Chris reaches over and rubs my knee. I push his hand away, not because I want him to stop but because this small kindness might precipitate a grossly decontextualized nervous breakdown. "I have to go."

"How about this weekend?" he asks. "I'll take you out. It can't be that bad."

"Oh," I say. "Don't bet on that. But it's getting better. Like lancing a boil."

"Or castratin' a pig," he says, taking on the most performatively hickified voice I've ever heard. "Just hold tight and lop it off, pig won't know what hit it."

"Please tell me you do not actually know how to castrate a pig."

"Darlin'," he continues, not breaking voice, "I castrate 'em so sweet they thank me for the service."

"Really?" I say, finally laughing a bit, trying to sound like a faux-farm-girl myself. "'Cause I know some other large mammals that might be in need of a good loppin'."

"Just pigs, ma'am," he says. "Night out. This weekend. Now go teach, you're late."

★ ★ ★

Okay, before I start in on teaching these past few weeks, I would like to say that I *wish* that I lived in a world where high school teachers were paid a million dollars every year, and bad teenage actors on shit sitcoms got minimum wage for their efforts. I wish. If that were the case, I might not go home at night, shaking my head in disbelief at what my students haven't learned. They don't understand to break long passages of text into paragraphs. They have no baseline recognition of the difference between "their, they're and there." Or, God forbid, the more intimidating "its vs. it's." Subjects and verbs do not agree, prepositions regularly end sentences, and the computer thesaurus is so misused as to madden the most generous of readers. Try explaining to Claus that "a hard-knock life" and a "difficult rap existence" really don't mean the same thing to your average reader, and risk being looked at like you are God's original dumb bitch, because his computer told him so.

And this is not unique to TROOPS. In fact, during the school year I've had such hooked-on-phonics moments as reading "Ruffly tend percent" or, my personal favorite, "manageeter," which, in conference with the student, I realized was a sound-it-out attempt at "ménage à trois." I'll get to why my students might be using such a phrase, but for now, I'll stick with the class at hand. Claus is tap-dancing on my very last nerve. Luckily (and I never thought I'd be saying this), he listens to Zach. And Zach, I must begrudgingly admit, is a darn good teacher. When I finally arrive at the classroom this afternoon, atypically late, Zach has arrived miraculously early and is talking to them about their final paper.

"You get to analyze advertisements," he says. "Find out how the media, these big corporations, manipulate your desire so you want things that you don't even need."

He's back in prototypical Zach-wear: a ripped T-shirt and cutoff jean shorts. Because he's male, and the tutor, he can get away with this. I still have to dress "teacherly" in my black pencil skirt and white eyelet blouse because I am female and because I assign them their actual grades. But I've added my beret to the outfit. Because I like it.

Claus makes a gigantic yawning motion. His hair is shaved close to his head, and he has on a black tank top with a thick, gold chain around his neck anchoring a giant gold-and-rhinestone C.

"You're above that, eh, Claus," Zach says.

"Yeah," Claus says.

"Don't be disrespecting Zach," Sharelle says, thumping Claus on the back of the head with her folder. Sharelle has dark, almost red-brown skin, but she wears bright blue "fashion" contact lenses. Unsettling, especially since she fished one out of her eyeball during the first class and sat there, unfazed, with one Technicolor-blue eye and one honey-brown scrutinizing the rest of the group. She's thin, with a tangle of braids piled atop her head, and if I had to guess, I'd say from the amount of banter between her and Claus that there might be something going on outside of class. Sharelle's first paper was a C minus, but she raised her last paper to a B, thus her enthusiasm for the final paper. She's gained steam and is ready to roll.

"You don't think any of this has any practical application, do you, Claus?"

Zach doesn't say it like it's an attack, but like Claus is just too smart for the rest of us.

"Nope," Claus says.

"You think the media influences the way you dress?"

"Nope."

"You think Doris woke up this morning and thought 'Hey, I'm going to look like a French stewardess this morning,' or do you think it's because she's seen that look in some magazines, on some actress or something?"

Claus turns his head and looks at me. I smile. He doesn't smile back. "You seen what else she wears?" he asks. "I think she thinks that shit up herself."

"Thanks, Claus," I say, moving to the front of the room. "And you decided to get that tattoo, and pierce your ears, and wear those jeans solely because you like them."

"Yeah," Claus says. "I look good."

Sharelle rolls her eyes from behind him.

"What brand are your jeans?" I ask.

"Tommy," he announces. "Ain't no white-boy Abercrombie shit. Tommy Hilfiger."

Will, whose face I can barely see from beneath a St. Louis Cardinals baseball cap, shifts noticeably in his seat.

"Can we try swearing less," I say. "Just for today. And why did you buy those? Would it make a difference if you were wearing Wrangler?"

Sharelle laughs, "I'd like to see you in some Wranglers, cowboy."

"Wranglers are some punk-ass, bitch jeans," he says.

"Okay, this is where I want you to start, all of you, in thinking about this next assignment. Why does Claus wear Tommy, and why are Wranglers 'punk-ass, bitch' jeans? You notice how he uses homophobic language to talk about the jeans, it makes it 'more masculine' to wear Tommy, and in the same way, marginalizes women and gays, since 'punk-ass bitch' implies homosexuality and femininity. Wranglers are for bitches and being a bitch is baaaad. But Tommy jeans, who do you think of when you think of Tommy jeans?"

"My boyfriend from high school," Tina pipes in. Her shirt reads, "Stop Looking At My Chest." Normally, Tina's part of the fashion-priestess trinity, but today she has her dark hair back in a short ponytail and no makeup. She looks like a fresh-faced kid, like she probably looks in her baby pictures.

"Mine, too," Linda says. Linda's in full makeup, blond hair lightened and blown straight down her back.

"How many of you own Tommy jeans?" I ask.

Two-thirds of the hands go up.

"And what about Abercrombie? Any of you wear those?"

Will doesn't speak, but raises his hand tall and defiant.

"So at least one person—Will—wears Abercrombie."

"Figures," Claus says, barely audible but *audible*.

"Excuse me," I say.

"What?" Claus asks.

"I like Abercrombie," Tina interrupts a bit reluctantly. "I think they make nice shirts."

"What if I told you," I say, "that ten years ago Abercrombie was about as hip as Wrangler, but they got some folks together, found some hip kids to advertise it, changed the image, and now their business is booming. In fact, their ads are often considered 'controversial,' which is another way of selling things. So I'd like for you all to think about that, why you want the things you want. Do you buy things because a celebrity endorses them, or because they seem sexy or powerful? Everyone bring in an ad of your choosing to the next class, and we'll talk in greater detail about the final paper."

Zach and I have taken to meeting after class in the coffee shop to go over grades and plot teaching strategies. Ratty clothes aside, I think that dating Mandy is shaping him up, as he manages to keep his hands off his feet, and he looks *cleaner* somehow. His hair has even grown out, and with a slight tan, he's almost, almost, almost got that whole Harvey Keitel thing happening again. It's a good thing there's no pink wine at the coffee shop.

"Thanks," I say. "Great idea to use me as an example, really give Claus something to sink his teeth into. Just pin a target over my chest next time."

We're quiet for a minute because the important undergrad behind the counter is grinding coffee.

"I was trying to get him involved in the ideas," Zach says, opening a third packet of sugar. "He's a really smart guy. In tutorial, when he can keep the mouthing off to a minimum, he's the best reader of other students' work in the group. He's probably been bored his whole life. At least in school. And you did a great job setting up the assignment. I don't think he hates you, I just think he likes to pretend that he does. And the rest of them are enjoying the class. They say so in the smaller groups."

"I just wish he'd tone down the smart-mouth. He made a comment about Linda's breasts the other day," I say, nursing my latte. "In class, and that's the last thing she needs. Claus may have been bored in school, but Linda needs a lot of help. She doesn't need Claus pointing out that her shirt is white, and he sure hopes it rains. What she *needs* is to learn the function of topic sentences so she can break a D on her next paper. I almost walked across the room and clocked him."

"So what'd you do?" Zach asks. He keeps his eyes on me while reaching into his backpack and pulling out a wad of blue yarn and two thin silvery needles.

"What," I ask, "is that?"

"Mandy's teaching me to knit," he says. "I can do it while we're talking. It's harder than you think. You ever knit before?"

"No," I say while he deftly loops the yarn in place. "Looks like you're a natural."

"Do I detect a note of sarcasm?"

"What would Claus say?"

Zach smiles. I try not to let my own preconceived notions about "masculinity" get the best of me, but there's a huge portion of me that's thinking, *Oh, God, Zach. Don't knit in public. You're not Rosie Grier. You look…*and the word I'm thinking is *girlie,* which at the end of the day, makes me no different from Claus.

"I think it's cool," I say. "You can make me a hat when you get good."

"Don't lie," Zach says. "You're the worst liar, Doris. It's okay, I'm comfortable with my sexuality. Knitting doesn't make me less of a man. Real men knit their own sweaters."

And I'm thinking that Mandy must be trying to turn him into a lesbian, but know that's the sort of comment best kept to one's self, even if it would be directed to Zach.

"No they don't. I swear, I am actually trying to think it's cool. But maybe you should do it in front of a mirror and look at yourself, and tell me if it doesn't look just a little crazy."

"Claus," he says. "What'd you tell him?"

"I kept him after and told him that just because he's intelligent enough to find other things to do in class besides listen to me, it doesn't mean that other students don't need all the help they can get, and he should respect that. Then I told him that if he disrupted class like that again, he'd be cordially uninvited back for all eternity."

"Good," Zach says. "You think it worked?"

"Who knows? I'm just glad that Linda came back. I think that I was more mortified than she was."

"You look at their papers? I think they're getting somewhere. Ali's was really good, an A minus easy in any freshman comp class. And Sharelle is really sharp. She's good at keeping Claus in his place. Keep her as your secret weapon."

My latte is cold but I'm too tired to get up and reheat it.

"She's supposed to be absent tomorrow. Doctor's appointment or something."

"Do you ever wonder," Zach asks, "what they've been doing the past twelve years?"

"Probably driving some poor, underpaid, overworked soul who thought teaching would be a noble pursuit out of his or her damn mind. I can't even imagine five classes like this in one day. The hormone levels alone might send me into perimenopause. I just wish they'd all read a few books or something between episodes of *Jackass* or *The Real World,* or whatever they watch."

"Sometimes I wonder if I might not teach high school after all of this is over," Zach says. "I like the kids better at this age. I think I'd just have to get a master's in education."

"Education?" I say. "After ten years working on your Ph.D. in English? You want to grow old and die here?"

"Thanks, Mom," he says. "It just seems like a good thing to do. I never taught TROOPS before, and it reminds me why I liked teaching in the first place. At least they're excited to be at college, ready to learn."

"So you'd still finish your Ph.D.?"

"Why not?" Zach asks. "I started it. Why not finish it?"

"But it's so much of your life. Doesn't it feel kind of like that soap opera, the 'like sands through the hourglass' kind of thing. I can't imagine starting another degree."

Zach stops for a moment and undoes his last three rows of knitting. Rehooks the needle and begins again.

"That's the difference between us," Zach says. "I don't really see what I'm doing out here as separate from another life. I like this life. If it goes on like this five more years, I'll be grateful. Maybe by the end of my education degree I'll want to be a fireman, or join the peace corps. You gotta roll with your life."

And although I am never quite able to let go of the fact that this advice is being given by a man who is knitting, who is dating a lesbian, no less, he just might be right.

Two nights later, Paolo, Ronnie and I are thick in our weekly Office Saloon decompression. Earl makes us a whole pitcher of martinis, mostly to impress Ronnie, but they taste so good that I'm almost thinking of trading in the bourbon for vodka. When Earl is making martinis, I do a mental digital enhancement of his image. I try to picture him with a slightly better haircut, at a hipper-than-thou bar in the Village, with a classy, vintage BMW instead of the canonical Langsdale Harley-Davidson. His cheeks are sunburned a warm red-brown, and I can tell by the way he looks at Ronnie, that from where he's standing, she doesn't need any "enhancing."

"What was I smoking," Paolo asks, "when I signed on board to train these little hyenas. I cannot get them to shut up. Giggle, giggle, giggle at the barre. Giggle in the center. Giggle as they *pas du chat* across the room. It's ballet. Ballet. Ballet is *not* funny."

Paolo has just started teaching a summer camp for high-school girls who want to be ballerinas.

"It's kind of funny," Ronnie says. "When Doris used to do it, it was funny."

I got to know Paolo first semester when I took his ballet class for elective credit. Paolo would make the women in my class wear dance skirts and pink tights and black leotards, just like we were little girls. Only we're all hauling at least a hundred fifty pounds of woman-flesh on our frames, so the girliness got lost pretty easily. And he made us do a recital at the end, wherein I hobbled through some bastardized "Dance of the Sugar Plum Fairies," which Ronnie attended, and which I shall never live down.

"They probably just think you're cute," I say. "And what I was doing in that class may have been called ballet, but you shouldn't have that in mind when you hear the word ballet."

"Of course they think I'm cute," Paolo agrees. "They're ballerinas. They're genetically programmed to fall in love with only gay men until they're twenty, sometimes thirty, but that's the malnutrition kicking in by then. But they're giving me a headache."

"Don't talk to me about headaches," Ronnie says. "I still have the sound of machinery ringing in my skull."

"No better?" I ask.

"It's okay…" Ronnie concedes. "I like this one woman, Mona. She's funny in that real practical way, like she doesn't mean to be, but still knows she is. And I did have a legit good time on my last break with her and Ray. They were killing each other over what Mona saw the other day at the Winn-Dixie."

"Oh, God," I say. "Do I want to hear this?"

"Seems that Mona was running in to get some chuck for her kids when this whole scene erupted in the soda-pop aisle."

"What did she say?" I ask.

"Only that some foreign man was chewing out this lady, calling her a whore. And the whore-lady was just staring at him, in her high heels and short skirt. Then Mona launched into a bit about how her first husband 'lost his way' at one of the massage parlors in town, and now it looked like there wasn't a safe place left. Out of the back alleys and into the supermarkets."

"So she didn't know I was from the university or anything?" I ask.

"Doris," Paolo says. "Hello? She thought you were an actual hooker. How is that better?"

"She thought I was an actual hooker?"

Ronnie grins. "'The Dixie Ho,' Ray said."

This is officially one of the top-ten worst weeks of my life.

"Did you say that I wasn't?" I ask Ronnie. "Did you say that in fact you know me, that I am not an actual hooker?"

"I know you?" Ronnie asks with a straight face. "Them's respectable folks at Valtek. I ain't telling them nothin' about the Dixie Ho."

"Not funny," I say.

"Kind of," Paolo adds. "The Dixie Ho."

He's cracking himself up so hard that he's practically rocking off his bar stool.

"I hate my life," I say.

"You'll love this," Paolo states. "You know that bottle blonde who cuts hair in town—the one who looks like a drag queen, but isn't? Well, she and Luis seem to be an 'official' item now. Saw them the other night walking down the street, arm in arm."

"I think I'm going to be sick," I say. "Poor Armando."

And later that night, I am sick. Sick to my stomach from the martinis, sick of Luis, sick of the fact that the world seems to be full of folks who get away with all kinds of nonsense, yet I get to pay publicly and in real time for things I didn't even do. I decide that tomorrow, I'm turning over an entirely new leaf. Less alcohol. Less funny business at the Office Saloon. More writing, which is what I came to Langsdale to do anyhow. I am going to strap myself to my computer at least two hours a day and try to get something accomplished this summer—something other than garnering nonflattering nicknames at the local *tienda*. Further, I am going to call my sister and really help out with the wedding. Get on with planning her wedding shower, though I'm technically opposed to it since they generally only address the marital areas of cooking and fucking: pots, pans and lingerie. Mondo-retro in the gender department. Who am I to judge another person, least of all my sister, for sliding into the retro-bridal thing? After all, I rowed right onto Doris Day/Rock Hudson fantasy-island, and that's about the most retro shit playing this side of Nick at Night. And stop swearing.

★ ★ ★

When I tell Ronnie my plan for reform the next day, she says:

"You're gonna stop swearing? Didn't you try that for Lent one year and it happened for all of ten minutes?"

Professor Lind gave her seminar the day off, so Ronnie and I are able to take our "nature walk," ambling around the outdoor track while the more devoted runners lap us repeatedly.

"God's on my side this time," I say. "Did you hear that storm last night? It was the angels cheering for my dirty mouth coming clean."

Last night it rained something brutal. The sky blushed this crazy tornado-green shade in the late afternoon, and by nine-thirty in the evening it was hailing and the sirens were sounding off. One thing I learned about second-story apartments when I moved to the Midwest is that while they may be a city gal's idea of safe, being a greater challenge than ground-floor apartments for your average pervert and/or serial killer, basement apartments are the way to go in the event of a tornado. I think that I'm supposed to lie down in my bathtub with a mattress over my head if one touches down. To my citified mind, it seems like a "kiss your ass goodbye" kind of proposition, but I assume that the weather folks know more than I do. At any rate, you'd never know from today's sky that anything had happened. It's eighty degrees, no humidity, and it's so blue outside it barely looks real.

"I guess it did rain pretty hard last night," Ronnie says. "I didn't notice so much."

"You didn't notice?" I ask. "The emergency sirens were going off. How could you not hear that?"

Ronnie shrugs.

"Could be the lifetime of earthquakes, or being tired as a slave, or maybe I was listening to something a little more exciting."

"*Really,*" I say, appropriately baited.

"One La Varian called last night and left a message on my machine to ask if I might not want to attend a moving-picture show with him this weekend. All gentleman-like and proper-datelike and everything. That's got to be more exciting than some old tornado. Tornadoes we get all the time."

"Okay, given how very few human beings of the adult-male variety who we actually know, might I make the analytical leap that this is our Day-Glo-T-shirt man?"

Ronnie nods. "The more I think about it, the more I don't care about his odd-color shirt selection. Black goes with everythang."

"How'd you manage to pull that off?"

"Take a wild guess," Ronnie says. "Who, besides me, would be most frothing at the mouth over a real-live handsome specimen of African-American manhood? Who would be trying to 'out-black' him with her knowledge of Bessie Smith and Miles Davis and Duke Ellington and her whole black menagerie of jazz greats?"

"Iris."

"Only good thing to come of having that woman in class this summer. They were talking in the hall yesterday before we went in, and Iris had to introduce me because I was there and smiling. I knew she didn't want to. She had that crazy 'mine all mine' look on her face. He was running her up and down a pole, too. I swear, I don't think she has a damn bit of sense."

"So did you get a feel for him?" I ask. "Did you find out what he's doing here this summer?"

"Not totally sure," Ronnie admits. "But he's definitely intense. He did mention something about reading his chapter."

"My, my," I say. "Barely a conversation and already out with the chapters."

"Can't blame a brother for trying," she says. "Plus, I haven't seen a chapter in so long I'm not even sure what to do with one anymore." She fans a swarm of gnats away from her face. "Luis ever write you back?"

"No, but the hell with him. What's he going to say? 'Sorry, I can't figure out how gay I am?' I do have a date with Chris this weekend. He cheered me up in my hour of greatest need."

"I thought Zach did that."

"No," I say. "Zach fed me to the wolves. Then he knit himself a hat."

Ronnie laughs. "I still think you're getting a little sweet on him."

"I'm learning not to hate him," I say. "Let's not get carried away."

While the attempt to curb my swearing may be doomed from the outset, I am able to spend a quiet and productive evening at home writing. I start a poem about Luis, then I start a poem about the weather, then I start a poem for my sister's wedding. I'd like to have something special to read for Lisa and Marvin, my sister and her hunka-hunka-burning lawyer. The poem about Luis isn't so much about him as it is about voice: specifically finding it and keeping it. It's hard for me to stay mad at Luis, since a year ago, I couldn't sit down at a computer without feeling physically ill. One of the dangers of turning the thing you love most into your bread and butter is that you can make it pedestrian—take it for granted the way you might a really good boyfriend, or clean air, or doors you don't have to lock at night. After years of graduate school, and years of writing workshops in the city before that, I couldn't even hear my own voice through the clutter. I'd sit down at the computer and I'd hear *I'm not sure what the speaker means by that word*. Or, *That last line strikes me as inauthentic, manufactured. I'd like a greater sense of vitality*. Or, *I'm sure that I'm just not the intended audience for this piece*. I'd write two lines, and instead of seeing those actual lines, I'd see them the way the twelve other poets in workshop were going to see them: like legs dangling under the water's surface in one of those killer-shark movies. And I froze up. I couldn't write anymore.

Luis may be a pretentious philanderer, but he loves language in a way that no other poet I've met comes close to matching. Probably because he has that satellite dish in his house and embraces pop culture. He doesn't "rank" words the way some poets do. He'd get as excited about the way "bootylicious" could be used in a poem as he might "sinewy." For me, Luis's feedback was like the gates of heaven opening. I felt as if I'd been given permission to take in the whole world again, not just the arcane references and pretentious spin-offs. And if by taking in Luis as well, I took in a wee bit too much of that world, I'm glad that even though he's gone, I have this part of me back. The part of me that trusts how I see things.

# Ronnie

La Varian wears a lot of jewelry. I don't know how I never noticed *that* before. The simple gold chain I don't mind. It's even elegant. It's the bracelets and rings that are a little weird, a little…flamboyant. On the one hand, I like La Varian's flair—the wild colors and the jewelry—because it's a breath of fresh air in the land of Brooks Brothers. It's so not English department. For a *woman,* even, it's so not English department. So, because he's hitting on me as hard as he is, I'm filing my observations away and I'm just going to enjoy being out with an outrageously handsome black man. I don't pay attention to what he's saying half the time. I just nod. Though all the while I'm looking at his long delicate fingers and admiring the silky dark skin. My skin's always changing colors now that I've moved to the Midwest. Grayish and blotchy in the winter, but an even caramel in the summer. Thank God it's summer.

"So, Miss Veronica Williams," he says, stroking his impeccable goatee. "How's a sista been keeping herself in a town like Langsdale?" His index finger glances my knee, for emphasis, I guess. It's one of the rare times—in these days of Valtek—that I'm wearing a dress, and we're sitting outside on the deck of the Vineyard—one of the more high-end restaurants in town—at La Varian's insistence. I look down at my knees when I feel his finger, and when I look up at him, he's peering at me over his glass of Maker's Mark.

I give him a quizzical look and direct him around the deck with the arch of my eyebrow. He looks around at the all-white clientele and chuckles. "I *have* made some really good friends though, like Doris, and my friend, Paolo. You've probably seen Doris around. Tall, dark hair, fashionably fierce."

"Wait." La Varian leans into me. "Does she wear a beret all the time?"

"That's her."

"Ha!" He leans back in his chair and then crosses his legs. *So what, he's crossing his legs,* I say to myself. *It's Eu-ro-pe-an.*

"I see her all the time," he says, picking something off his pants and rubbing his fingers together until whatever it was has been carried away with the breeze. "What a character." He drops one hand atop the other on his lap so that he looks like a model casually reclining.

The smile I'd maintained all evening to appear amenable and eager so that the pretty man will like me fades just a little bit.

"What do you mean, 'character'?"

"No, it's just funny, the beret. She always looks like

Marcel Marceau or a guerrilla or something. It definitely takes…effort, that look."

I decide he's allowed to talk a certain amount of shit because he doesn't know Doris, and hell, if I saw her wandering around, I'd notice the outfits, too. Neither of us has managed to one-hundred-percent blend. Also, I don't allow myself to envision *his* past outfits, and I don't allow myself to look closely at the striped *billowy* pants he's wearing, because I'm drinking alcohol and I might say something my mother raised me not to say. I don't think a man should own billowy anything, but if you look like La Varian, you can get away with it—for now.

"Well, anyway, that's Doris," I say. "And there's Paolo. He's from California, too. Used to dance—ballet—but now he's just teaching it and trying to get his degree in theater."

La Varian motions to the waiter. "Are you ready to order?"

I shrug and then nod, but the waiter doesn't seem to notice La Varian's motion, and he wanders off inside the restaurant. La Varian's eyes follow the waiter and his mouth sets into a tight pucker. He swirls his ice cubes in his glass. "Dang. Theater *and* ballet. Must be gay."

This is the moment brought to me by God. My chance to finally know, Is he is, or is he ain't? I take a deep breath before taking the figurative plunge. I laugh, loud and phony. "Actually, I almost thought *you* were gay. Isn't that silly? Hee Hee," I say behind my hand. La Varian doesn't see the fingers crossed on my other hand underneath the table.

He flicks his wrist dismissively. "People always think that about me, just because I wear a lot of flamboyant things, jewelry and whatnot. I like gorgeous things," he explains, looking at me and giving me a slow grin. "I like gorgeous things, Miss Veronica Williams. But I am not gay. I'll prove that to you soon enough," he says. He runs his hand over his shaved head and stares me down.

I have to fan myself and shift in my seat after he says that. I blame it on the summer heat, but the truth is, I'm wondering, how soon is now?

"Can I offer you a drink?" I ask La Varian because, of course, he's in my apartment already. What can I say? Dinner was *good*.

"I better slow down," he says. "I've had a lot to drink already." I counted his drinks, and La Varian's "a lot" is my "just getting started." I should slow down, too, on both the drinks and on trying to get La Varian naked, but you can't show a starving woman a steak and expect her to count calories. Black men don't pass through Langsdale, and beautiful, black, *single* men, who happen to be Ph.D.'s are as rare as a goddamn leprechaun. Better believe it's time for a buffet.

He wanders around my apartment looking at pictures and pulling books from the shelves. "This is a nice place. Very grad school, writerly funky."

I scan the paintings and photos given to me by my friends in L.A. and am slightly self-conscious about all the little toys and pop-culture amusements scattered around my apartment. Like the Tweety Bird Pez dispenser and the Slinky framing Cornel West's *Black Matters* on my bookshelf. "Thank you?" I say and he laughs.

"No, I'm serious. This feels like you, this place. It feels how you *are*."

A line about him taking his hands and feeling how I am passes through my mind, but I decide not to be that damn easy. A hungry person can choke on a steak, too. So instead I say thank-you and ask him to pick out some music while I go get a glass of water.

I'm in the kitchen when I hear him laughing again. I come out swirling the ice in my glass. "What's so funny?"

"What are these CDs you have?" he asks. He's crouching and has two CDs in his hands. His striped pants sweep against my hardwood floor.

"What?"

"Who in the hell are The Smiths, and sure, intellectually I understand the significance of the Sex Pistols, but *please*. You don't really listen to this stuff, do you?"

I smile, but I don't like the way he makes me feel with that question. "Sure. I *really* like it. The Smiths are good eighties music. British and morose and all that."

La Varian shakes his head and puts the CDs back—not where he got them—but back. "You have a lot of crazy-white-folks stuff in here, but luckily you got some old-school stuff, too." He picks up my Isley Brothers CD and shakes it at me. "Good music."

I love the Isley Brothers. It's solid music, music I grew up on. But so are The Smiths and REO Speedwagon (I know, arguable), and thank God he didn't see *them*. I didn't like being made to feel glad that La Varian stopped teasing me about my music. I hadn't had this kind of conversation since I was in fifth grade. *Are you a surfer or a cholo? Surfers listen to rock, and cholos listen to black stuff.* Since I was clearly not a surfer and not one of the Mexican kids in low-riders listening to oldies, I never really ever made a choice. I listened to what I liked. This was all sociopolitical, racial-identity shit about which I didn't want to have no lengthy anthropological, historical, rhetorical "discourse" right now. I didn't give a good goddamn. That's for Professor Lind's class on Monday, now I'll undress La Varian to *make sure* he isn't a leprechaun.

The next morning I watch La Varian sleep, and stare and stare at him, as if I've never seen a black person before. I like that he's here, in my bed. It feels like the start of something. When he turns his back to me, I run a line down his back, wanting him to wake up, but he doesn't. Even though it's early in the morning, it's hot anyway, so I get up and turn on the air-conditioning, which is almost as loud as being at Valtek. My apartment is old, i.e., dilapidated by L.A. standards, and though the air-conditioning is loud, it feels as if someone with an ice cube in his mouth is just blowing really hard. Not cold, but better than nothing. La Varian sleeps like the dead, just like me, so I decide to leave him alone and make myself coffee. I put on some Dinah Washington, after deciding it won't wake up La Varian. I might actually be happy. This might actually be okay. I hum along with Dinah, singing about the world being a showplace.

Television will mess you up, because I have all the scenes, all the episodes, of my future life looping over and over in my head. I'll be like Debra Winger being lifted off her feet at the factory. Except it won't be the military that'll be my ticket out. It'll be my own book of fiction, and my hot-professor husband. The über-black couple, Cliff and Clair Huxtable—deluxe—if that's possible. All my life I've kept my eye on the prize, the ultimate brother, while dating just about anybody in the Rainbow Coalition. An Italian, fine. British, fine. Regular white American, fine. But La Varian, he was more than fine.

"Trying to pull an Iris?"

I was staring out the window and fantasizing about Theo and Denise and Rudy. I'd practically forgotten that I had the real thing in my bedroom.

"Pull an Iris?"

La Varian had put his clothes on from last night, but he walked heavy and barefoot toward me. He sat down on my couch and stretched his legs out over my lap.

"You know, Dinah, the jazz…"

I started arranging his pant legs, pulling them toward me because they looked bunched up and uncomfortable. They didn't look so, so *homosexual* in the light of day, and not after last night.

"What's wrong with that girl, anyway?" I ask.

He shakes his head.

"Your *girlfriend*." I wink at him and he pinches me.

"She's just another white person in love with black people of the past. Safe black folks. For people like her, black folks have to be from the twenties or some shit before they get invited into her house. Let my cousin J.B. come around with his pants hanging off his ass and see what happens. She'd run calling for the police if a modern-day brother—without a damn trumpet in his hand—tried to talk to her."

"She invited you to her house. *You're* a 'modern-day' brother."

"Yep, but I'm cleaned up, pasteurized, and—"

"So bright and articulate!"

"I hate that shit!" he says, laughing. He stares at me for a minute. "I had a great time last night. Thank you. I didn't know how I was going to pass the time this summer. I started thinking I'd just have to throw myself into research and just get the hell out when I was done. Now I've met you."

I smile and take his hand. Rudy, Theo, Denise! "I wish I didn't have to worry about going to work tonight."

"Work? What do you do at *night*? Aren't you teaching?"

"No, I'm not teaching. Long story. I work at a factory outside of town."

La Varian sits up straight. "No you *don't*."

I nod. "Yep. Through a temp agency. It's the only thing that this person, in this town, could find to do."

"I don't believe you," La Varian insists, staring at me. "I'm sure you could have done better than *that*."

"Not really."

La Varian blows out a short puff of air. "What about waitressing at least? Or working at some stupid store in the mall? Hell, the GAP is always hiring."

"There *is* no GAP in Langsdale."

"Yeah, right. That's funny," La Varian says.

"La Varian." I lock eyes with him. "Seriously. The GAP closed two years ago."

His mouth hangs open. "*Damn*. I never heard of that before."

"Exactly. This is not a city. There are no jobs for people like me, people who aren't genius in an office. And I've never waitressed or *anything* like that. Besides, the 'real' jobs go to folks who are actually *from* Langsdale, who *live* in Langsdale. Not folks passing through like me. I'm a student, a teacher and a writer. School is out, I didn't get a teaching assignment, and last I checked, nobody is paying folks to sit around on their asses all day and 'create.'"

He shakes his head and throws up his hands. "All right. Whatever you say."

I try to read his face but can't, really. I seem to see something like confusion and disappointment. It's been a month since I've been working at Valtek, and to tell you the truth, I'm used to it. I got used to it *fast,* even. That happens when you don't have choices. I actually enjoy it occasionally, with Mona and Ray and whoever else has turned into a familiar face. La Varian looks at me, and I think he's going to ask me about the job, and I really want to tell him that it's interesting to me.

"That coffee looks good," he says. He takes the mug out of my hand and swallows a sip.

"I'm sorry!" I quickly apologize. "Bad manners. Let me get you a cup." La Varian lifts his legs so I can move. I'll tell him about the job, eventually, even though he hasn't asked. But for now, I'll get him his coffee. When I stand up and tighten the belt on my robe, he reclines on my couch with his feet propped up on my coffee table and rests his arms behind his head. He looks as if he's lived with me, in this apartment, his whole life.

# Doris

Ronnie has, as the title of the song says, "The Ways of a Woman in Love." Sure she still answers the phone and makes the obligatory Office Lounge appearances, but her dance card has filled up mightily. Of course, she does have the night job, the Shakespeare, and with La Varian, it's a wonder she hasn't become a member of the actual walking-dead. I can't say my schedule's been that much more forgiving. Grading has hit nightmare proportions. I swear that I have students for whom it takes me longer to grade their papers than it ever did for them to write.

Today, I'm keeping Will after class. Will is my canonical "farm boy." He is in no way, shape or form an actual idiot, but after three and a half weeks of TROOPS, he still refuses to speak. He just glares at the rest of the class, rolls his eyes, huffs his shoulders, taps his feet, cracks his knuckles. It's like watching a silent movie where I'm waiting for the character's head to explode off his body. And, might I add, he is one of the students who most needs TROOPS. TROOPS is supposed to pick up the public-school slack for students of *every* color. It's just sometimes harder to convince certain white students, students like Will who've probably coasted through on good looks and not causing trouble, that they *really do need help.* In fact, while TROOPS is racially diverse, it's solidly working class. No tax base=no good schools, no matter what your race, color or creed. I think that out of an entire three-page paper, there are exactly three *sentences* of Will's that make literal sense.

So I keep him after class to talk about his writing.

Which doesn't exactly help.

Will is going to have a grand old time, let me tell you, once the semester begins. He's tall, broad-shouldered, with straw-blond hair and watery blue eyes. His face is equal mixture freckled-tan and sunburn, and his baseball cap might actually be surgically attached to his skull. The signature piece of every farm-boy's uniform.

"What did you mean by this sentence?" I ask him, pointing to something that reads: *He's got no point here with the things they're going after in the picture's selling what they thing you want.* It's actually written in English, but sadly, not a recognizable form.

He shrugs.

"Come on, Will, you wrote it. Who's the 'he'? Are you talking about a critic? What's your thesis?"

The "thesis" is basically the "argument," and while

every paper is *supposed* to have one, I'd say that about sixty-six percent of them actually *do*.

"You know," he says. "That article we read. The guy who wrote it. What he was saying about packages and things being in packages, how you buy the packages. *You* assigned it."

"I know what I assigned," I say. "And I know who the author is, but you have to assume that it's not going to be me reading your paper. That you have a 'reader' who won't know what you mean unless you tell her."

Will checks his watch. I can't tell if he doesn't understand or just doesn't care.

"So are you a professor?" he asks. "A real professor?"

This is the oldest trick in the book. Deflect attention from the problem at hand by shifting the potential head-flying-off-the-body from him to me.

"I'm a teaching assistant," I say. "I've been teaching writing for the past five years, so for all intents and purposes, I am your professor."

"But you're not a *real* professor," he says.

I'm about two seconds from becoming a *real* bitch.

"I'm assigning your grade," I say. "And it's going to stay low if you don't learn to focus your argument. Let's go back to the beginning. You're analyzing an advertisement for beer, and there are five men at a sporting event, here, with their faces painted, which sets up a homosocial environment."

Will lets out a pointed sigh. He's staring at his sneakers, which look to be a size eighteen, minimum, and have lightning bolts doodled on the side.

"You don't think so?" I ask.

"Everything in this class is *homo* or *racist*."

The second-grader inside of me wants to say *and would that include you?*, but the grown-up teacher-person wins and I bite my tongue. Literally.

"I said homo*social*, which, as I explained at length today, is very different from homo*sexual*. What would you call five men, in a group, half-naked, watching a football game?"

"Nothing," he replies. "I wouldn't call them anything. Just 'guys.' You read too much into things."

"Well," I say, "whether you agree with me or not, you're going to have to start doing some analysis, or you're not going to pass this class. For the next ad, why don't you pick one that really catches your attention. Choose something where you *do* think that you're being sold something in a manipulative way. Pick an ad that stands out to you, that catches your eye, and work on creating an argument that *you* believe. Worry about the critics later, and make sure you meet with me before turning in your final draft. And look at the places I've marked pronoun usage. If you write 'he' or 'you' or 'them,' be sure there's an original subject or object to which your reader can refer."

Will continues to stare at the sneakers. He's either being an autoerotic foot fetishist, or a full-blown pain in my ass, and I don't need a full summer of TROOPS to be pretty sure that it's the second option.

"Do you understand?" I ask. "I can go over it again if it'll help."

You could cut glass with the look he gives me.

"I get it," he says. "Now can I go? I have practice."

"Fine," I say. "And try to talk in class sometime. I think it'll help you feel more engaged."

But I'm talking to his back, and then I'm talking to myself.

TROOPS, like my sister's wedding, like Luis, like Langsdale, bothers me far, far less when I'm getting my own writing done. In the week since I swore off swearing, booze and Chilean frauds, I have had a mere martini, cursed twice and kissed no one. Chris blew off our date, rescheduling for this weekend instead, and I didn't even blink. I didn't even complain to Ronnie and Paolo because I was in the middle of a sonnet sequence and perfectly happy to work on end-rhymes instead. But tonight Ronnie is actually *available* for booze consumption, and Will's loaded me up with a blue streak's worth of curses, and the sonnets are finished, and even during Lent, one gets the Sundays off.

"Please tell me you're not teetotaling tonight," Ronnie says, but it's more like an order than a question. "La Varian's a drinker, but he's not a *drinker*."

"You should bring him here," Paolo says. "I want to meet him. Get him to wear his MC Hammer–pants."

"A man in a headband," Ronnie jokes, "is not one to be talking."

Paolo came straight from dance, and he has a purple bandanna tying his hair back.

"I love the way he dresses," Paolo says. "It's like Mardi Gras every day. Have him come here, and I'll bring some beads, or he can give me one of those fancy bracelets. I'll be glad to show him what *I've* got."

"Alas," Ronnie says. "All external markers to the contrary, my man ain't buying what you've got to sell."

*"Really?"* I ask. "Has it come to that now?"

"Oh, yes," Ronnie says. "Alleluia and praise the *lawd,* it has finally come to that."

"Is he fabulous?" Paolo asks.

"Paolo!" I say. "That's so rude."

"When did you become Miss Manners? I tell you all everything."

Earl's pouring the drinks tonight, and this time he sits down next to Ronnie when he brings her second martini. He's knotted a red bandanna around the top of his head, but it looks more badass than hippie. After politely acknowledging Paolo and myself, he puts his hand on Ronnie's shoulder, just for a moment, then moves his hand back onto the table.

"What're you telling, Ronnie?" he asks. "Y'all talk loud enough that half of Langsdale knows your business."

"Uh-uh," Ronnie says, and she purses her lips, makes like they're a lock and tosses her fingers as if she's throwing away the key.

"One of these days I'm gonna take you out on my hog," he says. "I think you'd like it. Summer suits you."

"It's not just summer that's suiting her," Paolo says, and I kick his shin underneath the table.

"Cut it out," he says. "Those are dancer's legs."

"And I'm still waiting to see one of those stories you're writing," Earl says, ignoring Paolo and myself, which seems entirely sensible.

"Next time," Ronnie says, and they give each other a pair of "knowing" winks.

"You look palsied," Paolo says after Earl leaves for his spot behind the bar. "What would LaVeryOne say?"

Paolo had nicknamed La Varian, LaVeryOne because he couldn't remember the man's name. *Whaaa? Varian,* he'd say. *Can't we just call him Mardi Gras?* Now he's settled on Franglish for "very one." Clever, that Paolo.

"Gotta keep my options open," Ronnie says. "Always the chance for a snake to show up in paradise."

"Is he snaky?" I ask. "La Varian?"

"Not snaky," Ronnie says. "Maybe a little teeny, tiny bit entitled. Feet up on the table without asking. Opening the refrigerator and just taking things. Nothing to call Al Sharpton about."

"I'm so jealous," Paolo says. "I think you should have to share."

Ronnie shakes her head.

"Mine," she says. "Mine mine mine."

Earl is polishing the beer glasses, still looking at Ronnie. If the whole of Langsdale isn't listening in on our conversation, Earl most certainly is.

"I didn't know Earl wanted to read your work," I say. "That's really cool."

"I know," Paolo says. "He's *asking* to see a *chapter.* That can only mean one thing."

"That I have to *write* something," Ronnie says. "But I don't want to talk about that. I want to drink my Jack and Coke and enjoy my one night out for the week."

"Amen to that," I say, and the three of us clink glasses.

I didn't say anything at the time, but I know that it bothers Ronnie that she doesn't have the summer to herself for writing. Virginia Woolf was right when she talked about the need to have "a room of one's own" in order to get any decent work done. To hear Ronnie tell it, at Valtek, she doesn't even have a *station* of her own. I probably have Virginia Woolf on my mind because tonight is J.J. Jones's Midsummer Night's Dream-Party. J.J.'s summer party is rivaled only in corniness and lack of fun by her annual Halloween soiree, which she hosted this past year in the guise of Virginia Woolf herself. She wore a formless dress (not exactly a costume, might I add), and put some gel in her hair so it would look wet, and weighted herself down with rocks in her pockets. Tacky, tasteless and literary. So *very* Ms. Jones. Also very J.J. Jones is the fact that she cc'ed Ronnie on the "party" invite, as if that even *kind of* makes up for not hiring her.

Anyhow, Ronnie can't go because she has Valtek, and frankly, I don't think she'd go with a gun to her head if she didn't have a thing in the world to do. Not that I blame her. I can't bail on the evening because I promised to give Zach and Mandy a ride, since Zach's car is in the shop. Paolo was supposed to be my "date," but he claims to have the voices of a thousand adolescents ringing in his head. *A Valium I need,* he leaves on my machine. *Lesbians who dress up as other lesbians. No. Fool me once, shame on me, you know the rest, and I'm so tired, Doris. Love ya.*

So I strap on some purple Mary Jane pumps, a denim skirt slit all the way up the side, a tank top that's just obscene enough to keep the outfit fun, and drive the block and a half between Zach's apartment and my own. I've never been in Zach's apartment, but I know the building. It's run-down, and Zach lives in the unit on the side, a basement one-bedroom that looks to me like a case of radon poisoning waiting to happen. He and Mandy are seated outside, shoulder to shoulder, and neither looks happy. Zach's wearing a pair of chino-style pants and a light brown T-shirt. Mandy has on a plain pink shirt and jeans. Mandy gets in the front seat, and Zach sits in back.

"Thanks, Doris," Mandy says.

"Yeah," Zach says. "Thanks."

I can see in my rearview mirror that Zach is sitting with his arms crossed defensively in front of his chest. Mandy fiddles with her hippie-bead bracelet. I turn the radio up and chastise myself for not having at least one tiny glass of wine *before* the evening started.

"So how's your class?" Mandy asks.

"The usual insanity," I reply. "I think they're coming around. How about you?"

"Fine," Mandy says. "They're fine."

"If it's okay," Zach says, "we were hoping to just stay an hour or so. Make an appearance and cut out fast."

"God, Zach," Mandy says. "Leave when you like, Doris. We'll be fine."

More silence. I never thought I'd be happy to see J. J. Jones's hippie-Mecca in the midst of the cornfields to the right of the cornfields dead south of Langsdale, but I am. It's close to sunset and she has a bonfire aflame in back of her house. Thankfully, we're late enough that it should be an inconspicuous easy-in, easy-out operation.

"Join the fun," J.J. says when we enter. She's clearly sauced and has wildflowers threaded into her hair. Scary.

"I'm going outside," I say to Mandy and Zach. "Find me if you need to go."

J.J. owns a good chunk of land, and the bonfire is about twenty yards from her home. Had I been think-ing logically about the evening, I would have worn something low-heeled, but I chose *poorly* and thus have to keep my eyes fixed on the ground in front of me so as not to kill myself on the trek from house to fire. I hear Iris's voice before I even get close. She's rambling on about film theory as though God brought it down to her on a pair of stone tablets. I'm still five yards from the fire, and I think about doing a deer-in-the-headlights kind of thing. Just stand very, very still and hope that no one notices I'm there.

"Doris," I hear. "What are you doing?"

It's Iris. And I've actually been standing still, looking like the fool I am.

"You have to meet La Varian," she says. "He's a visiting scholar from the University of New York."

"SUNY," he interrupts. "Binghamton."

He extends an arm forward and a series of thick, gold bands glint in the firelight. Even in my Mary Janes he's a good two inches taller than me. A ma-an, as Ronnie would say.

"I've heard about you," I say. "From Ronnie, I'm a good friend of hers."

"Yeah, I know," he says, and it's not rude-proper, but it's nothing to be confused for friendly. Of course, he *is* a New Yorker, and as an ex–New Yorker, I kind of understand, kind of chalk it up to cultural differences, but I also kind of wish he'd smile back. "You get stuck in those?" he asks, pointing at my shoes.

"No," I laugh self-consciously. "I was just thinking."

"About what?" he says.

"Nothing," I say, because I can't exactly say, *I was thinking that I wish I could click my heels, Dorothy style, and not have to deal with the rest of this evening.*

La Varian turns back to Iris. He has on the semi-parachuted pants that occupy so much of Paolo's fantasy life.

"Those almost seem like a fire hazard," Iris says, pointing again at my shoes.

"No more than those," I say, pointing at La Varian's pants. This time he *actually* smiles.

"We're talking about the studio system," Iris interrupts. "How in Hollywood, they kept blackface going for years after blackface proper, with *Imitation of Life,* or even *West Side Story.* 'Brownface,' technically."

"I *hate* that movie," La Varian says. "Hate that string *bean* of a Natalie Wood doing her white-girl shuffle."

"As though there weren't qualified Latina actresses," Iris continues. "Or Puerto Ricans." She pronounces Puerto Rican as if she's from the island, and I wonder a little about how much La Varian really hates Iris, since they're having a grand old time with Natalie Wood, who may have been a string bean but seems like a pretty easy target.

"Always taking the little white girls and giving them the leads," he says, looking not at Iris, but at me.

"Yeah," I say. "It's so nice to meet you. But I'm freezing, I think I'm gonna head back inside."

On my way to the indoor party, I'm thinking that I actually *like* La Varian, in a weird way, because even if he's half insulting me, it seems like he's half sticking up for Ronnie. Which makes him a good boyfriend and not a bad one. In the fifties version of Hollywood aka Langsdale, I *am* the Natalie Wood and Ronnie *is* the qualified Latina actress, turned down for the role *written* for a Latina. La Varian would be a little out of his mind to hear Ronnie talk about the factory, then see me "not thinking" in my purple heels, without getting hot under the collar. It's just that I sort of see it from Natalie Wood's point of view. She's probably thinking that she's *acting* Puerto Rican, not *passing*. It's a movie, after all, and she's an actress, auditioning and getting a part, and somewhere in Hollywood there's a J. J. Jones, and why not go after the "her"—not the "me." Or, to put it simply, I just wish it seemed like La Varian liked me a little more, on the human-specimen level.

Inside, Zach and Mandy are at opposite ends of J.J.'s living room. Zach's sitting alone on a bench with a plate of cheese cubes beside him, and Mandy (who now has two flowers in her hair) is talking up a storm with J.J.

"How's outside?" Zach asks.

"Cold," I say. "I dressed wrong."

Zach doesn't even bite.

"What's up with you and Mandy?" I ask. "If you don't mind. I'm not trying to be nosy."

Zach scrunches his mouth a bit and pops a cheese cube into his mouth, chews it, then answers.

"You know how sometimes people convince themselves that sexuality is all in their heads. Well, sometimes it's not. Let's leave it at that."

"Oh," I say. "Sorry?"

"Nobody's fault," he says. "We're working on it. It may work out. Mind over matter. What the hell is wrong with your leg?"

I have my leg crossed, and the side of my left thigh is completely exposed. It's a patchwork of unshaven white skin and tanned patches.

"You wouldn't believe me if I told you," I say.

"You have that Michael Jackson disease?" he asks, "but reversed?"

"Not even. My sister's husband-to-be, they're getting married in a couple of weeks, sent me a box of self-tanners with a swath of this beige color, and he wants me to *be* that beige color for the weekend of the wedding, so that I look right in the dress, which is champagne. So I sectioned off a few pieces of my leg to see which tanner matched the swath best."

"And I thought it was just shoes that the bridesmaids had to dye."

"Ironically," I say, "the shoes are the one thing we're allowed to pick ourselves. I hate the way I look tan. See that, if I want to look like some pink ghoul in a champagne dress, shouldn't that be my choice?"

"Indeed," Zach says.

"I'm not doing it," I say. "Screw Marvin."

Mandy comes up to say that she's catching a ride with a friend. She kisses Zach goodbye on the mouth, but the way I imagine she'd kiss a brother. Zach pats her on the shoulder. They look like a pair of sad little chimps.

"Ready to go?" Zach asks. "I'm just not in the mood."

It's the best piece of conversation I've heard all night.

# Ronnie

"Jimmy D. has done messed around and got himself fired," Mona says. It's ten minutes before starting time, and we're sitting at a picnic table just outside the entrance to Valtek. Mona's smoking her generic cigarettes and tapping the ashes into a paper coffee cup.

"What? When did this happen?" I frown because I've never seen Jimmy D. do anything that would get him the ax. He'd been a temp for a long time, a lot longer than me. He was also a definite Billy Ray, handsome and sinewy. Wore lots of T-shirts with American flags and eagles on them. He wasn't especially nice, but he wasn't mean, either. He was just a good worker who'd ask you, "What's life doin' to you?" whenever he'd pass by. I liked that about Jimmy D. Sometimes he'd come around and relieve me so I could take my break, and let me take just that extra minute or two to get back to work. Mona started calling him my boyfriend because I always had an extra pep in my step whenever Jimmy D. came around. What can I say? He was handsome in spite of the mullet.

Mona points her cigarette at my can of Mountain Dew. "I believe you gone turn into a can of pop the way you drink 'em one after the other."

"Who fired him? What'd he do?"

Mona stubs out her cigarette, checks her watch, and then lights another one. Five minutes," she says. She sighs. "I'm so tired tonight. Seem like I ain't never rested up."

"He steal something? What?"

Mona tightens her lips and tilts her head toward me. "Now, you know Jimmy D. ain't gone steal nothing. He'd be the last one to do something like that." She takes one more long drag on her cigarette, drops it, pinches the end of it with the toe of her sneaker, picks it up and puts it in her front pocket. "He just got to talking, making noise, asking why we don't have no more than a half hour and three tens and more pay."

I nod. "Shoot. That sounds good to me."

"To a lot of folks. But the head supervisor didn't want no trouble and told Ray to cut him loose." Mona takes a rubber band off her wrist and gathers up all her long black hair. "And he been working here for two months already, trying to get permanent."

"Man," I say, looking at my watch. It was time. "We need those breaks, for real."

Mona smiles at me. "Darlin', we need a lot more'n breaks around here." Why was everyone around here always calling me "sweetheart" and "darling"? "But you temp and don't got to be near as careful as a lot of other folks." She glances toward the door. "Here come Ray."

The man himself cracks the glass door open and sticks his head out. "College," he says to me. "Station eight and nine are singing you a love song, calling out your name. Better shake that leg, sweetheart." He winks at Mona. What is it about winks? I'm a sucker for winks. They even make Ray look like something when he does it. Reminds me of somebody, too, but I can't put my finger on it.

"He ought not to call you 'College' like that," Mona says, laughing. She heads toward the door.

I tried telling Ray once that I wasn't in college, that I was in *grad school*, totally different.

"Don't matter to me," Ray said. "Either one of 'em."

Three hours later I'm standing outside with another Mountain Dew in my hand. It's taken me a month to figure out that most folks don't leave their stations just to go upstairs to sit in that depressing break room unless you're just about drop-dead tired. It's nicer to hang around outside and talk shit, or talk about the weather, always the weather. It's two-fifteen in the morning, and so hot I think about heading back inside. Even if it's depressing and loud, it's cooler. You have to pick your comforts. But I like being outside better, even if it is sticky and the mosquitoes are sucking on me like I'm a chocolate shake. *Vampiric,* I think. I like thinking about the fact that it's two in the morning, and while most other folks are sleeping, I'm working hard. There's a factory full of workers, all day, every day, except for Sundays, of course. Nothing but worship going on in the Midwest on Sundays.

I stand around with two other guys I don't know, one

smoking and the other with a big chunk of tobacco in his mouth. I grew up with my grandmother, who was born and raised in the South, dipping snuff—discreetly. So, even if I *do* think it's a *little* 1950s Mississippi to see a white man chewing tobacco, I try not to let it scare me and try to just hang out casually and blend. I *try*.

One man glances my way. He's short and older, around fifty, I'd guess. He has what my mother would call salt-and-pepper hair. "Hot, ain't it? And it ain't even July yet. We gone be in for it, I tell you what."

"I know it," I say.

"They say it's gone get up to 88 tomorrow night."

"And that humidity will get to a person," I say.

The other man looks at me as if he's sizing me up. He's younger, around my age, with a crew cut. I get a little nervous and wonder if this might be one of those *Mississippi Burning* moments. Even though it's rare, I've had them in Langsdale, and you just never know where it's going to come from, and in what form. I look at him and offer him a weak smile before taking a drink of my Mountain Dew.

"Dad, 'member that time it broke 90 in the shade and on through sundown? That was a mess, what, back in '92?"

"Sure was," the man says. "Sure was." I look at them both like I haven't before and realize they must be father and son. The younger one walks toward me and I can't figure out why he's walking toward me until he veers off to the picnic table and sits himself down. I let out the breath I was holding.

"This yours?" he asks, lifting a section of the newspaper off the table and holding it out to me.

"No, it was just there."

"Hmm," he says, pulling open the paper. "I've been looking for a car. I keep checking the ads to see what all's for sale around here."

I say nothing. I hate when I can't think of anything to say back to something so simple. It's like trying to figure out the language first, and then translating the proper response, and then saying it in the right way. Before I do all that damn conversion, the moment's over. I watch the younger man skim one page then the next and wonder if you get any kind of a deal for working at the car-parts factory, and then I have to wonder what cars the speakers I package are supposed to fit. I never thought about what the car was going to be down the line, because all I cared about was my paycheck and not being tired.

I try to ask both questions without getting the look that Ray gives me when I have to ask him something. "You could probably find a cheap car, like the ones we make stuff for here."

The son looks at the father, and then the father looks at me. It's Ray's look. "Ooh-wee. These cars ain't cheap—not cheap enough for us, bless your heart."

The "bless your heart" is worse than "sweetheart, darlin'" *and* Ray's simple look that tells me I'm simple all rolled into one.

"I tell you what," the father says. "It's hotter'n hellfire out here. I'm gone have to get back inside. Break's up anyhow."

His son stands, finishes up his cigarette, and flicks it into the gravel. He looks at me and gives me a nod before he follows his father inside.

"We're wrapping up *Hamlet* this week," Professor Lind says. "And then we'll start *Othello* in a few days. We'll spend three weeks on *Othello,* and your final papers will be due after that. You'll remember that you have one week off before the last paper is due. My conference in London?"

We all nod.

"Some of your last papers needed a lot of work. Those of you who didn't stop by my office hours last time should see me this time." Professor Lind looks at me and crosses her arms. "There is no reason not to see me for these last papers, unless you think you've got it all covered," she notes finally. Her eyes skim over John briefly before she leans against her desk and picks up her copy of *Hamlet.*

I know she wasn't talking to me, because I had gotten a B plus on my last paper, which is an F, by inflated grad-school standards. I wrote an okay paper on Shakespeare's Henriad and quoted the shit out of Žižek and Peter Sloterdijk's *The Critique of Cynical Reason.* The Sloterdijk knocked me out because it was so damn *relevant* and written in something that more closely resembled English. He seemed to say much better everything I wanted and needed to say about Bolingbroke, Prince Henry and that poor bastard Hotspur. What he was saying to me actually made sense in terms of the world, and for a change I didn't think reading all this theory was one big mind fuck. *Masturbatory.* I was actually interested in all the connections I could make between the theoretical criticism and the "primary texts," as they call books around here. I just didn't think I sounded smart enough in my own words. I'm still in the process of learning the lingua franca, which is twice removed from regular old white people's "standard" English. It took me years to break myself from saying shit like, "I seen her the other day." Now I have to learn words like *narratology* and *dialectical materialism*.

Professor Lind wrote in her curvy elegant handwriting "B+", and then wrote "A-(-)" next to the "B+." I went to her office to see what the hell that meant, and she sat me down and gave me a good long look before she started. Her looks didn't make me feel like Ray's looks—stupid—but they did make me feel like I was coming up short. I used to *hate* going to my professors' office hours when I was an undergrad because they were always asking me to, which made me feel as if they were trying to save the poor black kid. On the flip side, I had the teachers who just dismissed me outright—until I turned in a paper and then they realized I was "bright and articulate," and not coasting on "affirmative action." Never mind that half the white kids were affirmative action, what with their great-grandfathers—or whoever—who were "legacy," and had attended the university since the goddamn *Mayflower*. I didn't like being singled out, I didn't like being patronized, but I didn't like being ignored, either. It was just like in *The Autobiography of Malcolm X,* when he was in school. I didn't want to be oohed and aahed over like a pink poodle, but I didn't want to be told that I should be a carpenter when I wanted to be a writer. But now that I teach and *beg* my undergrads to come see me about their papers, because they'll actually learn something if they do, I don't hesitate to park myself in a professor's office—even if it's as scary as Professor Lind's.

When I'd gone to see her, she didn't ask me why I was there. She told me, "Sit down." She gestured toward The

Chair. It's huge and overstuffed and makes you feel like a kindergartner sitting in a grown-up's chair. "You want to know what I meant by ""A minus, minus.""

"Yeah," I said. "Yes. I guess there's a lot of room between a B plus and an A minus, minus, and I'm guessing…well…yes, what did you mean?" I sounded feeble-minded.

Professor Lind was wearing a dress with gold strappy sandals with a heel that I had to notice were very sexy. She got away with looking like an actual girl because she never apologized for it, no matter how politicized and policed something like toe cleavage could be in academia. She took off her glasses and twirled them around by one of the stems.

"You wrote something that was fine. It was capable. It was okay."

I started feeling *lilliputian,* which I learned the other day means small as shit. I sank down in The Chair.

"I don't know what you're doing," she said. She paused and waited for me to say something. I didn't. "You seem to be struggling between what you think is academic language, and a language that is actually much more engaging. I gave you the B plus for your execution, and the A minus, minus for your ideas and connections. You made very interesting moves in that paper. It was just a bit clunky."

I nodded and rubbed my hands along the arms of the chair. "Well," I said finally. "I guess I feel caught. We're MFAs in an English department, taking classes with Ph.D.s, and I feel like I *have* to write a certain way in lit classes—or at least, try to."

Professor Lind tucked some hair behind her ear. "You

do," she said with finality. "I'm not encouraging you to turn in crap."

I raised an eyebrow.

"I'm encouraging you to write well. I see that your syntax and grammar is flawless, when a lot of people in class are writing nonsense, bullshit, gibberish with twenty-five-cent words because they *think* it's good academic writing."

*Dang.* But I liked that someone was finally saying what I'd been thinking for a long time.

"Ronnie," Professor Lind said. "Let me see your paper."

I'd brought it along with me so she could show me how hopeless I was. She took it from me and started reading then, flipping through the pages. "Yes," she said, what seemed like to herself. "Listen, this is an interesting point," she says. She started to read from my paper:

"Because Hotspur was unwilling to make such sacrifices, he could only be unsuccessful in his attempt at kingship. Hotspur also makes the mistake of believing that he sees things as they 'really are,' and therefore strategy in attaining the crown is simple, in his estimation. One sees it, and one takes it through hard, honest, *masculine work* [emphasis added]. What he fails to realize, however, is what Slavoj Žižek refers to as 'the paradox of being' in *The Sublime Object of Ideology*."

Professor Lind stopped reading. "And then you interrupt something really interesting by dumping in this Žižek quote from out of nowhere. It's a good connection to make, that's why this is a decent paper, but I want more of your thoughts and observations before you give me the quote." She shoved the paper at me and I looked down at the page.

> The paradox of being can only reproduce itself only insofar as it is misrecognized and overlooked: the moment we see it "as it really is" this being dissolves itself into nothingness or more precisely it changes into another kind of reality. This is why we must avoid the simple metaphors of demasking, of throwing away the veils which are supposed to hide the naked reality (28–9).

I was trying to show how Hotspur screwed everything up when he tried to usurp the kingship, because he thought there was only one way to see things. Because he wasn't able to see that nothing was how he "saw" it, that what he thought was the right, real and true way to be was already changing into something else once he thought he'd had it all figured out. I loved this quote when I was inserting it because, to me, it just spoke to the complications of life. It was like listening to a Billie Holiday record. It made me think of Du Bois and states of consciousness. But I must have looked frustrated and confused when I was reading my own work, because Professor Lind said, "Listen. Finding your way of working will not be easy. I absolutely respect the primary creative process, and I know what I want, and can get, out of you, as a grad student taking a seminar on Shakespeare."

"Okay," I said. "I'll just have to figure it out."

"Yes," she said. "You will." And that was the end of office hours.

Now that we would be going into *Othello* soon, I was reenergized and actually looking forward to writing the paper. I still didn't know *how,* but I knew that I could. Professor Lind is asking us about the significance of ghosts in *Hamlet,* and I wonder what *I* think of ghosts and push Žižek and Sloterdijk out of my head.

I'm going to take a week off of Valtek and fly to L.A., compliments of my brother. He says he's tired of my mother and father "hollering" at him about how I ain't been home in a month of Sundays, a phrase I could never quite figure out because of its Southern ambiguity, and because it means a great deal of time way beyond a month of anything. But the real reason I need to come home is that my brother's worried about our father and trying not to show it. He's been having tests done to figure out why he's not been feeling well lately.

"So I have to pay for your college ass to come home with my hard-earned money," he'd said when he finally caught up with me. "You ain't never home, Factory Girl!" My brother is always loud, like he's an announcer at some sports event. "Where you be half the time I call you?"

I was going to answer that between the factory, school and La Varian, my time is hard to come by. But he didn't wait for me to answer.

"I feel sorry for you, slaving away in that country factory, so I'm a pay for you to come home," he said. "Plus, I miss you, too," he added finally.

He was trying to keep things light so I wouldn't be concerned. Always his style. "What do you think is wrong with Dad?" I asked, pacing around my apartment.

"I don't know, Ron. Don't worry, though. Just come home."

"Are you sure you can afford to pay for my ticket?" I felt guilty that I didn't even have half the money to get home.

"Please," he said. "My money situation is straight. It's your poor ass we all have to worry about." He made himself laugh, I could tell. He sounded nervous.

Poor, I may be, but proud, I ain't, so I took him up on his offer. At thirty-seven, he'd done good for himself by working in a factory ever since he graduated high school—a house with a pool, he had! Three kids and a wife! Money to buy his dopey sister a plane ticket! I had…what?

We're all out having drinks at the Office Saloon so that I can have one or four for the road to L.A. Paolo and Doris are trying to cheer me up. I'm leaving tomorrow night—Ray didn't seemed too troubled when I told him I'd be out for a week. "College," he said, "I don't know how in the world you make it around a big city like L.A. the way you stumble and carry on around here." He gave me another one of those winks.

It's the first time I've been out with Doris, Paolo *and* La Varian, and it's strange, not so relaxed for some reason. But maybe it's just me worried about my father. La Varian and I have just shown up and he's at the bar ordering drinks from Earl. Doris keeps drinking and adjusting her hat. It's not a beret, but it's summer appropriate and—I think—stylish.

"Meow," Paolo says, extending a claw-shaped hand toward La Varian. He sucks in his cheeks to give himself even more obvious cheekbones. "*Love* him!"

I laugh. "He *is* handsome, isn't he?"

"*Honey,* handsome doesn't do it, it just doesn't *do* it."

"Where are our drinks?" Doris asks, sighing. She smiles at me, at least it passes as a smile. "He's totally cute," she says, but she won't look me in the eye. "Drink. Now," she says. "I think Earl's punishing us for your showing up with La Varian." She sighs again and looks toward La Varian. "There's a long line, though. Poor Earl."

I caught Earl's eye when La Varian and I walked in together, but he smiled for a second, and then turned away when he saw me hanging on La Varian.

La Varian comes back with three drinks in his hands, all he could manage. "Ronnie, you want to go get that last one?" He tilts his head in the direction of the bar, and I stand up fast and nearly knock over the drinks on the table.

"Jumpy!" Paolo says. "Is Doris going to have to give you some of her Prozac?"

Doris glares at him and then flips him off.

"I'll be right back," I say.

I shove in between people at the bar and grab the drink. Earl's working hard—shaking and pouring and wiping his hands like crazy. I think he's too busy to say "hey," but when I turn away with the drink, I hear my name over the Doobie Brothers singing about the highway.

"Ronnie," Earl says, "who's that you come in with? Three-fifty," he says to a woman standing next to me. "Thank you," he says when she tips.

"Oh, that's La Varian here on a post-doc. We're just hanging out." I feel guilty and tight with any information I give to Earl. Why did I say "just hanging out," when the man's been in my house and bed more than a little bit? I barely even *talk* to Earl except for in the bar. But,

I have to admit that I spend a lot of time in the bar, which means that I do see a lot of Earl. We'd been talking about him taking me for a ride on his Harley before La Varian entered the picture.

"Quite a peacock," Earl says. He glances over at Doris, Paolo and La Varian.

"He's a nice guy," I say. I don't like his comment about La Varian being a peacock. It's called style.

"Nice?"

"Yeah, nice," I say. "What. You don't think so? You just met him."

"Ten-fifty," Earl tells the man who's standing beside me and holding out a twenty. He takes the bill. "All I know is that he wasn't none too friendly to me. Didn't like me putting his change down on the counter, mad 'cause I wouldn't put it in his hand. When you seen me or any other bartender do that? Money is always on the counter. It's easier that way." Earl cups his hand around his ear to hear someone else's drink order and then scoops up some ice.

I know La Varian thought Earl was racist for not wanting to put the money in his hand, and hell, around here sometimes you're right, sometimes you're wrong about that sort of thing. "I'm sure it was just a misunderstanding," I say. "See you around."

I turn to go. "Wait," Earl calls out. "When I'm a get you on my bike? You ain't backing down already, are you?" He wipes his hands on a towel and then wipes his forehead with the back of his hand. He stands there empty-handed, not pouring or mixing or taking money. Just waiting for me to answer.

"Soon," I say.

"You been saying that. What? You too busy playing tennis?" Earl grins good-naturedly and wraps a white towel around his hand like a bandage.

My eyes get big. *"What?"*

"I got a brochure in the mail. Saw your picture. You on an athletic scholarship or something?"

I feel something like a thundercloud forming in my head, I'm so pissed. I'm mad that Earl would assume I'm at Langsdale for sports, and I'm mad that even I misinterpreted the picture: at least tennis is a glamorous thing, I told myself, to get over my desire to shoot up the place. But no. It's a picture of just another black athlete on scholarship.

Earl looks confused. "What's wrong, Ronnie?"

"Hey, man," one of the regulars say to Earl. He's still in his deliveryman uniform. "You pouring drinks or talking to ladies?"

"Nothing's wrong," I say. First, I wonder why he's getting a Langsdale brochure in the mail, and then I try to give Earl some credit. It's not his fault—he's just reading into what the brochure is telling him—but I'm fresh out of credit right now. "See you around," I repeat, and weave in and out of the crowd, trying not to spill what's left in the glass.

La Varian is sitting on my couch with his notes spread all over the place. I do it all the time, but why is it bothering me now? It must be the drinking earlier that's got me annoyed. When we got home he made fun of the Saloon and asked me, Couldn't I find someplace better to hang out? "Langsdale is fucking you up," he insisted, "if that's the best place a sista can find to chill in."

"I like the Saloon," I said. "A lot. People are great there." I was confused about why he'd pick on the place until I realized I nearly ran out of there the first time I went in. Now it was the most comfortable place to relax.

He shrugged. "If you like it, I love it," he said.

He's got his laptop with him because it's a habit now that he stays mostly at my house and he carries it with him wherever he goes. He's working on this chapter that he hasn't let me see because he wants it to be perfect. "I think this is done," he says. "Will you read it?"

It's two-thirty in the morning and I'm tired. I don't think I can read a comparison of Nancy Cunard's *Negro* and Alain Lock's *New Negro* right now. It takes energy to care about this stuff. *Negro* and *New Negro* ain't got nothing on Tired Negro. "I'm kind of tired and a lot drunk," I say. I rub his head. "Can I do it in the morning?"

"Well, I'm just so happy that it's done," he says. He looks disappointed. "I was hoping you'd read it tonight, even though it's late..." He seems to be waiting for me to say okay, to give in, but I don't. Tired is tired.

He sucks his teeth. "Fine," he says. "Let's go to bed."

So early in the morning, it's because I'm nice and trained to be a good girl, that I get up and read La Varian's chapter when I'd rather be sleeping—like he is. But I'm well rested and the sun's coming up and beautiful. I'm looking forward to reading something smart and interesting about the Harlem Renaissance. I stretch my legs over my coffee table and settle into my couch, the side where La Varian always sits, with La Varian's laptop. I turn it on and open the file that's labeled "Locke Chapter" and start in. He's so smart and interesting that I read everything, even the footnotes. When I'm nearly done with the chapter, I come across the last footnote, but I don't quite understand it. It says, *I'd especially like to thank my wife, Trisha, for her invaluable feedback, without whom this would not have been written.*

I blink at the screen, *My wife, Trisha,* and I try to figure out if "my wife" could possibly mean anything other than "my" and "wife." I've never heard those words come out of La Varian's mouth before, and yet, here they are. All this time I'm trying to name what he "really is." He really is straight, he really is a Ph.D., he really is Cliff Huxtable, he really is handsome, he really does like me.

And now I know that everything is different from just the moment before, before I read "my" and "wife." I know that I really don't know anything, except that he really is married.

# Doris

Teaching, Week Five: Glimmers of Hope

Once the halfway point of teaching is reached, the class locks into place. Good classes often begin like roller-coaster rides with the slow, painful, dreaded chug-chug-chug up the tracks, then the hands go up, and momentum carries you the rest of the way down. My class has improved noticeably. They did well the day we went over their early advertisement choices, the three of them that remembered to bring one in, at any rate. Even Claus kept his mouth shut, which means he was thinking, which makes me irrationally happy. Today, they're supposed to have finalized their choices, and we're going over the ads in class to make sure that they can yield a four-to-six-page analytical paper. Ali starts. He's brought in an advertisement where two Arab-looking men are standing in the shadows, while a nice, white couple strolls down Fifth Avenue. For deodorant, no less. "ODOR: Code Level Orange," it reads. Ali has on an orange and white T-shirt with Langsdale's school insignia across the front and a pair of blue-and-white gym shorts. His hair is spiked slightly in the front, and the cover-up he's slapped on a few errant zits is two shades lighter than his actual skin.

"I think this ad is messed up," Ali says.

I nod in agreement. Zach is out sick today, so I don't have to worry about his slipping into some cuter-than-thou routine.

"What do terror alerts have to do with deodorant?" Tina asks. "That's just stupid."

"It's racist," Ali goes on. "I hate it when they use guys who look like that, who look like *me*. I can't go to the airport without getting held up an hour. It's not funny."

"So you think they're trying to scare people into buying deodorant?" I ask.

"Hell, yeah," Claus says. "Make you worried you stink and everything."

"The motivating factor then," I say, "is shame. They're trying to shame you into buying their product."

"But what about these men in the background?" Ali asks.

"What about them?" I ask in return. "And what about the location. That looks like the Empire State Building in the background to me, way at the top of the skyline."

"I don't think that should be there," Ali says. "It makes it seem like they're going to blow something up. Like that's what they're trying to make people think."

"That's the danger," I explain. "They're conflating two totally different things. Two fears. Both, on different levels, irrational. Fear of 'the other'—the dark-skinned man lurking about, and the fear of stinking up your date."

"That's not right," Ali says. "It's just wrong."

"But you've got a hell of a paper, there," I say. "This ad is timely. It's using racial and cultural anxieties to sell a two-dollar-ninety-nine-cent stick of whatever it is that goes into deodorant. And that *does* have ramifications outside the classroom. You know firsthand every time you go to the airport."

"Or walk down the street," Ali says. "Yesterday, I'm just walking back to my dorm, and some guy leans out a truck window and yells 'Osama' at me."

"Damn," Claus says, shaking his head.

"You're not even from Afghanistan," Tina adds.

"And if he were," I ask, "would that make it all right?"

"Uh-uh," Sharelle says. She's been doing her nails for part of the class, flexing them wrists and fanning the sunset-orange tips of her fingers. I've been ignoring it, so it's nice to see that she's actually paying attention. "That's no different from what I been called by some ignorant people in my day. But I don't think I need to be repeatin' that in class, Ms. Weatherall."

"And do you think that advertisers have a responsibility for the way they represent people in their ads? Do you think that your average viewer would look closely at this ad, to see the two Arab-looking men partially hidden, or do you think they'd just flip by?"

"I didn't notice it at first," Linda chimes in. "But now that you say so, I totally see what you're talking about."

"So that's another danger," I pointed. "That it's something unconscious. You see it, but you don't really analyze it, so it just slips somewhere into the back of your brain without you even knowing it."

Will has yet to join in the discussion. He isn't doing the whole eye-rolling, foot-tapping routine, but he looks abstracted—focused on something outside the classroom.

"Do you agree, Will?" I ask.

He doesn't seem startled, but without looking at me or anyone else, he says: "That sucks."

From Will, at this point in the semester, "That sucks" might as well be Noam Chomsky's critique of material-ist culture.

"Let's see your ad," I say. "Why don't you tell the class about what you picked, and how you intend to write about it."

Will unfolds the piece of paper in front of him so slowly you'd think he was defusing a bomb. Then he straightens out the ad and holds it up for the class to see. Featured prominently are a pair of blond women, more than half-naked, heads tilted back and mouths open, hold-ing something between them that is decidedly *not* just a cigar, to paraphrase Freud, and above them is the caption "Keep It Up," in white, dripping lettering.

Claus whistles.

I feel vaguely ill.

"It's for Vitagra," Will says. "It's like natural Viagra. From herbs or something, and there are these two twins, and this 'Keep It Up'—"

"I can read," I say. "Dare I ask where you found this?"

*"Penthouse,"* Will replies.

Tina scrunches her face like someone forgot to sweeten her lemonade.

"That's *nasty,*" Sharelle says.

This is one of those classroom moments where about ten thoughts are flying through my head at once: Shouldn't it go without saying that when I say pick an ad from a magazine, I mean one *without* a brown-paper wrapper? It's entirely possible that Will actually doesn't know any better; this is the first time Claus has looked at anyone with even a shred of approval; the women are going to mutiny, and rightly so; and where the hell is Zach when I could actually use him?

"Agreed," I finally say. "I'm not sure it's entirely appropriate, in fact I'm sure it's not entirely appropriate to get ads from porn magazines for this kind of class."

"Why?" Will asks. "You said get an ad."

"Yeah," Claus adds, "it's an advertisement, got a slogan and everything."

"All right," I say. "For the sake of argument, supposing that Will really did get to use this ad, which he can't, why wouldn't it make a good paper? Can anyone think of a reason that it would be hard to get four pages of analysis out of this?"

Will looks redder than usual, and Claus is staring me down.

For a good thirty seconds we all listen to the grass grow.

"I know," Claus finally says. "Because you can't use sex to sell sex. It looks all tricky with the twins and shit, but it's just sexed-up blondes selling sex to some old dudes who can't get it up anymore. Too straightforward."

"Yes," I say. "Exactly. Whereas Ali's ad is using shame and, arguably, racist imagery to *sell* deodorant. This is using a pornographic fantasy to sell a pornographic fantasy."

"Tacky," Sharelle says.

"Do you see?" I ask Will.

"I get it," Will mutters. He's looking at his desk and folds the paper sheepishly back into his pocket. Then he eyes Claus and says, "Thanks."

"No problem, dog," Claus says in return, reaching over and giving him a high-five.

On my way home I make the computer lab my first detour. I'm supposed to "check in" with Chris and firm up plans for the weekend, and Ronnie swore she'd write as soon as she reached L.A. La Varian was supposed to give her a ride to the airport, but I haven't heard from her in a few days. I assume if there had been any sort of real catastrophe, I'd have read about it in the paper, but I'd like to know what's going on with her father. Ronnie describes her father as this stoic, silent type, especially where his health is concerned. *Doris,* she said to me, *I just hope it's nothing serious, because unless they can treat it with tequila, I'm not sure my dad will go along.* She was joking, but she wasn't smiling. I ask intermittently, but Ronnie really isn't any more open on that particular topic than she describes her father as being. But I'm going to check my e-mail again, just in case.

"Hey sex-ay," Chris calls out to me. The lab is air-conditioned to subzero temperatures, but he still has on a thin, tie-dye T-shirt and cutoff shorts. "You ready for Saturday?"

"Ready as I'll ever be," I say. "Take me somewhere I've never been."

"Isn't that *implied,*" he says, leaning into the sentence. Ah, the promise of an NC–17 encounter in my deeply PG–13 life.

"Seriously," I say. "I gotta get out of this town. My sister's wedding is still a week away, and I'm stir-crazy."

"Back to the big city."

"Not even. Her fiancée, Marvin, he's got parents who are richer than God, so we're all going up to their 'family estate' in upstate New York. It'll be nice and everything, but rural is rural. It's just rich rural as opposed to poor rural."

"I'll think of something cool," he promises. "Pick you up at your building?"

"Yeah," I say. "I'll buzz you in."

"Let's say seven-thirty."

"Great."

The computer lab is pretty much deserted. There are always a few über-geeks who hole up in the corners and surf porn, but over the summer, like most of Langsdale, it's a bit of a ghost town. Suits me fine.

Of course, the first six e-mails are from Marvin:

Did you get the package I sent? Call immediately if color is off or you need more.

Delete.

Registry glitch online has been fixed. Please advise relatives to DOUBLE-CHECK items already ordered. We have EIGHT silicone pot holders and only FOUR hands.

Delete.

Doris, Please apprise me of your "poem." Lisa says you are writing one? Would like to approve draft and, if necessary, select alternate.

Etc., Etc. Delete. Delete. Delete.

Marvin has created the registry of an Enron executive for himself and my sister. I can barely afford to buy them a couple of napkins. No wonder folks are snapping up the pot holders—they're *only* thirty dollars apiece.

Ronnie's message is short:

```
Got home safe in spite of weather. Guess
who's married? I'll give you a hint—it
rhymes with "Bavarian." Call my brother's,
have quite a story.
```

"Holy shit," I say out loud. One of the porn freaks gives me a dirty look.

I write back:

```
Will call as soon as I'm home. You may have
found the one man in Langsdale next to whom
even Luis has integrity. Is he CRAZY??? Be-
side the point. Chris seemed enthusiastic
about date—will hope for no manic crash by
Saturday.
```

"Unbelievable," I whisper, closing out my account.

My second detour en route to *chez moi* is Zach's. He called this morning to say that he wasn't feeling well, and I promised to stop by with some soup on my way home. Even though he has a basement apartment, he's fancied up the stairwell with three plants potted on alternate steps as you walk down. There's a garbage can at the bottom of the stairwell, and it looks as if a ball of yarn and a half-finished swath of something sweaterlike have been abandoned there with the coffee grinds and crushed milk cartons. There's an empty bottle of Dewars next to the garbage, probably for recycling.

I knock softly. No answer. Then again, a bit louder, before leaving the carryout bag hooked to his doorknob.

At home, I comment on half my TROOPS final-paper proposals, then get to work on the poem for Lisa and Marvin's wedding. I start by reading some Neruda and e.e. cummings, for the sake of their lover-ly-ness. Problem is, by the time I get back to the poem I'd started, it reads like "Hop on Pop" by comparison. Marvin will string me up and tan me (quite literally) if I don't have something that *sounds* like a wedding, so I close out that file and type up the Neruda instead. Chicken, yes, but the draft of *my* poem at present rhymes "truly" with "groovy," and doesn't look as if it'll be making any detours to "art," on the slow train to "shit." That's part of writing: knowing what to keep, and what to throw away.

Instead, I open a file that I started after the bonfire: "La Varian Poem"—under which I've noted *whiny white-girl material,* and started with the line *I'm at a party, see…* There's something there, I can tell, but it hasn't gelled yet. Beneath the line, I write: *Married! Fraud!!* I then try Ronnie's brother's place twice. First time, no answer, and second time her brother tells me that she's meeting up with her ex. Interesting. At least she *knows* that he isn't married.

Once upon a time, long, long ago in a galaxy far, far away, I wrote a poem about Zach—composed in the brief interval after the pink-wine make-out and before finding out that he hadn't *exactly* broken up with his girlfriend. Two things I remember about it: first, that it wasn't very good. Second, that I wrote a line about him having hands the size of a King James Bible. A keeper.

I think about calling Zach's place to make sure he got the soup, but decide instead to walk by and check. The doorknob is unadorned, and Mandy's bike is locked against the iron railing beside his entryway. Instead of heading home, I keep walking. It's just after sunset, and the air has cooled down to around seventy. I can see every single star in the sky, and crickets have started their low evening lullaby, with the occasional frog or owl harmonizing. Ronnie's probably in some smog-induced euphoria, buying shoes and visiting relatives and purging herself of LaVeryBADone. Paolo's prepping his ballerinas for recital, so I sneak by the dance building where I can see him through the window, pulling one twiglet of a dancer's leg as high as it will go into a first arabesque. He's stately when he teaches, clapping his hands next to his face in mock anger, holding his own head and arm to the side with impossible delicacy to show his students how it's done. I wish I'd seen him dance in San Francisco. I imagine he was spectacular.

Mandy's bike is still at Zach's when I pass by again, and the lights are out in his window. Probably because I'm lonely, I wish that she weren't there, that I could knock on Zach's door and tell him about class today, give him a hard time about his knitting and eating habits. Because I'm lonely, I feel almost jealous that it's Mandy who knows him best. Chris, I say, focus on Chris, present-and-*not*-accounted-for, single, available, in-the-now Chris.

★ ★ ★

In-the-now Chris rings my buzzer at 7:50 Saturday night. He's decked out in a wifebeater that's yellowed slightly beneath the arms and a pair of overalls. I'd have to say that it's almost too casual even for the Office Saloon, and we look horribly mismatched. I'm wearing a casual but flirty pink sundress with thin spaghetti straps and white thong sandals. I even have my hair back in two low ponytails for a chic Daisy Mae appeal.

"Great dress," he says with such perverted enthusiasm that he almost redeems himself for tardiness and an unacceptable level of squalor.

"You're late," I say. "I was getting ready to put my plan B into effect."

"Plan B?"

"Gotta have alternatives."

"I had to meet a friend," but the way he says "friend" is cagey. "It wasn't anything I could cut short. I figured you'd understand."

He smiles and runs his hand up my shoulder, and goose bumps crest my skin.

"You need a sweater?" he asks, dragging his eyes over my shoulders and across my chest. "You look a little cold."

"Indoor or outdoor date?" I ask.

"A little of both."

I go back in my bedroom and select a thin white cardigan. Chris is whistling a song I don't know, and I can still feel the warmth of his hand against my skin, the firm pressure. His hands are smaller than I'd remembered, like two packs of cigarettes.

Chris drives a blue Ford pickup truck. A totally serviceable, functional vehicle that he uses to haul large

objects from place to place, rather than some bastardized
SUV used to tote toddlers from piano to soccer: it's a
down-home homage to the union of form and function.
I slide onto the passenger seat, pushing a stack of dog-
eared maps to the side, and buckle myself in. It feels more
like an adventure than a date.

"You want to see authentic?" he asks. "I'll show you
where I grew up. It's about thirty miles south, no 'college-
town pansies' there is what my Pops used to tell us. He
can't stand that I live in Langsdale with all the Commies
and liberals."

"What if they wear really pretty sundresses?" I ask.

"Jane Fonda wore pretty sundresses," he says. "No can
do. He's a purist."

We make small talk along the two-lane road that snakes
down to Clarksborough, which looks less like a "town"
to me than thirty-some houses in the middle of nowhere,
a gas station and a run-down Wal-Mart. The homes are
spaced far apart, two-level units with basketball hoops in
the driveways and large pastures out back.

"That's mine," Chris says, pointing at a darkened home
with gray, woodsy-looking paneling on the sides. The
shutters are painted a deep blue, and the lawn out front
is small and well maintained, with a ceramic goose
dressed in miniature overalls and a plaid shirt just outside the front door.

"Wow," I whisper. "There's *nothing* out here. I mean, I
thought there was nothing in Langsdale, but this is real,
hardcore nothing. No wonder my students look at me like
I'm from Mars. Compared to this, I am."

Chris puts his arm behind my seat to back into the
driveway.

"Good thing my pops isn't around to hear you talking like that. They've all gone to Lake Michigan for vacation. Dad's lived in Clarksborough his whole life. My mom, too. She's from a few towns over, but you'd probably think that was even more nothing. Spaced-out, wide-open nothing."

"I didn't mean it like that," I say. "I have this student, Will, and he drives me crazy, but when I think about this being the sort of place he's from, I don't know. It makes more sense."

"And I'm sure that if poor Will took an aer-o-plane out East, you might make a bit more sense to him."

"Don't count on it," I say, checking the clasp on my charm bracelet.

"Want to sneak in?" Chris asks.

"Let's stay outside, go round back. It's so beautiful out."

Chris goes into the house and emerges with a sleeping bag and a box of shortbread cookies.

"This is some white-trash wooing, here," he says. "Authentic."

The sleeping bag is a deep green and smells like mothballs with a faint trace of mildew. Chris spreads it across the grass behind his house, which makes up a small backyard that gives way to rows of corn silhouetted against the moonlight.

"It's amazing," I say. "So quiet."

Chris kisses me softly at first, like corn silk floated against my lips. He smells faintly of tobacco, although I've never seen him smoking. His hands glide over my shoulders, pulling the straps of my sundress down, and he nuzzles his head in the space between my shoulder and neck, biting gently against the skin.

"You're beautiful," he says.

I kiss him back, looking at the moon behind him, a harvest moon out of season, so big and bright it's almost like a second sun.

"I have to tell you something," he whispers, pulling back slightly. "I know you're pretty progressive and all, so it probably won't matter, but I still, well, I think it's something you should know."

No good has ever come of a conversation begun with those words, but I swallow hard and brace myself for the inevitable.

"Okay," I whisper back, my hand still tentatively grazing his forearm.

"It's part of the reason I was late," he says. "I got a call from this friend. She's just this girl I've been sleeping with, casually, you know, and she just found out—"

He's pausing, even though that's a subject-verb combination that takes only a very finite and predictable combination of objects—none of them good. Yet, the first part of the sentence rolled out so casually, "this friend I've been sleeping with," as if he was quoting the *Farmer's Almanac.*

"Yes," I say, doing my damnedest to fake "progressive."

"Well, she's *tainted,*" he confesses. "A rash, something, some lump. And I need to get checked, I think. Or she thinks."

I so do not need to get diseased for a *polygamous* relationship.

"Oh," I say. "I totally, totally understand."

His entire face relaxes.

"I knew you would," he says, reaching into the top pocket of his overalls and pulling out a condom. "I figure if we're safe…"

"Oh, no," I say. "I understand that you're *upset*. I'll definitely need to think about this one. I'm generally used to monogamous relationships. Really bad monogamous relationships, but definitely the 'just me' variety."

Chris leans back, sucks his breath in hard, exhales slowly.

"I see your point."

We drive back mostly in silence, not totally uncomfortable but nothing to be confused with the ride out. It's ironic that he probably thought that the East Coast gal would be a swingin' single, and I just assumed that he'd have the down-home training to take one gal at a time. Not worth pitching a fit over, but probably not worth following up on, either. I only wish there were some other soul to whom I could bring my computer disks.

"Thanks," I say, leaning over and kissing him on the cheek before I get out of the truck.

"See you 'round," he says, "Lula Mae."

"So long as I cannot work a computer."

"Then see you tomorrow," he says, faking a grin before backing the Ford away from my apartment complex and disappearing down the street.


It's easier to put the Chris incident behind me when the rest of my week is like an extended episode of *Beat the Clock*. I have approximately eighteen hours between my final TROOPS class of the week and leaving for the airport. Zach said he'd cover for me on Friday, God bless him, since the checklist that Marvin sent of "THINGS TO MAKE SURE GET DONE" is longer than *War and Peace*. I've packed my dress, two copies of the poem, a shower gift, a wedding gift, rehearsal-dinner wear, *alter-*

*nate* rehearsal-dinner wear, potential trip-into-the-city (please, God) wear. You'd think I was moving back East for good from the suitcases packed and ready to go by the door. Chris called and left a message on my machine, which I have yet to return for sheer lack of time. The only call I answer comes at ten-fifteen, since the caller ID reads J.J. Jones, and although she might be the devil's troll princess, I can't imagine she'd call me at home unless it was an emergency.

"Yeah," I say, in my best busy-but-listening voice.

"Doris," she says. "How you doing?"

"Fine. What's up."

"Well, we've had a little situation arise. I'd prefer to talk to you in person."

A situation. Code for catastrophe.

"Did something happen? Is one of my kids in trouble?"

"No, no," she says. "Nothing like that. I'd really rather talk about it in my office."

"I'm leaving for the airport this afternoon," I say. "My sister's getting married this weekend. I have, like, maybe twenty minutes out of the next two hundred that aren't totally accounted for."

"That's all it'll take," she says. "If you come by at noon, I'll have you out by twelve-thirty. Promise."

The tone of her voice lets me know that "if" means "when," and I'll be doing eighty to make my flight on time.

I'm practically packed by the time I get to J.J.'s office at 12:10 p.m. Her office reminds me of corporate America, not academia, with cheesy "Aim High" and "Succeed"-type posters on the walls, with pictures of mountains, or surfers, and inspirational sayings in cursive. She has her hair in a loose bun and is eating a sandwich.

There's a little piece of slaw clinging to the corner of her mouth, and I feel as if I've been kept after school, waiting for the principal to call my parents.

"Doris," she says, like she's just meeting me for the first time. "How are you doing, Doris?"

"Aside from trying to get six hours' worth of work done in four, and not look like dogshit when I arrive for my sister's wedding, just fine."

I wouldn't normally swear in front of J.J., except that she is *wasting* my very precious time.

"We've had a bit of a situation come up," she starts, leaning back in her chair and pulling a manila folder from beneath a stack of the same. "One of the parents called last night."

"What parents?" I ask.

"The mother of one of the young women in your TROOPS section. It seems she's quite concerned about the content of what takes place in your classroom."

"You're kidding," I say. A clammy sweat starts to break across my arms.

"I won't read you the exact content of the exchange."

"The exchange?"

"It's just a series of phone calls for now," she says, stroking the folder like a delicate piece of china. "The young woman is very upset, not about your class, but about her mother. She's worried about her grade."

"Excuse me," I say. "But what *is* the problem?"

"The mother is under the impression that you've been using pornographic materials in the classroom, specifically, a page from *JUGS* magazine."

"*Penthouse*," I say. "I mean, it was *Penthouse*, but I didn't bring it in. It was part of the advertising assignment, and you know how some of these kids are. This guy, Will, he brought in this porn ad, and I *told* him that it wasn't appropriate. It's not like I'm passing out girlie magazines."

J.J. looks at me without smiling, then opens the folder, but tilts it away so that I can't get a look at what she's reading.

"She goes on to say," J.J. continues, "that the language used in the classroom is also inappropriate. Quote, the teacher says things like 'bitch-ass punk' and 'shit,' which should not be said in any classroom, unquote."

"You've *got* to be kidding me," I say. "Is there a context for her complaint? Does she even listen to how kids talk today? Why am I getting singled out? I'm so careful about how I teach."

"But you're not," J.J. says, "careful about your mouth, now, are you, Doris?"

"I am *thirty* years old," I state. "I should be able to say whatever I *damn* well please if it helps get my point across."

"That's precisely *the point*," J.J. says. "If this is the sort of complaint I'm receiving, then you're not getting your point across, not in the most effective manner. I'm going to let you finish teaching the class, and I'm going to let you do your own grading, and hold off on disciplinary action, which, please know, I am on your side about, to keep you from losing your teaching contract."

Now I really might throw up.

"Losing my teaching contract?"

"Forget I said that," J.J. says. "It'll never happen. Just finish the class, as usual, and we'll straighten all of this out after grades are in. I don't want you taking anything out on this student, because as I said, she's made it known that *she* likes the class and that her mother is overreacting. You know Langsdale policy, though, we have to write down everything and take the mother's position seriously, even if she doesn't have the support of her daughter."

J.J.'s mouth is still moving, the lone piece of slaw has crept down her chin, and I close my eyes, wishing to God I'd had the sense to leave town without answering that damn phone.

I now have two hours and forty-five minutes to catch my plane, and with a two-hour drive, twenty minutes for parking, and eight hours' security to fly into New York, there's a good chance that I'm going to miss my flight. On the way out of my meeting with J.J. I run into Zach, who looks red-eyed and groggy, but is in super-chatty mode.

"Doris," he says, "thanks for the soup."

"I can't talk," I say. "I've got to get myself to the airport, and I'm not even sure I packed right, and my plane leaves in two hours and forty minutes now. Ronnie's gone, Paolo has rehearsal. I'm not going to make it. And I might get fired."

Then, even though it's the last thing I want to do, I start to cry.

"I'll drive you," Zach says. "I owe you. You'll make it." He pats me on the shoulder. "Stop crying. They'll pick you up at the airport and think you're some red-faced alcoholic."

"Oh, Zach," I say. "They already think that."

On the way to the airport, I fill Zach in on my conversation with J.J. He's stone-faced, properly scandalized both at the mother in question and at J.J.'s evasive nonsense.

"I loathe her," I say. "If they don't fire me, I'm quitting."

"But it's not the student, right? The student stuck up for you."

"I hate everyone," I say.

Zach laughs. There's a toy hula dancer glued to his dashboard, and she's gyrating spastically. He's doing eighty and unless he gets pulled over for speeding, I'm going to make my plane.

"You're a good teacher, Doris. It's all going to work out, so you can't let it ruin your weekend. Your sister is getting married."

"To a fascist."

"To your fascist-in-law, and you're going to have a blast. Maybe they'll have some pink wine and you can make those city boys remember what they're missing."

"I hate boys," I say. "They're lunatics."

"If it makes you feel any better," Zach says, clenching the steering wheel tight and pulling himself slightly forward, "Mandy called it quits."

"I'm sorry," I say. "You'll find someone else, I'm sure of it."

"It's impossible to date in a college town," Zach says. "Unless you think Sharelle or Linda is open to earning a little extra credit."

He gives me a wicked look.

"You're preaching to the choir."

"I smoked half a bag and watched twenty-two hours of television straight. *Animal Planet* marathon. Did you know that there's an animal called a humanzee? It looks like an ape, but it can walk upright and it likes to smoke cigars."

"Is it single?" I ask.

We're finally at the airport, and Zach drops me off curbside with thirty-six minutes to catch my plane.

"You saved my life."

"Just forget about this place," Zach says. "Forget about J.J. and everything because it's all going to blow over and in two weeks you're not going to care. But if you pout through your sister's wedding, you'll hate yourself later."

"Okay."

"Just don't forget about it so much that you don't come back."

He's not smiling, but his eyes are squinting slightly and a flush rises from my chest, to neck, to face. I exit the car as quickly as possible, hoping he won't notice, and lug my duffel bag to the curbside check-in, make small talk with the attendant while I watch the reflection of his silver-blue sedan linger, linger, linger, and then pull away.

# Ronnie

I'm waiting curbside for my friend, Bita, to pick me up. I watch cars that aren't hers pass me by while I fight the urge to sit down on top of my bag. It was a rough flight. Turbulence that had me always looking to see if the flight attendants had any form of body language that might read, "Jesus will be meeting you at the gate. The pearly one." I didn't used to be a bad flyer. I've flown to Europe three times with my old boyfriend, Sammy, been flying back and forth from L.A. to Langsdale for two years now. But the world is full of weirdos with crazy ideas about who's better than who, and who to blow up or invade because of such ideas. Being in a plane makes the mind play tricks on you—especially if you're flying in crazy weather. I've never seen a tornado up close and personal, but Indiana's been hit with a lot of them this summer, lots of *Wizard of Oz* nasty weather. As I rode on the airport shuttle, because needless to say, I fucked up my ride with La Varian, the weather reminded me of the tornadoes that hit last summer, right after Doris dropped me off at the airport. Last summer, leaving Langsdale, the sky looked a little too green for me. Even though it was warm, we got hit with a storm that rained hail so hard on Doris's car that she'd checked for scratches when we finally got to the airport.

To get a better look at her car, Doris had pushed her sunglasses on top of her head because, of course, ten minutes later there wasn't a cloud in the sky, the sun was blinding, and it was steaming. "Does everything about the Midwest have to be a total disaster? A train wreck? Armageddon? No, I take that back. It's classic Freudian over-compensation—this is why they have to have *biblical* weather, when it is *so* not necessary. It's summer! How does hail figure into summer?"

I stood with my duffel bag on my shoulder and watched her rub her thumb over a speck on the hood of her car.

I was just glad it wasn't snowing, which is black-people kryptonite, if you ask me. Africans are genius, and ain't no black folks in Utah for a reason. "So unnecessary," I'd agreed. "Like trees and nature and birds and shit. What's the *purpose* of squirrels, anyway? Or chipmunks? I mean, what do they *do?* What's their *point?*"

Doris gave me a big hug after she was satisfied that her car was no worse for wear. "You're totally deranged," she'd said. "Don't forget to check the MAC counter for that new pink gloss. Saw it, want it, and won't ever get it in Langsdale."

"Done," I said. "Anything else you need?"

"Help," she had said, walking to the driver's side of her car. "Help."

I'm wishing I'm up in the bar, Encounter, across the way, having a drink, and just when I am about to make a chair out of my bag, Bita pulls up next to me in a car I don't recognize. It's a big car, one of those huge Jeep-truck-van-combo–type things. She waves at me with a big grin on her face.

"What's this?" I give her a clumsy half hug from my seat. "When did you get this thing?" I take a deep breath. I like the new-car smell. Bita shakes her head but keeps her eyes on the road. "You look so good!" I say before she can answer me. I touch a section of her long brown hair and then tug on it a little bit. She smiles and absently scratches her light brown cheek.

"Thanks," she says. "Charlie. He insisted on this thing because he thought it was safer, better for me to be bigger, or as big, as everyone else on the road. Besides, Charlie's making so much money now, he's practically *nervous* if he can't spend it."

"That sounds like Charlie," I say. Bita's been married to Charlie for five years now. I've decided I like him, though I never would have pictured her with him: a slick, midlevel TV writer. Used to be midlevel, I should say, because now he's really raking it in. He's always working. He's a good Midwestern boy from Chicago's South Side. Charlie Flannigan. I still get a kick out of thinking of her as Bita Flannigan, because her last name used to be Gupta. "Nice Indian name," her mother said at the wedding. She'd adjusted the draping of her sari and then shook her clasped hands at me. "Flannigan," she said again, a little bit sad. She looked at me as if *I* had something to do with it. I stare out the window and think about my mom and dad.

"Hey," Bita says. She knows me well. "Your dad's going to be fine."

"Sure."

"I'm glad you're staying with us tonight." Bita's trying to sound cheery. "Charlie'll be home late, as usual, so we can sit up and get shit-faced, and you can tell me about this La Varian."

*La Varian.* I'd tried to push him out of my head because it hurt whenever I thought about him.

"Idiot!" Bita says. "Motherfucker." She shifts in her seat and leans into the steering wheel the way kids do when they're racing each other. She keeps checking her side and rearview mirrors for the best time to accelerate. Another driver, in what looks like an even bigger car, isn't letting her merge onto the 405.

Sure I complain about people who are insanely rich with no understanding of what money means to folks who don't have it, but I also know that staying in Bita and Charlie's house last night felt *good*. Better than the fanciest hotel I could ever imagine. Bita made steak, which I ate like it was going out of style, and while we sat on the deck drinking forty-dollar bottles of wine, I took in the twinkly lights of L.A. from their outrageous view, and she and Charlie laughed at my stories about Langsdale and La Varian. I almost missed Langsdale when I talked about it, but the La Varian humor was a mask, a performance.

It was hard to get up and go this morning because I would have really liked to hang out on Bita's sunny deck for the rest of the day. The air was good and the sky was clear. Charlie was already up and gone, but Bita'd stay home, maybe garden, maybe go shopping, read, rent a movie if she felt like it. What must that feel like, to have no obligations to anyone or anything? I've borrowed her "old" car—a Mercedes—to get from L.A. to my brother's house out in Riverside. It would take one hour and twenty minutes if there was no traffic, so I had a lot of time to think about my ending up the clichéd floozy of a married man. I find a hip-hop station—nonexistent in Langsdale—and drive.

After I'd read La Varian's chapter and stared at "my" and "wife" for a very long time, I decided to wait until he got up and simply ask him about it. My confusion was such that being "angry," i.e. "going off," wasn't even part of my reaction—yet. I waited until he woke up and came looking for me in the living room. He grinned at me, happy that I was finally reading his work and would give him feedback.

"What part are you on? Did you finish?" he asked. He leaned into me so he could get a better look at the screen flipped open on my lap. "I think the Cunard section can be tighter, but I've looked at it so much, I don't know anymore. What do you think?"

While he was sleeping I'd thought up a whole lot of dramatic-soap-opera, Erica Kane shit to say to him, but for once, wasn't so interested in words. "I read in your footnotes that you thank your wife. What's that? You're married?"

La Varian's face changed like one of the homemade cartoon books we used to make when we were kids, the kind where you sketch different expressions on a happy face and flip the pages fast so it looks like the face you've drawn is changing. Happy, confused, sad. Happy, confused, sad. "Oh." Silence. "I forgot that footnote was in there." He stood there stroking his goatee.

"*That's* your answer? You forgot the footnote was in there? What about the wife part? Did you forget you had a wife, too?"

"No, now wait a minute. Ronnie, I swear, I am *not* married."

"You're not married."

"No."

"*Not* married."

"No."

My eyes wandered around my apartment while my brain tried to take in what La Varian was saying. They stopped on a black Barbie that was propped up on one of my bookshelves. She was wearing a red party dress. I was too old to have that sort of shit in my place. "So what does 'I'd especially like to thank my wife' mean then?" My conviction wavered a bit. Could I be wrong and acting like a stupid insecure girl? There is always an explanation for these types of things, things that seem quite plain and self-explanatory, like the missing item from your home that you swear someone must have stolen, only to find it where you looked ten times before.

La Varian leaned his back against the arm of my couch and folded his arms over each other. He looked around the room, and I could see him thinking, "*Okay, I should say,* 'technically' *I'm married.*" He rushed on when he saw my twisted-up face. "But I'm separated, we're separated right now."

"So how can you sit there and tell me you're not married? You said, 'No, not married,' those were your words."

I wasn't even that concerned with the news of him being married anymore. It was the lying, the lies he was spinning, the relativism bullshit that was blowing my mind. He kept talking and talking. *Since they were practically divorced, he didn't feel the need to tell me, he didn't anticipate meeting someone like me, and he was afraid I wouldn't go out with him if I knew, he was still married on paper, but not in his heart....* The sad thing was that I was trying to figure out a way to make all this okay with me. Hell, the ironic thing was that if he'd just told me the truth, the *whole* truth, I wouldn't have cared. It was the whole making-the-decision-for-me thing that was hard to swallow.

"If you'd just told me," I said. "That's not how you treat people. You are so fucked up."

La Varian frowned at me. "*I'm* fucked up?"

"Um, *yeah?* I'd say so."

Now La Varian's face went from worried to pissed. "I may not have told you straight out that I was married, but look at this ring." He shook it at my face. "You could have noticed it if you wanted to."

I looked at the ring. I'd seen it a hundred times. It was ornate, a silver-and-gold braid with diamonds in the crevices. Very Las Vegas. "*That's* a wedding band?"

"It's on my ring finger isn't it?"

La Varian wore so much jewelry, had so many rings, that he walked around looking like a black Liberace half the time. How was I supposed to notice *that* one? "Please!" I said. "Look at all the shit you wear. Besides, it's not supposed to be some sort of investigation, clues I'm looking for to know if a motherfucker is married. Don't turn this around." I was finally getting to one-hundred-percent angry. He was a jerk.

I carefully placed his laptop on my table and stood up. "This is so not going to work," I said.

La Varian busied himself by closing down his computer. "You're right." He snapped it shut. "We are very different people."

I shouldn't have cared, but I had to ask. "What does *that* mean?"

"It means, Sally from the Valley, that you have just let Langsdale fuck you up, running around with your little dress-'em-up friend, hanging out in hick bars, working in a goddamn factory next to a bunch of Bubbas. You're not doing anything but slumming it. And the first thing they send me when I apply for the fellowship is that ridiculous brochure with your ass holding a tennis racket. You're like a commodified apologist for white folks, making Bubba, Buffy and whoever else feel good about themselves."

My mind raced to catch up with La Varian's point: he'd lied about having a wife, but *I* was the problem.

"What's Oprah got to do with you lying about your wife? And since we're getting real, your ass wouldn't be here getting a post-doc, furthering your academic career at a top university if you hadn't seen my picture on the brochure, Mr. Pasteurized. It made you decide that Langsdale wouldn't be so bad after all, and it wasn't—until I discovered you're a liar."

La Varian didn't seem to have anything else to say after that. He blew out a breath. "I'm leaving," he finally announced and went into my room. I could hear the change jingling in his pants, the creak of my bedsprings while he sat down to put on his shoes.

But I wasn't done. The fact that he had nothing else

to say made me know that he thought I was right about some things, if not all things.

"I'm glad you're leaving," I said, standing in my doorway. "You've practically been *living* here. You've moved in, been worrying me to death about helping you work on your chapter, to read it and edit it for you, lying in *my* bed, fucking me in more ways than one. And then you have the nerve to think you know what's best for me, when all you're really thinking is what's best for you."

La Varian stood up. "Let me by, Ronnie, before this gets out of hand."

"You know what that makes you?" I pulled all of my dreadlocks to the front so that they were resting on one shoulder. They suddenly felt heavy.

"Let me by." He pulled down my arm because it was blocking his exit. I put it right back.

"I *said,* do you know what that makes you?"

La Varian looked away and waited for me to finish like a parent waiting for a tantrum to come to an end.

And then I said something that officially made me an academic. It was something so mortifying and horrific to a person who defined herself as "us" (regular people, not overly intellectual) and "them" (academics). But I couldn't help it, because then and there I understood that it was *so* true. "That makes you a *colonizer.*"

La Varian's jaw dropped. Then he laughed. "Colonizer. Now, that's funny," he said. "Can I go now, before you really tell me off, make me cry by quoting Achebe?"

I lifted my arm and dropped it, heavy at my side. La Varian walked past, didn't look back, and was out the door.

How did this happen? How did Cliff Huxtable suddenly change into something else altogether? How did I turn from normal, to someone who'd drop colonial discourse, the colonization of *anything,* into a regular conversation? I could hear myself now, talking to my family who I hadn't seen in at least half a year: *Oh, yes, my time has been colonized by having to work in the factory. The colonizing factors stemming from graduate school work are demoralizing...* Michel Foucault, Frantz Fanon and Edward Said might find the gap between rhetoric, discourse and consciousness interesting, but I should have said to La Varian something succinct, straight and to the point; what my brother, Mona, Ray or even Bita would say to me if I tried to drop a little colonial discourse in between the Lakers going all the way this year, record heat in the Midwest or the best shoe store in the Beverly Center: "You are full of shit."

The 60 freeway goes on forever and ever, but I finally reach the exit and it's only five minutes before I get to my brother's house. I check my watch. One hour and fifty minutes it took to get here. In Langsdale, I thought I missed driving, the solitude of me and my music on the freeway. Interstates just don't cut it. But now I wonder, what's so great about freeways? In Langsdale, you can get from one end of town to the other in twenty minutes and be done with it, any errand can get done in less than an hour. Why is it only now dawning on me that that's a really cool thing?

There are a lot of cars parked in front of my brother's house and across the street. He's barbecuing today, and always likes a houseful of people when he has a gathering. I notice my dad's Lincoln Town Car in the driveway, and my brother's new Mustang. There are two other cars that I don't recognize. I never really paid attention to cars before, and now I can't look at a car without wondering where it came from and who built the pieces inside of it.

"Factory Girl!" My brother, Joe, shouts at me from inside the garage. The garage door is always open if somebody's home. He's always been a big dude, so he walks slow, takes his time walking around the pool table in the middle of the garage and meets me out on the driveway. He gives me a strong one-armed hug because the other hand has a Corona in it. After he lets me go, I bend down on one knee and bow, waving my hands dramatically.

"Props," I say. "I'm giving you your props. You've been doing this for fifteen years? It sucks," I say. "Hard."

He laughs a hearty laugh and then gestures toward his home. There's a little sign hanging out front that says "The Williams House" and a sprinkler running in the yard. "Yeah, but it's worth it. Come out back. Mama and them been asking about you all day."

"Wait." I grab his arm. "What's the news on Dad?" We were supposed to hear today.

"Oh!" My brother's face relaxes. "Good news. Not the best, but good. It's not cancer or nothing like that. His doctor's pretty sure it's diabetes."

"Are you sure?"

"That's what they say." He puts his arm around my neck and pulls me toward him. "He'll be all right. Still a pain in the ass, so you know he not worried about too much. Come on."

I follow the plastic runner that my brother has leading from the den, attached to the garage, all the way through the living room, to the sliding glass door. My mom jumps up from her lawn chair when she sees me opening the door.

"Veronica!" She gives me a hug for what seems like days before she lets me go. She's a tiny woman with the biggest hands I've ever seen. Her hoop earrings pinch my neck until she releases me. My dad gets up slowly and gives me a hug, too. "Good to see you, Ron." He's huge like my brother and moves stiffly, like some animatronic creature from Disneyland, the kind of man where every move is deliberate, but never a surprise. My-sister-in-law, Janice, is in the hot tub with a margarita in her hand, and two guys I don't recognize tread water in the pool. "Hey, sister-in-law!" she calls out to me. "This is Allesandro and Javier, your brother's friends from work."

"Hello. Hi," they say. Allesandro is a big guy, with long hair in a ponytail, and Javier's smaller, with hair cut close to his scalp. Javier pulls himself out of the pool to sit on the edge and take a sip of his beer, but Allesandro stays in. *Hot,* I think, looking out at Allesandro, who stares at me while he pinches his nose to get the water out. I notice his brown skin, which is flashing in the sun.

"Let me look at you," Mama says. She tugs on my hair and tells me to turn around, so I do. "You're tore down," she says. "And your face is puffy."

"Ma," I say. But too much alcohol and too much work, one crazy man, plus no sleep, does, in fact, equal "tore down."

"Your brother says you're working in a factory this summer?" my dad says in a *tone.* "Why is that?"

"Let the kid have a seat at least," my brother says. "What are you drinking?" he asks.

"Got any Jack Daniel's?"

"What?" My brother looks amused. "Since when? You were sipping wine coolers before you left for the country. The only thing you could hang with."

"Thangs done changed," I say.

"I guess so," he says. "Hard living, girl. Hard living." He laughs. "That's what a job, a real job, will do to you."

"A margarita, Joe," my sister-in-law calls out.

"Alex, Javier?" my brother raises his eyebrows and points at Javier's empty Corona bottle.

"Yes," they both say. "Yes."

It's later in the day and more people have shown up. Nieces and nephews, some of Janice's family. Some people are in the garage playing darts and pool, some are in the den watching TV, and a lot of folks are out back playing cards at a fold-up table, or swimming.

My father's been like an annoying fly with his questions. Buzz around, buzz around, land, I swat the question away, thinking it's gone for good, but then it inevitably comes back. Any questions about *him,* of course, he dismisses with a flick of his wrist. I'm only able to get out of him that my brother's right. He will be fine. He'll just have to lay off the ham hocks and fried chicken and start taking insulin. So we settle all that. I'm not *as* worried as I was flying out. And otherwise, it's been just the kind of day I need. I look out at the brown mountains from my brother's backyard. I recline in a lawn chair and check out the water shimmering in the pool. I look at Allesandro. More shimmering. I've been in the Midwest so long that I understand how beautiful California is. I'm sitting in a backyard with a hot tub and pool, a view of the mountains, the sun shining down on me. I've got a Jack and Coke in my hand listening to Stevie Wonder coming from the speakers my brother's rigged up out here. This isn't even Bita and Charlie, fancy-big-house-in-the-Hollywood-Hills living, this is regular, comfort-able, almost-anybody-can-have-this living. Once, when I first moved to Langsdale, another grad student asked me if I had a pool. "No," I said, "that's crazy." I was living in a tiny bungalow in Echo Park. The question seemed ab-surd. "But everyone in California has a pool," he said, snickering. Some Cornell bastard. A medievalist, which gave him *no* room to snicker. And now I was loving this, this life I moved across the country to get away from, be-cause it wasn't *enough*.

"So what are you doing?" my father says. "You leave a good job and a good man to go work in a factory?"

I knew he was going to bring up Sammy. A nice man, a good man, a man I didn't appreciate and love enough to stay for in L.A. I'd see him this trip because we were still good friends. "I didn't leave to go work in a factory, Dad. This is just for the summer. I teach, I write, I study, that's what I do."

"Well," he says, at a loss. I think he's finally going to leave me alone until he comes back with, "I just don't think school is the best thing you could be doing for yourself. I mean, look at Bita. She's living in a nice house, a big house, married…"

"I like that Charlie," Mama says. "He sweet."

Mama and Dad have not seen Bita since we were in college, years ago, and they only met Charlie once, at a going-away party Sammy threw for me at our house, but they were always asking me how they were doing. Sud-denly they were the new Cliff and Clair Huxtable, only

Indian and Irish. "Bita and Charlie are doing well," I say. "I'm glad for them, and I'm going to do well, too. I don't need a lot of money."

My father leans forward in his chair. "Don't need a lot of money?" He looks at my mother as if to say, *help* her. "Maybe you do need to stay in that factory a little longer so you'll see that life ain't no game, Veronica. Everybody in this family has worked too hard for you to be the only person to go to college and mess it up." He looks out at the pool and sips his tea. "What are folks studying that's so important anyway?"

Multi-limbed erotica. "Lots, Dad."

Okay, maybe everything is not meant to be "studied," but all I know is that I'm not some dude's baby's mama—or in jail—but Dad was making it sound like either one of those things would be better than grad school.

"She'll be all right," Mama says. "Get herself somebody like Charlie or Sammy when she ready."

Why won't my brother come out and save me? He's out in the garage talking shit and playing darts. I pull the back of the patio chair up until I hear it click two times and it rests at the angle I want. I look out at the pool, empty now because it has gotten a little chilly—predictable desert weather. Hot one moment and cold the next. I imagine that Allesandro is still out there, swimming his laps, his long hair trailing behind him in one neat fluid line. He is, as Prince says, a sexy motherfucker. Cue twangy porn music with exaggerated guitar licks, and I can see Allesandro climbing out of the pool, water pouring down his body. He's winking at me and asking me when the *carne asada* tacos will be ready. I don't know how in the world to make them—or anything else—but that's okay, he'll teach me. He's telling our daughter, little Alle-sandra, to get out of the pool because it's cold. *Salte de la piscina, Allesandra. Esta frío...* The warm wind stirs up lit-tle waves and the pool water shimmers and shimmers like fool's gold. I'm thinking I'll finally get in. Take a dip. But I hear my name.

"Ron!" my brother calls from inside the house. "Come play darts. Allesandro and Javier can't play worth shit."

Mama and Dad are preoccupied by one of Janice's aunts, so I take my chance and run while I can.

Inside the garage they have a ball game on with no sound—Dodgers versus Braves—and the stereo blasting. They make jokes about women, trash their foreman, trash the president, drink tequila and make fun of me. *Allesandro gets all the ladies... Stavinsky's a racist who rides them too hard at work... President Bush doesn't care about us... Do a shot, Ronnie, do a shot, now that you're hanging with the big boys...* They make me laugh, and I like that Allesandro shows me how to hold the pool stick. I have the best time that I've had in a long time, but I can't stop thinking about essays and articles and theory that seems to speak to every little thing they bring up. Javier keeps losing at darts and talking about another foreman who doesn't like black people, even though he's Mexican and has only been in the States for five years. He asks me if I know about a Mexican poet who's famous in Mexico, but I've never heard of him. I'm dying to tell him about this Noel Ig-natiev book, *How the Irish Became White,* which talks about white privilege and what's gained when ethnic folks try to get in on the privilege and point a finger to designate someone else as "other." It's exactly what he's saying he's seen with his own experience, but I don't want to sound as if I'm trying to teach anybody anything. I just want another drink, and I think—I know—that Allesandro needs to show me how to hold that pool stick again.

"Like this?" I say, and I turn my head just a little bit so I can get a glimpse of his face. A strand of his hair tickles my neck.

"Yes," he says. He's got a serious, heavy voice. "I think you've got a good feel for it."

"Allesandro now?" Doris says. "I guess your dad must be okay."

"Yes." I tell her about the diabetes.

It's my second-to-last day in L.A., and I'm calling her from my brother's before I drive out of the valley and back into L.A. to hang out with friends. She says she's sitting in the dark in her apartment because of yet another storm. "I shouldn't even be on the phone," Doris says. "If I get electrocuted, you owe me."

"Allesandro was just a nice distraction," I say. "Have you seen La Varian around?" I sink down lower into the hot tub because my shoulders feel cold. The Santa Anas are blowing, dry and electric. They make me feel a little off, a little nutty.

"What's that noise?"

"I'm in a hot tub."

"You *are?* Your brother has a hot tub? I *hate* L.A." She sighs. "I hate *Riverside,* or wherever the hell you are. I get some crazy siren going off warning us about tornadoes and you get a hot tub. La Varian, by the way, has been seen out and about with Iris *a lot* these days."

"Shut up."

"Oh, but yes."

"What a fucking cliché."

"Yep."

"He attacks me for being an apologist for white people, and then he goes *out* with one?"

I had told Doris about La Varian's and my insane exchange the last time I saw him. She thought "colonizer" was a laugh riot, too.

"Wow," I say. "Iris."

"Things fall apart, indeed," Doris says. "I suppose being a pretentious pseudointellectual is color blind. At least it's not some mousy eighteen-year-old white gal from the Dairy Queen."

"I *guess*," I say. "What. Ever."

"And Sammy? How did that go?"

"Well—"

"Shit," Doris says. "Did you hear that? I just saw *insane* lightning and the building shook. I'm off this phone. Call you later."

Dial tone. Doris is convinced that she's going to go up in a blaze of glory because of the electrical storms and weird weather we've had all summer. She thinks we'll be swept up by a tornado if we don't keep a lookout. I'm a jaded earthquake veteran though, and I'm not half as worried.

I didn't get to finish telling her about Sammy, which was okay. Sammy, to me, was the nicest guy I ever fucked over. Handsome, sensitive, understanding. Black, even. I didn't know how good I had it until I moved to Langsdale, and confused the packaging of La Varian with someone like Sammy. But he didn't want to move, didn't want to do much but edit film and travel. I *had* to move, I wanted *knowledge*, which sounds corny as hell now, even though Langsdale was the smartest choice to make at the time. Now it was too late. Sammy and I loved each other, but weren't *in* love anymore. And every La Varian did not a Sammy make. All black men are not created equal, to paraquote Jefferson with all the grad-school irony I can muster.

"I'm worried," I said to him the other day. We were downtown, in Chinatown, having dim sum. "Maybe I made a mistake about grad school." He leaned back in his chair and twisted one of his short dreadlocks around his finger. He studied me with his hazel eyes, eyes I used to get lost in.

"You're worried?"

I nodded. I tried not to tear up. I didn't know why I was feeling sorry for myself all of a sudden. I was having my "Auntie Em, Auntie Em, there's no place like home," moment.

"Look," he said. "Who knows you better than I do?" He tipped the canister of sticky rice toward me. There was one neatly wrapped rice pouch left.

I shook my head. He pulled the container closer and began to carefully unwrap the banana leaves.

"Nobody," I said, and teared up again, because it was true. "Nobody knows me better than you." More evidence that I was an idiot who'd made the biggest mistake of her life.

Sammy put his chopsticks down and reached across the table. He grabbed one of my hands. "Then you'll trust me when I say that you didn't make a mistake. I think you need to do this, Ron."

"But I'm not even writing anymore," I whined. "All I do is work and drink and waste time on weird guys. I'm a goddamn Movie of the Week."

He laughed. "Sorry," he said, tightening his lips to get rid of the smile. "What you said is funny but it's not true. This is just a chapter in your life, that's it."

"Chapter" made me think of La Varian, and Nigel, and whoever else lay ahead. I sighed and poked at my lunch with my free hand.

Sammy let go and went back to the rice. "You can't know how sad I was for you to leave, and you can't know how I know this is right for you. So what, you're not writing now," he said. "You will."

I shook my head. Sammy made everything seem simple. "But I'm not even sure I'm interested in creative writing anymore. Lacan is actually more interesting these days."

"So?" Sammy asked. "Write about that."

"You don't understand," I said. "Things keep changing. What I want keeps changing, and I don't want to make bad choices. And Mom and Dad are getting older… I should be here. I should be home." I'd never forgive myself if something happened to my family while I was in the Midwest, nose deep in Derrida.

Sammy scraped the rest of the rice grains off his banana leaf. "Look. Remember when you first got to Langsdale and you were looking for an apartment?"

"'Course I do."

"You called me from a pay phone, freaked out because you saw some clowns waving a Confederate flag from the back of their truck."

"Insane."

"Right." Sammy held his hands up in front of him, as if he was getting held up. It was his don't-get-me-started pose. "But the point is, even though you wanted to get in your car and drive straight back to L.A., you took the time to get used to some things and you made an okay life for yourself. You made a choice, and it's still playing itself out. Let it. You can't make decisions about life based on anticipating something that may or may not happen. Let your life unfold."

*Let it,* I thought. Just the kind of hippy shit Sammy was prone to say.

"So." Sammy had finished, crumpling his napkin and putting it on top of his plate. "Let's hit MOCA. They're exhibiting Miró."

Bita, Charlie and I are walking around South Pasadena after dinner, and I'm not in a good mood, not even close. I'm not looking forward to getting on a plane tomorrow morning and going straight to Valtek after I land. On top of that, Charlie got on this riff about tobacco-chewing hicks and the Klan in Indiana, while we ate a two-hundred-dollar dinner. All I could think about was Mona and Ray. And Earl. It's always entertaining to make fun of a type until you realize you actually know someone who's supposed to be *so* hilarious, just because they exist. It's everything, though. The weather, the sunshine, all of that, I still love, but the woman who bumps into me because she's talking on her cell, the cars, cars everywhere big and shiny, stores lined up on both sides of the street with people going in and out like ants, ten-year-olds dressed like hookers, it depresses me. I know, though, that the minute I'm in Langsdale, I'll be complaining about the Midwest, so I make myself take all of it in, because I do miss it all: the suburban track homes, the obscenely big houses in the distance of Hollywood Hills, Echo Park and China-town, Santa Monica Pier, South Pasadena in its elegant tackiness. It's a city, though Doris, the true New Yorker, says it's not. I don't care. I'm glad for it, I'm glad that I fit, and I'm mad that I'm letting Annoying L.A. get in the way of Fabulous L.A. But it can't be helped.

"Here's the bookstore," Bita says. She's had a gift certificate from Charlie that she's been wanting to cash in. He gave it to her on Valentine's Day. We wander around while Bita tries to find something, and as I'm flipping through a book on post-colonial theory, I feel a tap on my shoulder. It's Charlie.

"Here's something for you, Ronnie," he says in what he thinks is a hick accent. He runs a hand through his black hair and squints those green eyes that Bita adores. "For you and that Earl fella a yourn." He holds up a book. It's a cookbook by Ted Nugent and his wife "She-mane." I laugh, because it *is* kind of funny.

"'Kill It and Grill It,'" Charlie reads aloud. "'A guide to preparing and cooking wild game and fish.'"

"Look at him," I say, pointing to Ted Nugent in his shirt with the arms cut out. "He's totally crazy." He's holding a rifle (kill it), and his wife is holding a knife and spatula (grill it).

"'Includes recipes for deer, elk, wild boar, rabbit, bear, wild turkey, duck and *more*,'" Charlie reads. "Better fire up that grill, Becky Sue," he says to me.

"Charlie!"

We both turn around when we hear Bita's voice. She's shaking.

"What's wrong with you?" he asks.

"This bitch at the counter won't redeem my gift certificate. She says it looks forged and she won't take it."

I frown.

"What?" Charlie puts *Kill It and Grill It* on the shelf next to a book on narrative theory. "Where?" he asks, following Bita.

In the end, it was a young, cream-faced, self-assured woman who said she was sorry and that it was all a big misunderstanding because when Charlie showed up demanding to know why his wife couldn't get what she wanted, suddenly she and her boss, Pat Boone's double, agreed to redeem the certificate. Charlie even shook hands with Pat Boone's double after joking with him to smooth things over. And that was all. We left.

We're driving up the hill to their house, and I can't wait to take a nap, but Bita keeps going over what happened, turning it over and over in her head. "You should have seen how she shoved that certificate back at me like I was a criminal," Bita spits out, fuming mad. From the back seat, I can't see her until she flips down the sun visor and checks her makeup. "I even asked to see the manager, and he came, said he agreed with her and left. That's not even good business." She stares at her image in the mirror, wipes away a smudge of eyeliner with her finger. When Charlie tries to stroke her hair and call her "honey," she knocks his hand away.

"Geez, Bita," he says. He puts both hands on the steering wheel and grips it tight. He looks hurt. "Why are you getting shitty with me? It's not my fault. I didn't do anything."

"Exactly," Bita says, and says it again. "Exactly."

## Doris

Poetry is full of meditations on absence, how a person is constructed not only in relation to those around her, but in opposition, as well. Flying out to my sister's wedding, that's sort of how I feel, identitywise. In Indiana, I am the absence of the East Coast, but when I go back East, I suddenly find myself becoming vaguely, self-righteously hickified. I take actual offense when my sister's lawyer, husband-to-be, Marvin, asks me when I'm leaving the "flyover" states. Traffic irritates me. Everything seems dirty and overpriced. The fact that a double bourbon at a nice bar can run me twenty dollars becomes a harbinger of capitalist apocalypse—the literal height of insanity. I don't even want to get into discussions of how much my sister will spend on new shoes or a nice handbag—let's just say that it's close to my rent. Also, while trendy fashion knockoffs may fly in the absence of actual designerwear, once I hit New York, I feel self-consciously cheap and a little dumpy. My Target flip-flops are no longer the height of kitschy-cute, they are merely $7.99 pieces of Taiwanese plastic which look to be exactly that. And everyone's wearing stilettos, or Adidas slides, or whatever style is the height of "now" and at the same time decidedly "six months from now" in my actual world. In the presence of style, I am the absence of style. I arrive to make everyone feel that much hipper. Because the thing is, all of my sister's friends *notice*. I almost miss the academic hippies.

Marvin picks me up from the airport because my sister is getting her nails and toes done, and all her personals waxed and buffed like some spiffed-up automobile. And I, the hygienic equivalent of a dirt bike, with chipped nails and a Miss Clairol dye job that has left me looking like heat-miser from the Christmas special, am stuck making chitchat with Marvin, who has gelled-back blond hair and a deep caramel tan, like he's been lounging at the beach and auditioning for a swimsuit ad. Once in the car, he two-fists the cell phone and drives like a meth freak. I try not to think about the fact that his Cadillac SUV is nicer than my apartment.

"Doris," he says, looking at me closely, "didn't you get my package?"

"I got your package."

"And?" he asks, pointing at my fleshy, pale arms.

"I'm not into that chemical stuff on the body," I explain. "I'm not totally convinced that it won't give you cancer in ten years, or twenty, or whenever people have been wearing it long enough to see what goes wrong. And even if it doesn't give me cancer, I can pretty much guarantee it would give me acne, since everything on the planet gives me acne."

"You're not going to match," he says, grouchy but resigned.

"No," I say. "I'm not."

I'm tempted to play with his newfangled Global Positioning System (since rich people evidently can't even read their own maps anymore), but am afraid I'd get my hands slapped. Marvin stews a few more minutes.

"Doris," he starts, "so how much longer you gonna be out there?"

This is the question all Ph.D. students dread. The well-intended yet slightly patronizing inquiry into our well-being, a tsk-tsk for daring to absent ourselves of the race for Versace suits and summer homes. Beneath it: a veiled "screw you" for all the leisure time they fancy graduate students have. I know that Marvin imagines me lounging on my couch, eating bonbons and composing sonnets between episodes of *The View* and *All My Children*. Trying to convince him that teaching is hard work, that research and writing is exhausting, and that relative poverty gets less cute with each passing year: utterly useless. His question does hit that deep-seated fear every dissertating human being hides from, even me: *Oh, my God, I might never get out.*

"Next year," I say.

I've said that for the past two years. I don't even know whether to believe me anymore, but my unmitigated loathing of J.J. has given me a certain devil-may-care insouciance. As TROOPS porn-guru-cum-potty-mouth, heck, I might even be done next week.

"Thought you were going to be done this year," he says.

God, I hate this guy. Of course, if I said to him, "Yeah, and I thought you'd be a partner by now at your silly-ass law firm," *I* would be the bad guy. Since it is my sister's wedding, and this is the life-form she's chosen to unite with, I bite my tongue.

"Your family all here yet?" I ask.

"No," he replies. Then the cell phone squawks again, and I'm back where I started—bottom of the list of the least of his priorities. Three phone calls later, I'm almost impressed with Marvin, listening to him on the phone is almost like riding with Sybil, maven of the multiple personalities. Marvin has perfected his important voice: *That's right—have it tomorrow. At the latest* and his lovey-dovey voice: *I got her, honey, wuv you, too.* And his oh-God-I-have-to-endure Lisa's troll sister voice: "So you dating anyone?"

"I don't want to talk about it," I say, because it's the truth. Explaining Chris or Luis? I'd rather explain semicolon usage to Claus *and* Will.

Marvin snickers, a little half snicker. I would pay actual money, yeah, I would add two months to the completion of my degree to get out of this car right now. My only glimpse of New York City was from flying into it, and I felt a bit like Moses—granted a vision of the promised land but given no chance of entry. Now we're headed an hour and a half upstate to chez Marvin's clan. They're the "dueling cellos" sort of hill people, not like my parents, who are a teacher and guidance counselor at the same school in Brooklyn, to this day. My parents are like me: educated, but not even remotely moneyed. Lisa's a different story. We all knew she'd get herself a rich 'un, and she most certainly has. Even as kids, she wouldn't use

Barbie clothes that my mother made for her; she had to see the outfit come out of the pink cardboard and plastic box to deem it worthy of her doll. I love my sister, but she's cut from a different cloth than the rest of us. Expensive, high-thread-count cloth.

Fortunately, Marvin's on the phone most of the way to his parents' place, and I lean my head against the window and pretend to sleep. There's hardly any traffic on the road, and Marvin's SUV doing eighty is as smooth as my Toyota doing thirty. A violin piece is playing at a low volume on the car stereo, which has better sound quality than my actual stereo. When I close my eyes, all I can think about is J.J.'s slaw-riddled jaw and the fact that I might not have a job. No job.

"Pull over," I say.

Marvin glares at me, but then looks worried.

"Jesus," he says. "You're green."

One hour outside of New York, I hold the guardrail for dear life and lose the half ounce of pretzels and six ounces of cranberry juice I'd forced down on the plane ride. Marvin gets out of the car and makes a halfhearted attempt at patting my back, whispering *it's okay* until I can force myself back into the vehicle.

"Lisa's going to freak," he says, turning off the cell phone that's ringing beside him. "She'll freak out. How can you be sick? Please don't be sick."

"I'm not sick," I insist. "I'm airsick and carsick but not real sick. I swear. I'll be fine by the time we get there."

Marvin turns and looks at me harder than he has in his entire life.

"I think you're right," he concedes. "You look better already. You look good."

I know, as unspoken fact, that Marvin finds me categorically and canonically repulsive, so far am I from the Upper West Side vision of beauty that he had bought into: the is-she-or-isn't-she anorexic thing, with a dose of Betsy Bloomingdale and Jackie O, and whatever über-WASP super-twig is passing for Jesus at the moment. This, I must add, is one other thing that I like about the Midwest. I don't worry all the time about my person. If I even slip into "I'm so fat" mode, Ronnie (who proudly and automatically goes for thirds at any meal) will say "You're stupid." Not "No, Doris, you look great," but "You. Are. Stupid." I've lived in Langsdale long enough that I don't really think so much about my body. That given, I know what *effort* it takes for Marvin to compliment me and keep a straight face.

I feel decidedly better by the time we reach the Marvin Mansion, a tasteful estate with beautiful woods and rolling hills surrounding it on all sides. Nothing nouveau riche about Marvin's family, this is old, old money: money that's so rich you have to know what you're looking for to see it. I'm guessing that nothing in the house is less than two hundred years old, except, perhaps, the Chagall hanging in the entryway. It doesn't take *Antiques Roadshow* to know that said painting is *not* a print. An actual Chagall of three birds adrift in a sea of otherworldly blue. I would almost marry Marvin myself to look at that painting every day. He doesn't seem to notice it's there.

"You look better," Marvin repeats. "Really."

He puts my bags down in the foyer.

"That," I say, pointing at the painting, "is so, so beautiful."

"That," he says, still not looking at the painting, "is real."

He shows me to my room, then points me in the direction of Lisa's. I can hear my parents' voices downstairs, mingled with Marvin's extended family. My dad, of course, is louder than all of them put together. I give myself the once-over in the full-length mirror in the hallway before going in to see my sister. I do look better. Good, even. I have enough hubris to get me down the hall, head held high—that is, until I am faced with the super-fit, super-tan, super-slender twin visions of my sister and her best friend, Theresa. They're holed up in Marvin's sister's old room, chattering like wildfire.

And it's not even about how fat they look.

It's about how old they look.

Following semipoetic logic, I wonder if her marriage isn't just the absence of being single: an arbitrary but temporarily preferable state. My sister got engaged all but seconds after her twenty-ninth birthday. When I walk in on her and Theresa, they're comparing engagement rings and joking about how they're happy they "snagged one" before their looks ran out.

"I'm doing Botox," Theresa says, pulling at the skin around her eyes. "Just a touch, to take the edge off."

They talk about aging like it's a nervous breakdown.

"Hey, bridal lady," I call out, entering the room and pretending that I love Marvin and think that he and Lisa will be the happiest couple on planet Earth. I do want my sister to be happy.

"Look at you," Lisa says, gesturing for me to spin around. I rotate my Target flip-flops, sarong and white tank top a full 360 degrees before stopping, flipping my hair for emphasis. "So cute."

I love my sister. She looks the best I've ever seen her, and she's always been a knockout. Her hair is dyed a rich chocolate brown that's almost black, maybe two shades darker than natural, and she has it swept into a practice updo for the big day. She and Theresa both have on tan cotton shorts and light blue pin-striped sleeveless blouses, and the same style of shoes: petite heel with an elegant sandal that makes their feet look like they're floating. My feet look anchored. They're redoing their nails, since Marvin didn't like the finish that the manicurist used, and they remind me of a couple of kids playing dress-up, the way Lisa and I used to do.

"Mom and Dad are driving me nuts," Lisa announces. "They're in one of those holier-than-thou modes where everything at our wedding is, like, getting mentally translated into the equivalent of school lunches for poor kids. And don't even get me started on Marvin. He's like the opposite, bleeding money. Did he talk you to death on the ride up?"

"No," I say, making a snap decision not to tell my sister about my little vomit break. "But I think he talked the rest of New York to death."

Theresa, my co-maid of honor, rolls her eyes. I'm probably the only person on earth who thinks Theresa is less-than-attractive. To me, she looks pinched and weathered, in that used-to-be-a-pretty-blond kind of way that can happen anytime after puberty to those with fine features and cold hearts. She's always been jealous that Lisa has an actual sister, and she's polite but gives me the eye to let me know that I don't quite match her exacting standards. Truly, I have no idea why my sister likes her. I think they tortured fat kids at Girl Scout camp together once upon a time. Which Lisa has outgrown, which Theresa has not.

"He was on his cell?" Lisa asks. "I'm going to kill him if he doesn't lay off that thing. You know he has two now? As if call waiting weren't enough. It's like he needs four-way call waiting. Yet, when I need him to confirm seating for the reception, he's mysteriously out of range."

Theresa leans back onto her elbows, legs posed in front of her like there's some hidden camera recording her every move.

"So what's new in Idaho?" she asks.

"Indiana," I say. "Totally, totally different."

"Whatever." Theresa musters up a bony, indifferent shrug.

"Teaching's almost over," I say. "Just waiting for the next semester to get started. Trying to write every day."

"You published yet?" Theresa asks.

The second most dreaded grad-student-type question, but thankfully one that I can answer in the affirmative.

"Yes," I say. "In fact, I am."

My sister squeals and jumps up and down.

"It's so cool, Theresa. I have the two magazines that took Doris's poems. And there are going to be a million more, I just know it. She's going to be faaaamous."

Theresa looks at me blankly, but hard. Now is not the time to point out that there's no such thing as a famous living poet—unless you're counting Jewel.

"Your skin," she says finally. "God, you have really, really good skin. How old are you anyhow?"

"Almost thirty-one," I say.

Theresa gestures for me to come closer. Flattered, I oblige.

"Seriously," she says. "Lisa, have you really ever looked at Doris's skin? She has, maybe, a few deep lines starting across the forehead, but otherwise, baby's bottom. What do you use?"

I rattle off a list of drugstore products: Cetaphil, Neutrogena, whatever sample they're handing out at the mall, and Theresa listens skeptically.

"I don't know," I say jokingly. "But I don't have the figure that either of you has. Maybe the old face/ass choice is true. I chose face because it's easier and tastes better."

"Guess so," Theresa says, looking at my ass, which could be the size of Idaho and Indiana combined given the way I feel now. "Interesting."

"Stop it," Lisa warns us. "You're both beautiful. Everyone's going to be beeeautiful for my wedding. I'm getting maaaaaarried."

"Lisa?" I ask. "Have you been hitting the sauce?"

She laughs her very-bad-girl laugh, a staccato burst of glee.

"I'm so stressssssed," she hisses. "And Marvin is Groomzilla. He and his family, they're like hemorrhaging money over this wedding."

"Forty thousand dollars," Theresa chimes in, "and counting."

I can hear the words *that's disgusting* curling up in my gut, gathering steam in my windpipe, ready to burst out in one unchecked, self-righteous burst. No wonder my parents are biting their tongues. They got married at some little Catholic church, with ten guests and a reception at the local diner. Lisa and I were taught by our parents to want and to live with less, materially speaking. All through grade school we wore hand-me-downs

from my cousins (with many a half size and season between our lives and theirs), ate truckloads of spaghetti,
and macaroni and cheese, and a not-so-healthy amount
of low-grade beef, none of which I ever really minded.
However, Lisa was constantly unlearning her childhood,
adopting the American mantra of "more is better," because more is *more*.

It reminds me of a conversation I had with Claus last
week, when he asked, *So, how much you make anyhow, Ms.
W.?* I told him twelve thousand dollars a year, including
my tuition waver, a decidedly less-than-bling-bling salary.
Did Claus respect me for choosing less money and a job
that might actually make the world a better place? Nope.
Instead, he looked at me befuddled, as if he'd thought
until that exact moment that I might actually have *some*
smarts. *Not me,* he said. *I'm a make me some money when I
get out of this place.* Looking at my sister and Theresa, they
don't seem so miserable, and they certainly don't look
poor and frustrated. Not like me, wondering how much
money I'm going to make when I get out of grad school,
or if I'm even going to make it out at all.

"You seem so happy," I whisper to Lisa. "Really, truly
happy."

And whether it's the alcohol or the truth, Lisa beams
back, "I am. I really, truly am."

Once upon a time, long, long ago in my early teaching days I taught a composition class where the students
had to analyze movies. In order to keep their attention
and (hopefully) get them to learn, we watched *Pretty
Woman,* the Julia Roberts/Richard Gere vehicle in which
Roberts plays the stylin' Cinderella-hooker who helps

Gere learn to open his heart as well as his wallet. Pointing out the *improbability* of such a scenario to my students *(No, really, how many of you know hookers who married millionaires? Anyone? Anyone?),* one of the students, an open-faced girl from the mid-Indiana farmland said to me: "Don't you believe in love?" My response at the time was: "Yes, I do. But not like that."

In a way, that's a little how I feel about my sister and Marvin. Two years ago, Lisa was burnt-out on dating. Eroded shell-of-a-human-being. Totally burnt-out. One night she called me to tell me about her latest date from hell. Her last pre-Marvin date.

"He started in by telling me that he doesn't like wearing condoms," she'd said.

I think I said something along the lines of, "you've *got* to be kidding," but with a bit more judgment and expletives.

"Then," Lisa'd said, "he gestured around the bar, and was like, 'And I'll bet I'm not the only one. I'll bet if you polled every person here, they'd all say, at least the men, that they didn't like wearing them.' But, Doris, it didn't end there. I told him he ought to watch out for social diseases, and there's not enough liquor in the bar, in the world, to numb my head, and then he says, 'It just kills the mood. You get things going, then you can't get them back,' wink wink. But it's even *worse,* he then says, 'But I'm working on it. Now, when I'm looking at porn on the Internet, I practice putting on a condom. I think it's working. Kind of.'"

Marvin came next, and after the first few dates I would ask Lisa what she thought, if there were any sparks, if she felt that something in the pit of her stomach.

"No sparks," she'd say. "I don't need sparks, Doris. And that feeling in the pit of my stomach is just the bile rising for when I realize what a perfect ass the spark-man really is. I like being with Marvin. He's a gentleman, and he's very handsome. He has a good job, and he's crazy about me. At this point in time, that's worth a whole forest fire's worth of sparks."

Marvin was the guy she settled into, and she seems happy. But the sweet little latent-farm-girl romantic voice inside of me just doesn't want to call that love. Of course, my sister is now getting married and I am merely, as Theresa is quick to point out, getting older. I miss the days when it was just fat they talked about. At least fat, technically, could be helped. But aging? Good luck.

I wait until the house is quiet before sneaking down to the kitchen for a glass of milk and the blandest food I can find, something to calm my stomach for good. I hadn't been consciously avoiding my parents, but I just wasn't up for meeting the whole extended Marvin gene pool, not with a shower and rehearsal and actual wedding all crammed into the next three days. I almost cried, I was so happy to see my father in the kitchen, backlit only by the refrigerator bulb, foraging like some deranged raccoon.

"Tacky," I say. "Poor relations."

"Dori!" he says, closing the refrigerator door. "I heard you were sick!"

"Shh. Inside voice."

My father has two pieces of salami in his mouth, which he keeps there while pulling me into his flannel robe and hugging me tight. My dad's a big man, six-four slouching, and it's work for him to whisper. It always takes me a minute to get used to the gray in his hair, denser every visit, and the ever-shrinking fringe of it like a low-slung halo round his scalp. But after thirty seconds, he looks like my dad again, big smile, big nose, big eyes. All face and personality.

"Get a load of this place. Your mother went to bed. I think she was worried that if she stayed up too long, she'd break something and we'd be out our retirement."

"But, Dad," I say, "did you ever really think Lisa would marry anything else? She's not exactly a punch-and-cookies kind of girl."

My dad shakes his head.

"Marvin's a nice fellow," he says. "We went together to get haircuts. I don't think he trusted my barber. Eighty dollars he spent. On me. To trim this."

He points at his six square inches of hair.

"It looks good."

"It looks just as good for twelve," he says. "Counting tip."

We sit down at the wood-block table in the center of the kitchen. My dad pours me a glass of milk and makes us both a pair of salami sandwiches with Dijon mustard imported from France.

"This is so good," I say, talking with my mouth full. "Good thing Marvin's not marrying me. I'd get totally fat with a spread like this."

My dad reaches across the table and wipes mustard from my cheek.

"What about that?" my dad asks. "You seeing anyone special? Your mother thinks that you need to start eating lunch at the law library, or the hospital, somewhere you can meet a nice man. I'll bet that Marvin has some eligible friends."

"Dad," I say, "do you really think that Marvin's friends are going to be lining up to meet me? 'She's published two poems *and* dresses like Goodwill is Prada.' If they wanted that, they'd visit the East Village, which they don't, I guarantee it. I'd rather die alone in a cardboard box. They'd put me in a cage and starve me like some veal calf."

"They stuff the veal calves, Dori." My dad laughs. He brings out my melodramatic streak, more so than usual. "Wonder what you'll end up with," he says. "Not in a box, you're too scrappy."

"Probably with some guy who knits," I say, not really knowing where it comes from. "And I may yet die in a box. A cardboard one. Because it's all I can afford."

"If the man who knits loves you, remember that at least it's a trade. Honest work. And all this," he says, gesturing at the house, the imported mustard, the Chagall in the distance. "You know what Aristotle said, or Socrates, 'Call no man happy until he's dead.'" Morbid, my father, but accidentally so.

I try to imagine Zach here, and realize that he and my father would get along like a house on fire. They'd get twelve-dollar haircuts together and open the wedding reception up for the homeless and unemployed, and probably make fun of whatever I was wearing.

"Get some sleep," my dad advises. "Marvin has a schedule."

"Marvin has a schedule" turns out to be the understatement of the weekend. If Marvin ran my life, I would probably have three books published by now, a tenure-track position, a socially acceptable and presentable husband and a *bambina* on the way. And he does it without breaking a sweat. I've got to hand it to Lisa, if that energy translates into *all* areas of their relationship, she may have done quite well for herself. Regardless, he makes J.J. seem straight from Bedrock as managerial skills go. Theresa, queen mother of snippiness behind his back, is positively geishalike in his presence. *That Marvin,* my dad elbows me at the rehearsal dinner, *something else.*

I'm so happy to be eating lobster, I can barely respond.

"You go," my dad says, tousling my head like I'm ten years old. "That's it, you show 'em you're an eater."

Tonight is possibly the only time outside of funerals that I've seen my father in a suit. My mother is wearing a pretty peach-colored pantsuit that picks up the gold in her hair, and she's even quieter than usual. My dad's always been the talker of the two.

"Shut up, Dad," I say. "Aren't you supposed to be making a toast or something?"

Marvin has seated me between my father and some stockbroker named David Arthur. My students think that I'm so "New York/East Coast" because I'm one of the few Yankee specimens they've observed up close in the bug jar of Langsdale, but David is what I think of when I think East Coast. Square jaw, sun-blond hair, clothes just evah-so rumpled, perfect table manners, perfect grammar, like a grown-up Ken doll with distant *Mayflower* relations whom he'd have the decency *never* to mention. And I could tell you what his next girlfriend will look like without even asking. Like Theresa.

"I like that you're eating," he says, looking at my plate, which I've all but licked bone dry. "It's cool."

I could give him a hard time, but what would be the point?

"It's incredible," I say. "And you wouldn't believe it, but I've been doing it my whole life."

"My last girlfriend," he confirms, and points a finger down his throat, making a discreet gagging noise.

"Oh, no," I say. "Totally, totally defeats the purpose."

Rather than apologize for my voluptuous derriere, I decide to lean into it. I'm Anna Magnani, Monica Vitti and Sophia Loren rolled into one Midwestern tomato. Mr. Arthur, with his lifetime of yakking stick insects, will not know *what* to do with himself. I regale him with tales of the Midwest, my life there, my friends, the Ronnie and the robin story (always a winner), and you'd think I was Christopher Columbus himself, bringing news of a new and distant world.

"I've been to Chicago," David says. "Guess it's not the same."

"No, David," I say. "It most certainly is not."

At the end of the evening, David lets me borrow his cell phone to give Ronnie a call. When she picks up, she sounds exhausted. It's almost ten o'clock, and I was thinking she'd just be going to work, but it sounds as if she's been jolted from a cycle of REM sleep.

"Is it fun?" she asks politely.

"It is," I say. "Even Marvin is less on my nerves. I just wanted to see if you could get me from the airport. I didn't get to drive myself. It's a long story."

"No problem" she says. "Or I'll send Paolo."

"And the rest of L.A.?"

"I'll tell you on the ride."

The next afternoon, Lisa and Marvin get married. They exchange vows in a small church made of marbled rock, and sunlight streams through the stained-glass windows like something out of a fairy tale. David and I walk down the aisle together, and I feel like the star of an old movie in my long, champagne-hued dress. At that exact moment, it almost doesn't matter how Lisa and Marvin are going to feel about each other tomorrow, or in three years, or ten. Who could stand in a church like this, dressed like them—Lisa in my mother's antique lace gown, Marvin in tux and tails—and not feel like it's going to last forever?

Lisa's eyes are tearing, and Marvin shifts her hands in his. He clears his throat. Even David looks misty. And though it's the last thing I should be thinking about, my mind wanders to Luis, to La Varian. I'll bet the last thing CityBlondBarbie ever thought, standing next to Faux Che on some beach or in some chapel, was that somewhere down the line there was a Winn-Dixie in Indiana, a state she'd probably only seen on a map, with her future husband's lover's name on it. Or La Varian's mystery wife reduced to a footnote.

"I do," Lisa whispers. Her face is angelic, backlit and radiant.

My parents watch from the first pew, and my father holds my mother's arm close to his body. Thirty-five years, and not once do I remember my father making excuses, coming home late or "just looking" in some other woman's direction. Not once, not one day, did he and my mother seem anything but a team, anything but two people in love. Not once.

Marvin slips the ring on Lisa's finger and they kiss. I don't just love my sister, I admire her. Technically, I'm eleven months her senior, but right now I feel as though she has a lifetime on me. There's no prenup between her and Marvin, it would never occur to my sister to look at a marriage and see a divorce. Marvin, either. In a field, my sister would be part of that field. She'd find wildflowers, watch the sunset, wander as far as she could without getting lost. She'd look around her and say, *Yes, all this and me, too.*

Walking back down the aisle, David links his arm in mine and offers me a tissue.

"It's okay," he says. "They're going to make it."

And I hope they do. I really, really hope they do.

# Ronnie

"Look," Mona says, holding up a *People* magazine that someone left behind. "It says here that Marcus Montgomery and that Dakota Triplehorn bought each other matching Rolls-Royces and platinum his-and-her watches *and* a private jet so they can get around to wherever they want to. Did it for their fourth anniversary, been dating for four months."

I don't even know who these people are, because for the first time in years and years I'm out of the popculture loop. It's not even ignorance on purpose, like people who always say, *Well* I *wouldn't know.* I *don't have a TV,* all superior and elitist over the blind masses. I happen to love TV—in all its entertaining, horrifying beauty. Hell, for *Roots* alone TV has been worth all the other crap mixed in—even the "reality" bullshit they've been peddling these days. I actually miss TV, now that I've not been able to afford cable all summer. I wouldn't have the time to watch, though, even if I could afford it, and for some reason, I'm angry about idiot Marcus Montgomery and *Dakota,* and all their Hollywood bullshit, even if I don't know who they are.

I say, "Who in the hell's that?" I'm sitting across from Mona and have my head propped up on my two fists stacked one on top of the other. We have four more minutes until we have to go downstairs. It's raining outside, so we've had to stay in.

Mona shoves the magazine at me. I pick it up, put it down, shove it back toward her and shrug.

"*Previous Engagement?* You ain't seen that picture?"

"No." I yawn. "I hate stupid films."

"Films," Mona says. "La-di-da. They ain't pictures no more?" She checks her watch. "Man, I hate to go downstairs right now," she says and picks up the magazine one more time. She looks again at the picture of the happy— Hollywood happy—couple. "Well, I don't care. I think that Dakota is pretty."

"If plastic is pretty," I say, but then lay off because to my own ears I sound like one of those I-don't-like-TV people. It's too easy to be the jaded Los Angeleno. Once you've seen one Botox/bulimia combination, one man with plucked eyebrows and a fake tan, you've seen them all.

"You see anybody famous when you was out there?" Mona asks. She gets up and starts making herself one more cup of coffee and puts three packets of creamer in it. I perk up when she asks the question. I did see one of my favorite actors, one of the character actors that no one has ever heard of. Joe Torey. I get excited telling Mona about being behind him in the checkout line. He bought Frosted Flakes and deodorant.

*"Who?"* Mona screws up her face.

"You know. The one with the crazy teeth? Always plays losers?"

Mona just shrugs.

I love that guy. I was so excited to be behind him in the checkout. I almost told him what a big fan I was, but decided that was too stalky. "He was just in the small art film *The Lightbulb.*"

Mona's finished her coffee and crushes the cup. She stretches. "I wouldn't of seen that picture," she says. "I hate pictures like that. Nothing ever happens." She stood at the door. "You coming or what?"

Downstairs, I took my time walking to my stations. The night seemed longer than it had ever been my two months here. I went to them, though, and started working, because I had no choice. Work, or leave. Ray came around checking in like he did with everybody every night.

"What's wrong with you, College?" he calls out over the noise of the machines. "You working right slow tonight. This ain't no California, now. Ain't no time to be 'mellow' or whatever you call it."

I smile and hold up a speaker cover to inspect it before I answer. It isn't perfect. You're supposed to be able to see through all the tiny holes in it, but this one's tiny holes are mostly covered over in plastic. "Machine's off, Ray," I say. I show him the speaker.

He holds it up to the light to get a better look. "Dang. It's been giving us trouble all week. Lots of damaged ones coming through. Let me go turn this dadgum thing off." In a minute, it's slightly less noisy because Ray's turned off the machine. "You can go work on eight until I get this figured out. I'm gone have to reset the controls, get that plastic coming through right."

"Okay." I look in the direction of station eight and suddenly I'd give anything to be doing something else. Ray's turning to go fix the machine, but I stop him before he gets too far. "You think I can work on another station, Ray?"

He puts the speaker cover down on the conveyor belt. "Another station?"

"Yeah, I mean, I've been doing this one for a while. Two months now." I'd gone from needing to take notes on every little step, to being bored, so bored that much of my entire shift was always one big daydream. Me sitting on Bita's deck, me and pre-asshole La Varian, me trying to compose arguments for Professor Lind's final paper, me sleeping or sitting on my couch watching hours of TV. It's a wonder cars all over America don't have shitty speakers.

Ray scratches his head. "We got you trained good on these two things, Ronnie, and everybody's doing their jobs at their stations already...it don't make sense to pull you off these here and retrain you on something we don't need you for."

I nod and try not to look sad. But I give it one more shot. "I guess I'm just bored, Ray." I shove my hands into my pockets.

Ray picks up the bad speaker cover from the belt. He turns his free palm up, like, what do you want me to do? He stares at me, and I get the feeling that I'm one of the most bewildering people Ray has ever met. "Well, hell, College," he says finally. "A person can be a lot more worse off than bored." He points to station eight with the speaker cover, then walks away.

We've waited too long to take our walk around the outside trail at the Y. I didn't wake up until two in the afternoon, so now the sun is blaring and the humidity is ungodly. It rained all morning long, so now there are little worm carcasses everywhere. I try not to look down while we trample all over them and mash them to shit. Doris and I shoot for five laps, which is five miles, but sometimes, depending on the level of hungover, sleepy, tired or hot, we don't quite make it. We alternate talking with no talking, just walking, and now I'm thinking about how I'd like to be back in my bed sleeping until it's time for me to go back to work tonight. I change the channel in my head because there's no need thinking about work if I'm not working.

"Professor Lind is throwing an end-of-class gathering at her house," I say. "You have to come. It's not just for folks in the class, either. I can bring a guest. She's doing one big summer thing and inviting a lot of different people."

Doris adjusts her yellow sun hat and pushes her white sunglasses back up her nose. "I think I have something to do, like, watch a whole lot of TV and paint my toenails."

"Okay, that *is* more fun than another academic party. I'm not arguing that. I'm just saying, pretty please. If you're thinking karmicly at all, you'll come with. It'll all come back to you."

"Fine," Doris says. "Gross, something just bit me." She slaps her shin. "Which one are we on?"

"Three."

"Damn, it's hot. Why can't we be on lap four?"

We walk for a bit and stop to pet one of the familiar dogs on the trail, a brown Chihuahua named Eddie. His owner's a big guy with a sandy beard who always stops to let us pet Eddie, but he never says much. We don't even know the guy's name, but we always say hello to Eddie. When Eddie's owner gets out of earshot, Doris says he reminds her of Earl.

"He does," I say. "Totally."

"Cute," Doris says. "He's cute, just like Earl."

"Y-es," I agree slowly.

"He asked about you last night, wondered why Paolo and I had been at the bar three times in a row without you."

"What'd you say?" I fall behind Doris to let a jogger pass us on our left. I never told Earl that I did anything else but go to school and write. It never came up. I don't know how I feel about him knowing. I think I prefer him thinking of me as the glamorous, half-naked, drunken flirt who's always stumbling in and out of the bar, rather than "a factory worker." I'd started Valtek not really thinking about it much, other than it was just another job, but other people's reactions had me thinking these days, like the times I used to wear my fishnets proudly without even thinking about them, until people kept giving me looks that said "inappropriate." Doris waits for me to catch up before she answers my question.

"I told him about Valtek," she says.

"Oh." I envision my Jack and Cokes not being so generous anymore. I keep walking in silence.

"He said he had a cousin at Valtek."

"Oh, no," I say, slowing down. "Who?"

"I don't know, I didn't ask," Doris says. "Why 'Oh no'? Why do you care?"

I shrug. "I don't know. It's just weird, I guess."

Doris doesn't say much for a good fifteen minutes. We complain about the bugs, pet a few more dogs that come around the trail and laugh about Allesandro, on whom my crush lasted all of one day. It was the *Any wife of mine is going to give me eight kids and be a better cook than my mother* that turned me off. Cute only goes so far. I'm lost in my own thoughts again, when Doris clears her throat.

"Okay," she says. "Don't kill me."

"What," I say. I stop walking. "Don't kill me" can't be followed by anything good.

"It'sjustthatEarlkeptaskingaboutyou," she blurts in one breath. "He looked so sad until I told him that you and La Varian weren't hanging out anymore." Doris covers her hat with her hands and bends forward as if she's waiting for me to hit her over the head with something.

"What," I ask slowly, "did you do?"

"Gave him your number?" Doris winces and closes her eyes. She finally opens one and looks at me.

It takes me a minute to hear—and understand—what she's saying. "Are you *crazy?*"

Doris starts walking again. Fast.

"He's going to *call* me?"

"I don't know," Doris says, biting her nails. "He said he would?"

"You say that like you're asking *me*," I say. "Man," I say, "if you weren't so goddamn shocked yourself, that you'd do something so *crazy,* I'd *kill* you. I'd kill you *dead.*"

"What? I don't know why you're flipping out," Doris

says with resolve. She's adjusting her hat, since she crushed it earlier. She picks up the pace. "You know you like him."

"Kidding," I say. "I was kidding."

Doris looks at me out the corner of her eye. "Oh, *no* you weren't," she says. "Drunk half the time, yes. Kidding, no."

I walk and don't say anything. What am I supposed to do with someone like Earl? Yes, I think he's handsome. Yes, he's awfully nice. But he's a good ol' boy. Me dating Earl would be beyond interracial. It would be inter*planetary*. Inter-common-damn-sense. Clair Huxtable and Grizzly Adams. Together again.

"What lap is this?" Doris asks matter-of-factly.

"The last," I say, and wipe the sweat from my forehead with the front of my T-shirt. "*Your* last," I correct, and shoot her a look.

"I'll stay for *hours* at Professor Lind's party," Doris offers. "I'll make like the Brie and couscous is barbecued pork ribs, and I'll never ever give your number out again, I swear."

One thing I hate more than a lot of things about academia is arriving at a "party," only to be met by silence—meaning no music—and folks hovered over a platter of dried-out carrots. And that's what Doris and I get when we step into Professor Lind's house. It's a beautiful house, brick with a red door, and slick hardwood floors that echo when you enter the foyer. She's got lots of art hanging on her walls, eclectic stuff. African masks, Shakespeare prints next to Andy Warhol prints, lots of beautiful plants. At least the lighting is nice, too. Soft, with lots of candles placed on countertops and windowsills.

Only three rooms are open to the guests, and I wonder what's in Professor Lind's other rooms. A lot of faculty are standing around, predictably, the vegetable platter. I skim the room to survey the potential damage. Then I have to grab Doris's arm.

"La Varian and Iris are here," I whisper too loudly, like a kid.

"No. Way. Where?"

I tilt my head in their direction. I can't look again—not until I have time to get used to the idea of seeing them together.

"*What* is La Varian thinking?" Doris says, cupping her mouth and leaning into me, even though they're across the room and probably can't hear. "And can you believe that tiny college he's going to next? Compared to it Langsdale is Yale, Harvard and Howard all rolled into one. And what is she wearing? She looks like she just came from an archeological dig, and he looks like Christmas and Kwanzaa had a head-on collision."

"And we were worried about the way we dressed tonight."

Doris makes a face. "Let's go get something to drink, like immediately. *This* without alcohol is not even an option." We weave through various clusters of people until we make it to the kitchen, where we think we'll be safe. Professor Lind is pouring ice into a bucket and looks up when she hears us laughing.

"What's so funny?" she asks. She smiles and nods toward Doris. "Hello."

"This is Doris," I say.

"Already amused?" Professor Lind sits the ice bucket on the counter and fishes a pack of cigarettes from her blazer pocket. "Help yourselves," she says, motioning toward the bar. Doris gets us cups and pours the wine while Professor Lind stares at me. "I like to know the dirt."

"Oh, it's just this guy I dated for a little bit. He's in there with Iris. I guess they're together now."

Professor Lind lights her cigarette and takes a puff. "That *you* dated? *With* Iris?"

I nod.

"Hmm," she says slowly, and blows out her smoke. She looks up at the ceiling and squints her eyes, trying to make the connection. "Is it La Varian Laborteux you used to date?" When she says his name—La Varian Laborteux—I actually get proud for a second. I'm the kind of woman who deserves to be with someone named La Varian Laborteux. It just reeks of elegance. Not the kind of woman to be with someone named Earl. It occurs to me that I don't even know Earl's last name, and the pride leaks out of me and is replaced with sorrow for myself. I can hear my father lecturing me about Sammy.

"Drink up," Doris urges, handing me a plastic cup of Chardonnay. She touches her cup to mine and takes a sip.

"That," says Professor Lind, "is a fabulous outfit." She reaches over to touch the ruffles of Doris's skirt. I'd told her she should *totally* wear it because it was very Carmen Miranda.

"Thanks," says Doris. She looks at me. "I think we're going to have to keep moving all night to avoid what's-his-name and what's-her-name."

"Or not," Professor Lind says. "Iris is an interesting choice for La Varian." She levels her eyes at me. "A confusing choice. Is there a story?"

"It's long," I say. "The story."

Doris keeps sipping and looking back and forth at me and Professor Lind.

"That La Varian is a very smart young man," Professor Lind states. "On his way to brilliant. I saw him give a paper last week. It was flawless."

"I'm sure it was," I say without much enthusiasm. I'm thinking about *Trisha, without whom this article would not have been written...*

"The *paper* was flawless," Professor Lind goes on, then pauses for what seems like effect. "I don't think you should have to keep moving to avoid anything. You should keep moving to *get* what you want."

"Amen to that," Doris says.

"Hell—" Professor Lind takes a long drag before stubbing out her cigarette "—I knew I forgot something. There's no music. I never intended to be..." Her voice trails off. "Like *that*."

Doris and I raise our eyebrows at each other.

"Any suggestions?" Professor Lind asks. We follow her into the living room and start to look through her CD collection. Lowell Fulsome. Aretha Franklin. Elvis Costello. David Bowie. My hands stop at Chaka Khan.

"We have to put this on," I say.

Professor Lind extends her hand and I place the CD in it. "This will keep the dryness and Derrida to a minimum," she remarks, smiling. "A party should be a party."

We've reached the cutoff point, Doris and I, but sadly, no one will. Cut us off, that is. And if no one else will cut us off, why should we do it to ourselves? Professor Lind has a houseful now, and we've managed to mingle and not get into much trouble—until now—because inevitably everyone on the Last-Person-I'd-Like-To-See list is here and accounted for: La Varian and Iris, of course; Luis; that awful know-it-all from Shakespeare class, John; and every other faculty member who has never learned to say hello nor learned to start a sentence without the phrase "I read somewhere..." I saw Luis come in a while ago, but alcohol, surprises and Doris don't mix, so I decide not to mention it. She'll see him when she sees him, and will be too drunk to care—I hope.

In the meantime, we think it a good idea to seek out people we would have avoided two hours and six glasses of wine ago. After a while, when we're standing in a tight circle talking to poor, jittery Professor Lee, who does Twentieth-Century American, Luis sidles up to Doris, asking, "How *are* you?" Some people will walk straight into a fire.

"How am I?" Doris repeats to Luis. "Like you care. Why do you even bother talking to me?" She shakes her hands at him. "Why?"

Luis looks around to survey what kind of damage is being done. We were all having a fun conversation before Luis slithered up. Professor Lee had let his hair down. He's bald but still. Professor Lee is a shy, older professor who is near retirement but has a sense of humor anyway. We were lamenting how, still, Carver is underrated, and how come the meanest and most idiotic person still won *Survivor* every time. It was maddening, wasn't it? Luis came up to us right in the middle of Professor Lee's one-night-I-was-so-drunk story. Professor Lee scratches his nose when Doris decides to acknowledge Luis's presence in a less-than-diplomatic way. "Why," she asks, "are you breathing my air?"

"Excuse me," Professor Lee says. "Restroom," he adds like an apology.

Now Luis is laying on the charm that always seemed to work on most people. I don't know whether to stay or go. I stay.

"Doris," Luis says evenly, "there's no reason to be antagonistic." She pulls at her skirt to smooth it out. "I'm just saying hello," he repeats, calm and even, as if he's trying to reason with a mental patient. He adjusts the lapels on his blazer and looks at me. I look away. Why is he doing this to himself? Earlier, he'd been talking to Iris and La Varian—mostly La Varian. Christmas collided with Kwanzaa was looking good to Luis, it was clear.

"You are a liar and a fraud," Doris says. "Figure yourself out. I can't believe we even dealt, and I'm glad I've moved on to actual heterosexual men. Making out with some random stockbroker at my sister's wedding was so much better than…than *whatever* it was we were doing. Hand," Doris holds her hand up in front of Luis's face. "And breast," she says, grabbing her right boob. "One feels the other. Got it?"

*Ouch,* I think, looking at Luis, who honestly doesn't seem too fazed. Could it be something like relief on his face?

"I guess I really can't talk to you," Luis says with the same measure, trying to play it off, but as my mother says, *I ain't buying what you selling.* He turns away and walks into the kitchen.

"*Hate* him," Doris says, and that's when she notices Zach who'd been standing behind Luis the whole time. We just didn't see him talking to someone else. Doris looks happy to see him and gives him a big smile, but he looks at her and doesn't smile back. He just turns back to the woman next to him.

Doris looks confused, but doesn't try again. "What's that all about?" she asks. She looks a little hurt.

"Ain't no telling," I reply. "But I'd go out on a limb right now and say it's time to go." I wonder about who heard what when Doris was going off on Luis, and I think it's time to cut our drunken losses and get out. "So let's go," I say.

I do what Professor Lind said. I don't avoid La Varian and Iris. I just don't have a reason to go near them. I look at them when Doris and I are leaving, though. Iris is standing close to La Varian and La Varian keeps his arms and hands close to his body. I know in my heart that he can't give a shit about Iris, but I know in my heart that people like La Varian don't like to be called out on their stuff, don't like to be wrong. Reaching for the doorknob, I hear the beginning of Rick James singing "Superfreak," and I think, *La Varian and I should be dancing to that.* We used to dance to music in my apartment all the time, and we were good, naturally good, like two ribbons intertwining, that's how well we danced together. I can just hear Iris making one of her heavily theorized points about how bad it is to make assumptions about black people and dancing. *It's so essentialist, reinscribing certain paradigms of blackness, that black people are naturally good at dancing.*

Maybe. She might have a point. But all I can think is that it was nice when La Varian and I danced and it would have been nice to dance with him again. Everything, all of it, would have been nice.

# Doris

Freud, to my way of thinking, was mostly a great big who's-your-daddy psychoanalytic nightmare. And if you think he was just worried about little boys wanting to sleep with their mommies, think again. Read "Dora," a case history about some poor teenage Viennese girl whose parents split and then her father's lover's husband (very *General Hospital*) started putting the moves on Dora like the late-nineteenth-century pervert that he was. Freud thought she was "ill" because she *didn't* respond to these advances. Further, Freud decided that Dora's "hysterical" (i.e., made-up) cough was the product of her thinking about, and I quote, "organs other than the genitals for the purpose of sexual intercourse." If that were the case, at least *half* the adult population would be hacking up a lung on a regular basis. Craziness. I will, however, on rare occasions, give the man his due—his thoughts on the unconscious, for instance. The idea that none of us really walks around knowing exactly what we want or doing exactly what we feel. No matter how much we think we're self-aware and acting accordingly, there's something lurking beneath—that seven-tenths of the submerged iceberg, just waiting to surface.

I say this not to be pretentious, but in defense of my own recent actions. Maybe I shouldn't have given Ronnie's number to Earl. I know he's not La Varian, but really, isn't that the point? And whether Ronnie wants to admit it to herself or not, Earl isn't just another Billy Ray. The week Ronnie was gone, Earl motioned me over while Paolo and I were at the Office Saloon. "Did I offend Ronnie?" he asked, concerned. Earl doesn't look concerned when he cuts off drunk bikers twice his size, but he was worked up, twisting a towel in his hand while he was talking. "I would *never* offend her," he vowed. He acts like a different person when Ronnie's around, tries to impress her, begs her to ride that bike of his (a death trap, if you ask my opinion). And Ronnie can't quite see how she acts around him. She held back on the La Varian thing with Earl, never told him *all* about it, which I can't but think means something, even if she doesn't want to admit it. I quote Dr. Freud here: "The person under analysis" (or for my purposes, trying to date successfully) "must overcome certain resistances—the same resistances as those which, earlier, made the material concerned into something repressed by rejecting it from the conscious." Of *course* Ronnie doesn't want to think about dating Earl and staying in Langsdale. Heck, I'd chuck that right from my conscious mind, as well. But if she can just separate Earl out from the Langsdale part, take the idea one little dose at a time, de-repress it, to bastardize my Freud, I think she just might have a nice six months or so. Or more? Or less? He's *not* your average Billy Ray.

I run this elaborate, dare I say insightful, theory by Paolo, while we're sitting outside at the Vineyard, waiting for Ronnie to show.

"So funny," Paolo says. "That's the longest explanation I've ever heard for the fact that you, yes *you,* have the biggest mouth ever. Ever."

Not nice.

"And now," Paolo says, "we can't even go to the Saloon until Ronnie gives us the go-ahead. I'll go broke drinking here."

For the local wine bar it's nice enough. You can sit outside the rare evenings it isn't pouring rain. But the service is worse and the drinks cost twice as much than at the Office Saloon.

Paolo swats a mosquito that's as big as a quarter away from his face.

"God almighty," he says. "They're nuclear bugs out here. I can't get West Nile, at least not until fall, when I'm teaching the grown-ups and have health insurance again."

He motions one of the waiters for a citronella candle and is summarily ignored.

"They're mad," I whisper. "We're bad customers."

"You're the one who ordered *water,* Doris. At least I've had the decency to nurse this glass of wine, which, by the way, is now the temperature of swamp water. White wine. Not good."

"Paolo, as of last night, I can officially no longer handle my liquor. You should congratulate me."

He shakes his head.

"Story first."

At that moment, Ronnie arrives, wearing a baby-doll sundress and her dreadlocks in two gigantic bunlike clusters on either side of her head with thin, gold hoops in her ears. Very summer chic.

"The force," Paolo says. "May it be with you."

"Don't be so *obvious,*" Ronnie says, laughing.

Paolo has on a white, ribbed tank and clam digger–style chinos. Nothing to make fun of there; he could step on a runway and not look out of place.

"So why isn't Doris drinking?" Paolo asks. "Did I miss the one fun, English department party of the millennium?"

"No," Ronnie says. "Just the funniest."

"So?"

"Long story short," Ronnie says. "Luis. Doris. Lots of wine. Doris taking her hand, grabbing her breast, showing Luis—and the rest of the department—how it's done. Luis walking away. Doris passing out on the way home and begging to go to Denny's."

"Ugh," I say. "I forgot about that part."

"Doris," Paolo says. "Shame on you. If I didn't know you better, I'd say that was gay bashing. Poor Luis."

"Poor Luis, my ass," I say. "I thought I was over all that nonsense, but evidently I have a lot of leftover Luisophobia. It just might have looked accidentally like homophobia. God, I hope that's not what people think."

"Professor Lind said she thinks you should be invited to all the parties," Ronnie adds. "For what that's worth."

"Fabulous," I say. "Abso-freaking-lutely fabulous."

The unconscious, if you really stop to think about it, isn't such a bad thing. I'm not sure I'd have made it through the past week without mine. My sister's wedding was great, lovely, fun, all of the above. I mostly forgot about Langsdale, and J.J., and my impending potential for unemployment. I even got a long, sweet good-night kiss from David-the-stockbroker—grossly exaggerated at Professor Lind's party, but for what I choose to think are obvious reasons. I came back to no resolution. Zero. No e-mail from J.J., no nice message on my machine telling me it was all going to be okay, the charges had been dropped, etc. etc. One from Zach, asking if I got in all right, asking to call, but he's since pulled a colossal Jekyll and Hyde. It's a biblical personality change, Saul on the road to Tarsus–type conversion. Last week he's driving me to the airport, this week he'll barely look in my direction. And it hurts my feelings more than I would have thought, and not just because it's hard enough to teach knowing that there's a mamma-Judas out there, one person removed from one of my smiley-smiley students.

The last week of class should be the best week. It should involve me patting them on the back for working so hard, and them turning in their best essays of the summer. It should culminate in some fun activity, a party, a reading of their work, a sense of closure and accomplishment. Instead, I just watch my language and wish that they'd all go away. Even Claus notices the change.

"Frosty," he said to me yesterday, tilting his head in the direction of Zach.

"Mind your own business," Sharelle warned. I didn't have the energy to engage.

I knew things were bad when Will smiled sympathetically at me before turning in his final draft.

Today, though, I decide that since it's the last day of

class, I'm going to put my own feelings aside and do the last-day-of-class dance that I've mastered over the past five years. What is it that they tell the real alcoholics? Fake it till you make it? They're each supposed to bring in a poem, a song or a piece of writing that speaks to them, tell the class about it and give each other a hand. I've selected Cavafy's poem "Ithaca," which says in so many words that life is a journey we barely understand. Sparse and clear. I thought about bringing one of my own poems. They even asked to hear one, but since I came back from my sister's wedding, I can't even look in the direction of my computer. Something unconscious happening there, too.

On the way to class, I run into J.J. She's jogging around the campus in a purple T-shirt with gaping rings of sweat darkening the fabric around her belly and beneath her arms. I wait for her to catch her breath while she gestures at me like a crossing guard, motioning for me to be patient.

"Doris," she pants, "just sent you an e-mail. Good news."

As much as I hate J.J., my heart starts doing a two-step.

"The mother. She read her daughter's latest paper, and that, plus some other documentation, made her decide to drop the charges. We can't get rid of the paper trail, not entirely, but there'll be no further course of action."

"Oh, thank God," I say. "Thank God, thank God, thank God."

"Thank Zach, too," she says. "He wrote you one heck of a letter."

I hurry on to class, and J.J. chugs off in the other direction.

I'm no longer faking happy, I'm officially euphoric.

The sky seems brighter, the grass greener, bluebirds on my shoulder and all that jazz. I'm off the hook, and even though I never believed I was on the hook, I feel like some wrongly accused innocent set free, free, free. That, and Zach wrote a letter. For me. On my behalf. Mr. Hyde himself. I must look totally spacey when I walk into the classroom. Zach is joking with Claus, and even gives me a half smile.

"You look so pretty, Ms. Weatherall," Tina says. I have on black capri pants and a peasant blouse, hair pulled slightly off my face. One of my better looks.

"What happened?" Claus joins in. "You get some? I think Ms. Weatherall be getting some when she's *supposed* to be grading our essays."

Zach looks down. I can't tell if he's still smiling or not. He walks to the back of the classroom and takes a seat.

"Can't I just be loving life?" I ask.

"Your life must be hella lot better than TROOPS," Sharelle says. She has on a bright red shirt and red ribbons woven into her braids.

"I think it's you and Zach," Claus says. "I think it's looooove."

I'm racking my brain for something to say, but Zach beats me to it.

"There's nothing going on between me and Doris. If she's happy, or getting some, rest easy that it's not my doing." He's looking at me as he says it, not angry but no mistaking the tone.

Snippy, *and* with Claus, *and* on the very last day.

Dead silence.

I pull out a stack of papers and switch to the business at hand.

"These were excellent," I begin. "There's not one person in this class who hasn't improved. You should be extremely proud of yourselves, and know that each and every one of you is better prepared than most of the other freshmen who'll be coming in this fall. I don't want to hear about anyone not making it through the next school year. You're too smart for that. You've worked too hard."

Back to the high fives and happiness. Zach mouths "sorry" from the back of the room. I nod in acknowledgment, not forgiveness. Since when has "getting some" with me become the single most reprehensible notion on this planet?

"We'll start with self-assessments, then we'll move on to our open-mike poetry/music/reading-slam-type thing." I ask them to evaluate their own performance over the course of the semester, looking back on how their writing has changed these past six weeks. It's better than a grade for giving each individual a sense of how much he or she has improved. They write intently for a good fifteen minutes while I swing my legs back and forth like some five-year-old, and Zach reads a book, not lifting his head until the last paper is turned in and we move on to the fun.

The reading goes well. Sharelle reads a poem that she wrote herself, an hysterically funny rant about TROOPS gossip that rhymes heavily and has everyone in stitches. Claus applauds with hands over his head. Tina's brought in an inspirational piece, something vaguely churchy and uplifting, and for his bit, Claus procures a CD player, pops in a CD and raps along. Another hearty round of applause. They clap politely for my poem, which is clearly too highbrow for the event.

"What about your poems?" Sharelle says. "I thought you were bringing your stuff, not some old Greek."

"I forgot," I lie. "And Sharelle, let me say that it's almost a good thing, since you're a tough act to follow."

Zach goes last and reads from one of my favorite books of poems ever, *Where the Sidewalk Ends* by Shel Silverstein. When I was in second grade, I had every word of it memorized. He does dramatic voices for each of the poems, and Claus is laughing in spite of himself.

"Don't be strangers," he says at the end of class.

Once we've finished all the goodbyes, Zach picks up his backpack and makes for the door.

"Zach," I say. "I heard from J.J. Those charges were dropped."

"Good," he says. "I'm happy for you."

He starts out the door again.

"J.J. says you wrote a letter for me."

"It was no big deal. Don't worry about it."

"She made it sound like a big deal. I just wanted to say thanks."

He puts his backpack down and leans against one of the desks. I think he's going to say something but he doesn't.

"Don't you want to go over their self-evaluations?" I ask. "That's the best part."

He thinks for a minute before looking up.

"Nah," he says. "You can just put them in my mailbox at school when you're done with them."

I'm at a loss. The only thing left to do is go full-out second grade on him.

"This sounds really stupid," I hedge. "But are you mad

at me? Did I do something that I missed? I thought we were getting along really well."

Zach doesn't dismiss me outright. He looks at the desk, looks at his shoes, looks at the ceiling, and lets out a sigh. I'm looking at his chest, at the thin tangle of hair showing through the V at the top of his shirt, at the deep brown his skin has tanned since the start of summer. Then my eyes follow a line down his arm, to his hands, which are clenching and unclenching, thick silver bands on his middle and forefingers.

"Okay, Doris," he says. "I'll be honest with you, if that's what you really want."

But I don't want him to be really honest. I want him to cross the distance between us and run one of those hands soft against my blouse. I want to walk over to him and weave my fingers through his hair and close to his skin. I want him to know that I've only just now, this very instant, realized that I've wanted this weeks longer than I've let on, even to myself.

"Okay," I say.

"I wrote this letter for you," he begins, making extended eye contact with me for the first time this week. "And while I was writing it, I was thinking about how much I've started liking you this summer. Not like Claus says, I don't know, maybe not that, but as a person. As a teacher. When you're in the classroom, Doris, I love being around you. You're funny and real, and not so self-conscious and stupidly obsessed with superficial crap…"

If this is the good part, I'm not sure I want to hear the rest.

"Okay," I say.

"And then the first time I see you out, it's at that stupid party at Professor Lind's house, and it's this other Doris. Three Stooges Doris, with you and Ronnie and that dancer guy."

"He wasn't even there!"

"That's not the point. I guess I'd thought when I took you to the airport that we were at a different place than we obviously were. And that's partially my fault. But as your friend, as someone who thinks there's a better person in there than you let on—God only knows why—you really shouldn't be announcing to a roomful of professors who you blew over the weekend. It's not good politics. Because not everyone sees you teach, Doris, and not everyone is going to bother getting to know you. And that stupid act you put on, that's what they're going to believe."

He's not even yelling. He's talking to me like I'm Claus, or Will, or Tina. Like he's explaining why the thesis statement I've written is never going to work, can't carry the paper I've intended to write. And it hurts, not like temporary probation from J.J., but a horrible too-late kind. I can feel it spreading across every square inch of my body.

"I didn't 'blow' anyone over the weekend," I say. I don't even think that's what I said to Luis, but everything from that conversation to my nontrip to Denny's is one big, hazy mess.

"Doris, that's my point all over again. If you didn't, why say you did to a roomful of people? Not just people, your professors. Your peers. It's just…frustrating." Then a long pause. "Disappointing."

After that, Zach leaves and this time I don't try to stop him. I sit down in the empty classroom and watch through the windows as Zach moves purposefully from my field of vision.

★ ★ ★

"That's some last day," Ronnie says.

We're at the Wing Shack, drinking beer and eating the super-hot special with blue cheese and celery. This is what we've been reduced to, one of the top ten dangers of small-town living. We can't go back to the Vineyard because it's overpriced and reminds Ronnie of La Varian. We can't go to the Office Saloon because of the Earl situation, and the fact that Ronnie still isn't sure what she wants to do about that. We can't go to the coffee shop because that's Zach's favorite haunt. We'd better find someplace fast, though, because the Wing Shack only serves beer and soda, and I hate beer so much that I couldn't get drunk on it if I tried.

"No Paolo?" Ronnie asks. "Our other, what was it, 'stooge'?"

"His fella's in town from San Fran. They're locking themselves away, but he wants us to go to the recital he's been putting together."

"The junior ballet league? Do we have to?"

"I believe we do. It's not until next week, so don't panic in advance."

"This beer," Ronnie says, pointing at the plastic cup in front of her that's only down a third. "*Something's* gotta give, because this beer tastes like *ass.*"

"Do you think I act like an idiot?" I ask. "Does no one in this department take me even remotely seriously?" I look down at my nails, painted the new 1960s "kitten" pink, preordered from MAC by my sister, who gave all her bridesmaids self-pampering packages as wedding favors. I can't decide which I hate more: the fact that I love this nail polish, its perfect, pastel pinkness, love the fact that I *have* it, the same way Claus loves having a pair of "Sean John" jeans. That, or the fact that I *know* better than to love this nail polish, *know* better than to talk about loving it, and *know* that if I were teaching the TROOPS version of me, I'd make myself *ashamed* to love this nail polish. Nail polish that I technically cannot even afford.

"I'm not humoring this," Ronnie replies. "Since when do you care? You want to stay up all night thinking about how Way Gay feels about you? Or if Iris thinks you're smart? Or J.J.? You'll never convince me you give a real good-goddamn, so don't even try convincing yourself."

"Zach hates me," I say. "It was the most disproportionate display of condescension that I've ever, ever seen. Ever."

"Well, you know what they say."

"What?"

Ronnie points a chicken bone in my direction.

"Hate is angry love."

"But I don't hate Zach," I explain. "Even after this afternoon. It's not like Luis. I'm mad and I'm sad, but I don't hate him. I wish I could go back and do it all over. From the party on."

Ronnie lets out a little sigh and pushes her hair behind her ears.

"I hate to be the one tell you, Doris. But if that's the way you feel, how you really, really feel. That's even worse."

I watch the warm beer in front of me get flatter by the minute.

"Don't tell me that," I say. "Because at this exact moment, I'd rather not know."

# Ronnie

That night, after Professor Lind's party, was the first time I ever called in sick to Valtek. I just couldn't do it. I told myself that I would just have to stay home and not spend money *out* this week. I'd sell some CDs if I had to, and I'd eat only two meals a day, two twenty-five-cent packets of ramen noodles would be enough to get by on. Eating less won't kill me. I'm certainly thick enough to keep from wasting away. That party was last week, and I've been at Valtek like clockwork ever since. I'm starting to feel numb, though, like very little, other than work, matters. I get excited about my Othello paper due in a week, but then I can't seem to focus on it. All I can focus on is sleeping. But for all my complaints about grad school, I've been thinking about staying. Not just staying, but on through a doctorate degree. What working in a factory for two months has proven to me is this: It's no kind of job to have if you can avoid it. And if I can survive the summer, I'll be teaching again in the fall, and everything will work out. I can go back to doing the thing I love—the only thing I know how to do. Besides packing up vents and plastic speakers from an assembly line. At her party, I found Professor Lind sitting on her deck alone. I talked to her about staying on after the MFA to do Ph.D. work, and I was surprised that she was skeptical.

"Why do you want to do it?" she asked me. "What do you think you'll get out of it?"

I was annoyed. I thought she was trying to discourage me because she didn't think I could do it. "Isn't this like the chapter in Žižek, in the discussion of *'Che vuoi?'* How everyone asked Jesse Jackson what he *really* wanted when he ran for president? Nobody asked white candidates what they really wanted by running for president. Now you're asking me what I really want by getting a Ph.D."

Professor Lind smiled. "You're right," she said simply. "I'm glad you've paid such close attention to Žižek. There's more to that chapter, though. The Lacanian formula of fantasy? Let's just play fast and loose with the guy and try to make sense of him vis a vis real life. *Your* life." Professor Lind extended one hand, palm up. "In this hand is your *'Che vuoi?,'* the question of what you really want by thinking about more grad school. In this hand—" she held her other hand up "—is the actual thing—at least five more years of grad school and an actual doctoral degree." Then she spread both hands wide apart in front of her. "The distance between these two things? That's the fantasy between what you desire and the actual object of desire. So." She picked up a wine bottle and poured some more into her cup. "I just want you to ask yourself what fantasy, what scenario, you see when you look at a Ph.D.?"

I sighed. A few fireflies drifted past us. And I took a drink from my cup.

"Look, Ronnie. All I'm saying is that I know you're a creative writer and a very intelligent woman. You don't need a Ph.D. to be either one, so when I ask you what you really want, I'm asking you about your desires, what you expect the Ph.D. to *give* you. You're great in the classroom and will be great in the classroom, whether you get an MFA *or* a Ph.D. Remember our discussion of your last paper," she said. "You ran into trouble when you tried to fit into something that really wasn't you." She slapped her arm. "Dammit. We're getting devoured."

I'd barely noticed.

"Bottom line," Professor Lind said, "you have to *love* academia, otherwise it's going to crush your soul."

I let what she said sink in, and then I realized that I was completely lost as to what fit anymore. Having my soul crushed didn't sound like a good time. School would be the answer, but what kind of school? Truly what I can say to myself—if not to anyone else—is that I *am* impressed by a Ph.D. It would be a cool thing to have, that doctorate, better than money, even. But why? Why am I impressed with it, what *do* I see it giving me? Professor Lind didn't give me any answers. She just gave me a lot to think about. Typical.

I hold the remote control in my hand and change the channels without really paying attention to what's on. I've slept all day, so I'm not really sleepy. I'll watch *Animal*

*Planet,* BET, or whatever else is on until I have to leave at 10:45. My phone rings but I debate with myself over whether to even go over to my caller-ID box and see who it is. I've been avoiding the phone because I'm afraid of a call from Earl. I don't know how to handle the situation yet. It's still a wild idea to me, treating Earl like anything other than a guy to flirt with at the bar.

My curiosity gets the best of me, so I get up to at least see who it is. The name reads *Bita Flannigan.* I pick up. "Hey, lady," I say, trying to sound peppy and not work-weary.

"I'm glad I caught you. You're never home!"

"Everyone always says that. I guess because I never am."

"That's what I want to talk to you about."

I say nothing because I can feel the whole factory lecture coming on.

"Are you there?"

"Yes," I say. "What then?"

"Just hear me out before you say anything," Bita says. "You know how crazy everybody thinks your job is…"

Here we go. "I'm listening."

"Well, I'm going to send you some money so you can quit it."

I've been standing and pacing around my small apartment, but when I take in what Bita suggests, I sit down. "That's crazy," I say, but I feel something like excitement when I think about not having to go back to Valtek. Almost right away though, "crazy" comes back to mind. "I can't take your and Charlie's money. Everybody acts like I'm selling my ass on the street or something. Summer's almost over. I'll be fine."

"Listen," Bita says in her hard voice that tells me she's

had enough. "This is bullshit. I don't know what you're trying to prove. You can work. You work hard. Good for you. But I want to help you now."

"I don't know," I say slowly. "It's weird, isn't it? For you to just hand over money?"

"I'm not going to go around and around with you on this," Bita insists. Then she adds, "It's just not fair that you to have to do that kind of work."

"Not just me. It doesn't only suck for me." I think of Mona and my brother. "It sucks for everybody who has to work that hard."

"Exactly," Bita says. "So if you had money to burn, and I was working like you are, working hard and making *nothing,* even if it was just for the summer, would you just let me keep working when I didn't have to? When you could just write me a check for money you wouldn't even miss?"

"Of course not."

"So why is this different?"

"I don't know. It just seems like I should suck it up. These are the cards dealt, it's only for the summer—"

"You keep saying that, 'It's only for the summer,' but however long you'd have to do this is not relevant. I know you *think* you're keeping it real—or whatever—by doing this kind of job, because you feel like you have to make some sort of penance for having it easy."

Bita is making me furious. I'm rarely furious. It feels like an interrogation, one where I can't answer before I'm fired another question, and even if I had time to answer, I wouldn't have a comeback.

When I don't respond, Bita keeps right on talking. "Listen," she says, "I believe you when you say there aren't jobs in Langsdale. Trust me. I visited you. I saw, I ran screaming. All I'm saying to you now is that the situation is easily solved, and this isn't news, but there will always be those who have, and those who have not, and when you have, you should give."

I keep quiet, partially to be annoying, to keep her hanging out there on the line.

She sounds almost as mad as the day the girl at the bookstore tried to call her a scam artist. "I'm putting the check in the mail, and you'd better cash it."

"You can send it," I say, "but that doesn't mean I'll cash it."

"Fine," Bita says. "You are getting on my nerves," she snaps, and hangs up.

I don't know what's wrong with me, because the truth is, I'm tired of Valtek. I want to spend the rest of my summer reading and writing. But I think of Mona and Ray and folks like the father-and-son combo, and I feel as if I'm leaving them holding the bag. But I hate to admit that Bita may be right. I said that La Varian was the type of person who hated to be called out on his stuff, who hated to be wrong, and now I realize that this might have been one of the problems between La Varian and me. We are very much alike.

The phone rings again. It's Bita calling back to say she's sorry for hanging up on me. But when I check my caller ID, I see the name Erardo Lo Vecchio. Who in the hell is Erardo Lo Vecchio? I consider letting my machine get it, but the Italian name gets the better of me.

On the final ring before my machine comes on, I pick up. "Hello?"

"Uh, Ronnie?"

"Yes?" I can't place the voice, which is *so* not Italian, not even close. It's got a soft twang in it, almost familiar, but not quite.

"Ronnie, this is Earl."

I pause. *Earl?* I'm confused by Erardo. "Earl from the *Saloon?*"

"That's right," he says. "How you been keeping yourself, Ronnie? I hadn't seen you around. Doris told me you were out in L.A., but I thought you were avoiding the place."

I can't decide what to concentrate on—the crazy name, or the fact that Earl's calling.

"You there?"

"Yes, I'm sorry, Earl. It's just the name on my caller ID. Is that *your* name?"

"Yeah." Earl makes a noise that sounds like half a laugh, and half a puff of air through his nose. "My great-grandaddy's name. I don't go by it, though. Never have. Cain't nobody hardly pronounce 'Erardo,' including me. Folks been calling me Earl since the first grade."

"Wow."

"Yeah."

Silence.

"So you're Italian?"

Earl clears his throat. "Yeah, on my daddy's side, and a whole lot of other things, too. My family's all mixed up."

"Wow," I say again, slowly. I sound like some stoner, one toke over the line. My love for all things Italian is well known. And here was Earl, *technically* fitting the bill. *Strange* as a three-dollar bill.

Earl clears his throat again. "Well, I'm calling because—"

"So have you been to Italy, then?" I can't let this go. "Do you know what part of Italy your family's from?"

"I don't know nothing about no Italy, Ronnie. Never have been. One of these days, though, I might take me a trip over there."

I think about all the trips I've taken with Sammy. "I've been," I say. "Three times. All over. It was amazing." As soon as the words are out of my mouth, I sound braggy and know-it-all.

But Earl only says, "That's real nice," in that soft drawl of his. Not a hint of smart-ass.

He waits a couple of more beats in case I figure out how to have a normal phone conversation with him, but he must not be able to take it anymore because he says, "Ronnie? I'm not good on the phone, so I'm going to make it short— I want to take you out."

"Oh." Shit. What do I say?

"And I know how you work at night and all, so I was thinking we'd get lunch or something."

"Doris told you about my job."

"Yeah, and Ray. I asked about you after I found out you were working over there."

"Ray is your cousin. Great." Every stupid thing I've asked or done flashes before my eyes. If Ray is Earl's cousin, and they've talked about me, it can't be good. "Oh, God, what'd he say? That I was the worst worker he's ever seen?"

Earl laughs. "No. Not exactly."

"Not exactly" told me that Earl had probably heard every story about me there was to hear. *And then, you know what College asked? She asked if she could take notes. Hell, ain't but four or five steps to remember!* I feel like I want—

need—to fill in the gaps of Ray's stories to retrieve some of my pride, so when Earl asks again if we can go out, have lunch tomorrow afternoon, I say yes.

Before I got off the phone with Earl, I managed to offend him—twice. He offered to pick me up, I insisted on meeting him. "You don't wont me coming to your house?" Earl asked. "It's not that," I said. "It's the bike." Truth: I was kinda weirded out about him coming to my house. "Let me take you to the Vineyard," Earl said. "No, let's go to Greg's Cafeteria," I said. "What, you don't think I can afford the Vineyard?" Earl said. "Of course not," I said. Truth: The Vineyard *is* very expensive—and reminds me of La Varian. "They just have lousy service there," I explained.

So we negotiated a couple of land mines to get to where we are, which is sitting across from each other at the cafeteria. I love cafeteria food. I kept sliding my tray down the line and picking up nearly every thing there was to pick up: two pieces of fried chicken, one bowl of macaroni and cheese, one stuffed bell pepper, one bowl of cheese potatoes. And one slice of apple pie.

"Whew," Earl says, watching me dig into my cheese potatoes. "You don't hardly mess around, do you?" He has a big grin on his face, and I notice—again—his dimples, one carved perfectly in the center of each cheek. He's still keeping his beard cut close, and I can see those dimples real good. In broad daylight he looks more like a mischievous kid, and not a, not a what? Redneck? Cracker? As soon as I think of both, I push them out of my head. I watch him cut his fried chicken with a knife while I pick mine up with both hands. Is he cutting the chicken for my benefit? Who eats fried chicken like that? It's weird, but somehow endearing. I try to keep my attention on just me and Earl, but the fact is that most of the people in the cafeteria are elderly, all of them white. Sometimes people look our way, but Earl doesn't seem to notice.

"I'm what they call a good eater," I say proudly. I wink at him and he winks back. *Now* I see it. It's Ray's wink, exactly. I'm surprised at how big my appetite is, because I thought I'd be goofy and awkward, unsure of how to act in front of Earl. He's not Earl from the Saloon anymore. He's Earl. Period. *Erardo.* But this is nice. This is surprisingly easy. We talk about all kinds of stuff, from bar stories to politics, from L.A. to Indiana. He's got an easy laugh and he makes me laugh easily.

"So," I say, "promise me that Ray hasn't called me every name in the book."

"Mama and Daddy told me never make promises I cain't keep."

"That bad, huh?"

Earl takes a long sip of his coffee. He puts the cup down and smiles.

"I don't know why it took me so long to get the hang of things." I cut a piece of pie with my fork and offer it to Earl. It only strikes me, as his eyes move from my eyes to the fork, that offering a piece of my pie is like offering him a *piece of my pie.* Earl blushes and shakes his head. He rubs his solid belly. "Lord, Ronnie. I got no room."

"Okay," I say. "Next time."

"I'm holding you to next time," he says, and holds my gaze with his blue eyes until I have to look away.

"And you ought not to feel so bad about the factory. Some folks just ain't meant to do some things."

Something about what he says makes me think of Bita, so I say something reactionary and stupid. I've turned into Iris. "That's classist," I say.

Earl gives me a serious look. "That's what? *Classist?* Like uppity? Is that what you mean?" He shakes his head. "It ain't about class. It's about the road folks end up taking, Ronnie. I worked at Valtek, too, for a good while. Lot of my people have worked at Valtek, but it just wasn't for me. I'd rather bartend than work at that factory, and I'm the same class as anybody else I know. You think I think I'm better'n Ray?"

I've offended him—again. "No," I say so softly that he may not have even heard me.

"Well, I don't," he answers his own question.

"I know. I just said you don't."

Earl leans back in his chair and strokes his beard. He crosses his arms and stares at me while I pretend to be so involved with my pie. "Ray says you think you're better than the folks at the factory," he says quietly.

I open my mouth to protest.

"But I told him that didn't sound like you."

"How would you know?" I put my fork down and look up and down those big arms of his.

"Well—" Earl keeps stroking his beard and staring at me "—I don't know. But a person gets a feeling," he says. He looks at me real hard. "That's a pretty dress you got on."

I feel my face get hot. He's a man who notices when a woman has on a pretty dress, and tells her so.

Earl picks up his coffee cup again. "All I know is, a job is a job, and you're lucky to end up doing what you love to do. That's why I'm gone go to law school at Langs-dale," he says, peering at me over the rim of his cup.

*Law* school? For *real?*

"See?" Earl says. "Now you're looking mystified as all get out. I cain't go to law school?"

"I'm sorry, I don't mean to look surprised." I push away my pie plate even though half of it's still there. I keep saying and doing everything wrong, and when I look at myself through Earl's eyes, I see a pain in the ass. I wonder why he keeps trying.

"Remember Jimmy D.? Got fired?"

I nod. I haven't thought of Jimmy D. for a long time. I'd totally forgotten about him.

"Well, he got fired behind some bullshit, excuse my language, Ronnie. It wasn't fair. He's a friend of mine and about to lose his house. Lawyers help people like Jimmy D. That's what I want to do." Earl looks down at his hands. "I got started in college a while back, but didn't nothin' stick. I got something I want to study now, though." He rubbed his hands and looked at me. "Some of my people do think it's strange. Ain't never been a lawyer in my family."

"Wow," I say. "That's great." I hadn't thought of lawyers as anything but assholes, since I worked at the legal magazine what seems like a lifetime ago. But I can see Earl in a suit, in court, trying to help people the best way he knows how. He'd look good in that suit, too. I can see it.

I can tell Earl's sizing me up, like he's wondering whether to pull me off the hook and throw me back in for something better. *Wow, that's great,* I hear myself saying, and wonder if I sound overly enthusiastic, like I'm praising a kid for his fingerpaints. Or do I sound overly amazed? *I didn't think your kind of people went to law school.* Maybe Earl *should* throw me back. I wouldn't blame him, and that's how fast the tables can turn: Clair Huxtable realizes she may not be a nice enough person to date Grizzly. "You look like you need some help with that pie," he says finally. He pulls my plate closer and takes a forkful, and then another, while I watch him eat. I watch this handsome man eat and grin at me, do everything he can to be charming and funny, and I understand that Ray and Bita are right about me. I *did* think I was better than Earl, I *did* think I was better than Mona, because I'm smart and I think that's supposed to mean something. I want it to mean something. And like Bita said, Valtek turned from something accidental to a pebble I refused to take out of my shoe. I intended to walk and walk on that stone, when all along I was someone who, unlike Mona, and unlike Jimmy D., was always a phone call away from someone who could bail me out, whether it was factory money from my brother, or Hollywood money from Bita. And Earl was right. It's all about roads. Working at Valtek would never put more money in Mona's pockets or anyone else's pockets. At six dollars an hour, it wasn't even putting money in *my* pockets.

Earl's saying that he noticed me the first time I walked into the Saloon because he'd never seen somebody so pretty. Charming as hell, that Earl, so I decide to tell the truth to myself. I'm here—with Earl—not because I need to defend myself against Ray, but because I want to be sitting across the table from him. I resisted because I was just scared of how this…sandy-haired, blue-eyed Earl in his biker boots and beard would look and feel. It's really not the white thing. Pasty-ass Nigel was fine. European

Italian is fine. But bartending, Harley-riding Earl gave me pause. *I'm classist,* I think. But I'm also attracted. Together, we might look crazy, but it also feels fine. So I keep telling myself the truth: I resisted Bita's offer for money because I was scared of how *that* would look and feel.

But here's some more truth: tomorrow Bita's check will arrive and I will go to the bank. I will sign my name on the back of it, and I will deposit that check, and I, most likely, will feel fine.

## Doris

A week after TROOPS ends, I come home to a post-card from Lisa and Marvin. They're honeymooning in Bali. The postcard shows a palm tree with two coconuts below, happy-faces drawn onto their shells with black-and-white paint: "Greetings from two love-nuts in Paradise." The back reads: *Having a great time. Wish you were here.* Clichés scrawled in my sister's gargantuan, curlicue writing look instead like perfect little sentences, greetings from a far-off land of sandy beaches, radiant sunsets and lovers walking hand in hand.

Here, it's rained three days straight. Paolo's gone totally underground, although Ronnie and I are supposed to meet up with him at the ballet recital later tonight. Must be in the air, since I've gone slightly underground myself. I called Zach a few days after our discussion, or fight, or whatever it was, but he refuses to call me back. It's turned me into a pseudo-stalker. I walk by his apartment slower than usual, making sure he's alive, hoping that he's checking his messages, or just watching *Animal Planet* and knitting himself stupid. The lights are sometimes on, and his garbage can is filling up, but my phone has yet to ring. I'm stopping all that as of tomorrow. There are worse things than being a grad student—such as finding yourself inadvertently acting like someone on the wrong end of a *Lifetime* restraining-order marathon.

So I rent a stack of movies, because after teaching ends, all that I'm even remotely useful for is watching television (not *Lifetime,* thank you very much). In the back of my mind, I'm thinking about rebooting my laptop and working, and I take out *West Side Story, Rebel Without a Cause* and *Splendor in the Grass.* That "string bean of a Natalie Wood" has had me thinking. Thinking mostly about how much Zach is right: that I don't take myself all that seriously, not in public at any rate. That Natalie Wood and I both have our own little version of the "white-girl shuffle," me with my Prada knockoffs and MAC nail polish, and her, getting drenched by her mother in a bathtub in *Splendor in the Grass,* hyperventilating about her virginity and chanting, *I'm not spoiled, Mother, I'm not spoiled.* If she'd sat up and quoted Freud, would anyone have cared?

The poem just flows out, even and conversational, within fifteen minutes of reviewing *West Side Story.* It's the talk I've been having with myself, only changed, made public and performative. It's what I didn't have the balls myself to say to La Varian, and when I finish reading it, I can't tell if it's an argument or just more whiny crap: *voila,* I have a title:

## White Girl Whine

I'm at a party, see, and someone mentions *West Side Story,* not my favorite movie, but I've been known to sing along. And Natalie Wood is so adorable—a kind of girl I'll never be, petite, demure, small-waisted with enormous eyes. Warren Beatty's *Splendor in the Grass.* A hyper little virgin. ("I'm not spoiled, Mother! I'm not spoiled!") So at this party, at the mention of faux-Latina Natalie Wood, someone goes ballistic. *It's like blackface* (and it is)—*Of course they take the "little white girl" and give her the lead.* A round of eye-rolls follows. This is when the prickly discomfort starts. Because the little white girl is somehow different from the little white boy. She's just slightly ridiculous. Not a threat, really. Last year's toy for little white boys, historically peaked and on the wane. Fragile. Complicit. Impotent. Isn't she in a bathroom somewhere with a finger down her throat? Who could possibly, possibly, in the face of Rita Moreno, take her seriously. Who but a little white girl would sing "I Feel Pretty" at the peak of her powers. Little white girls: with their Barbies, and ballet lessons, and pink rooms and pink shoes and pink lipstick. And really, for the sake of accuracy, aren't they more like little pink girls? Floating on pink clouds through life—taking all the good roles in the Latin Musicals. I'm at a party, see, and I just so happen to be a little white girl, and for honesty's sake, I do have on pink lipstick, and girlie bangle bracelets, and I'm probably more scarred from years of *Cosmo*-conditioning than I care to admit. That's probably a little pink scar, my mouth, which stays closed like a doll's. *It's not her fault,* I want to say. But no one wants to be disgusted with a casting director, or society, when there sits Natalie Wood, and she seems so very ridiculous. Besides—I'd just be whining. Which is what white girls do. Because Barbie's Dream House wasn't tall enough— and they didn't get that pony—and Jimmy Joe just never ever got around to asking them to the prom. ("I'm not spoiled, Mother! I'm not spoiled!") Natalie whining again—how very pink of her. Natalie in histrionics. Because she's supposed to be this perfect little present, a mute and pristine package. Look at how these white girls act—like you could possibly take them seriously.

I love the feeling of finishing a poem better than any feeling on this planet. I get up from my computer and walk about my living room, survey the bare walls and decide that no amount of feng shui or Faux Che is going to keep me from reveling in my hyper-girliness, not tonight. Ronnie convinced me to wait on sending the box of knickknacks and wall hangings to Goodwill that has been sitting in my closet since the Winn-Dixie incident. I take them out and restore them to their original spots throughout my apartment. The mermaid in the hall next to my bathroom. The 1950s movie print that says "The Perfect Sinner" in bold PG–13 type lettering in a tucked-away corner next to my bed. The only memento that gives me pause is a magnet that Paolo sent me from San Francisco: *maybe I want to look cheap,* it reads, and I'm back to thinking about Zach. *Hell with him,* I think. I put the magnet on my refrigerator, then I put it in the trash. Then I take it out of the trash and put it back in the box to go back in the closet. This might go on for hours, but the phone rings, temporarily pushing pause on my manic indecisiveness.

"You still going to this dance thing?" Ronnie asks. "Paolo wants us to get there a little early and keep James company."

"James's the man?"

"He is."

"Have you seen him yet?"

"Only from a distance."

"So?" I ask, removing the magnet again from the box and turning it around in my hand. "What's the verdict?"

Ronnie laughs.

"Let's just say he's hot, but he looks like a lot of work. Even for Paolo."

I'm too self-absorbed to push any further.

"I think I'm stalking Zach," I say. "He won't return any of my calls. But I know he's alive, or at least someone's alive and living in his apartment. And it's starting to make me depressed and mildly psychotic. But I did finish a poem and I actually like it."

"Good on the poem," Ronnie says. "Wait on Zach. He's probably being careful. Nothing you can do about it either way but wait. Still a free country."

"I hate that. I'm a love-fascist. He better not wait too long, or I'm gonna go out and find that humanzee."

"Doris," she says, "I don't even want to know. Just be at the auditorium at seven-thirty."

"You bringing Ear-rardo?" I ask.

"Let's count," Ronnie answers. "We already have a neurotic New Yorker, one homosexual dancer, his part-

ner and me at a ballet recital for teenage girls from Langsdale, Indiana. I think that's enough 'We Are the World'
for one evening."

"That reminds me," I say. "We have to go to the county
fair this weekend. They're having baby pageants, and hog
wresting and tractor pulls. I want to drown my sorrows
in corn dogs and cotton candy. And maybe buy a pet. Did
you know you can buy a goat for, like, forty dollars?
That's cheaper than a pair of shoes."

"You know how much it costs to feed a goat?"

"No. Less than a kid?"

"Lot more than a pair of shoes."

"I'm lonely."

"You'd have better luck with the chimpanzee."

"Humanzee," I say. "Totally different."

"You keep heading down this road," Ronnie says,
"you'll be lucky to get either."

Driving to Ayer Hall, a limestone building that
houses the dance studios and auditorium, the rain
comes down in sheets. Even crawling along the streets
at five miles an hour, I'm good as flying blind. I
brought my umbrella, but it's scant help. I'm soaked
and cold by the time I meet Ronnie and James, and I
know instantly why Ronnie was being so cryptic about
James's appearance. He's handsome, no question. His
hair is white-blond, cropped close to his head, and
he's tall. Six feet or so, easy, with trendy wire-frame
glasses and a perfectly sculpted body. He's one of those
men where even in clothes, you feel like you can see
him naked. He has on a simple lightweight black
sweater, linen pants and classy leather sandals. One sil-

ver band on his left ring finger, but otherwise, no jewelry other than his watch. He's like La Varian in terms
of style, only more understated. At the same time, he
stands as if he's waiting to be noticed, like a fine piece
of art or some overvalued only child. Friendly-level:
medium.

"I can't believe this is where you all live," James whispers conspiratorially after Ronnie introduces us. "On
purpose."

"There's worse," I say. "Truly."

"I'll have to take your word," James replies. "I've been
taking pictures of the billboards. I've never seen so much
antiabortion rhetoric in one place. Do kids just get
knocked up for fun? Is there nothing else to do?"

James isn't being pissy, he's acting pretty much the way
I did when I first moved to Langsdale. Ronnie, too. Like
he can't believe this is actually America. Paolo told us that
James is a "venture capitalist" taking some time off since
his dot-com went under. He's going to help Paolo finance
his dance company once Paolo's finished with his degree.
James points at one of the flyers tacked to a "student
events" bulletin board: "Dance Marathon for Jesus." He
gapes at me and Ronnie as if he's been let off from a time
machine and spaceship all rolled into one.

The scary thing is, I've been here so long that half the
time I forget about the billboards: TERRORISTS
LOVE GUN CONTROL. THIS IS THE SIGN
FROM GOD YOU'VE BEEN LOOKING FOR.
KORNFEST ON THE SQUARE.

"We make it fun," Ronnie says. She has on a red silk
wraparound skirt and white halter top. Her hair is twisted
in an elaborate bun secured with jeweled butterfly hair-

pins. "It's tougher to get knocked up around here than you might think."

"You're not from here?" he asks, but it's a pleading voice. "You do realize there are forty-nine other beautiful states out there?"

"You give Paolo this hard a time?" Ronnie asks.

"One year," James says, raising his index finger. "One year. One day more and I walk. He comes home with that arts degree and the children out here can have the corn back, all to themselves."

Ronnie laughs, and I'm still trying to process that this is Paolo's boyfriend.

"You two are good-looking," he says, looking me up and down in a deeply clinical manner. "How do you make do?"

"Local talent," Ronnie replies. "Doris is holding out for the county fair, see what she can scare up."

"There's a county fair?" James says, clamping his hands dramatically to his cheeks. "This trip is nothing if not anthropological."

Paolo bounds out in all his directorial glory. He looks exasperated, and James gives him a kiss on the mouth, which draws stares from a few of the junior-ballerina parental units, but they look away when they notice I'm looking back at them.

"I'm losing it," Paolo announces. "One of the mothers is trying to set me up with her hag-niece. An ex-dancer, she claims. She works at one of those Bible-shows in Branson, Missouri. *The New-New Testament Revue. Tap* dancing. Ugh. Even if I were straight, I'd be insulted."

"Say the word," James says. "I'll fly you home."

Paolo shakes his head dismissively.

"Nine more months. Think of it as my unwanted pregnancy. I'll survive. Now, go get seats."

James, Ronnie and I park ourselves front and center in the auditorium. The lights flicker, and everyone quiets dramatically. Outside, the thunder is loud and close enough that it shakes the building, rolling overhead from one side of the auditorium to the next. I'm rubbing my shoulders to keep from freezing in the air-conditioning.

"Poor Earl," Ronnie says. "He wanted to take me out on his bike tonight." She looks at me out of the corner of one eye. "Not that I was going," she adds.

By the end of the performance, the rain has slowed to a drizzle. We'd all planned originally to go out afterward, but I'm just not feeling it. I know it's my fault that I'm not instantly crazy about James. Were it not so deeply immature, I'd say that I'm almost annoyed with him for not finding one nice thing to say about Langsdale. That, plus the comment about flying Paolo back to San Francisco. Not fair. If Ronnie gives Langsdale the finger, and Zach continues to ignore me, what will I do if Paolo leaves? Selfish, selfish, selfish me. And selfish trolls who do not play well with others, not this evening at any rate, need to go back to their lairs and regain their humanity. It's probably just that I'm wet, and tired, and the immediate post–poetic composition bliss has given way to self-loathing and self-pity. Better just to sleep it off.

"That was great," I say to Paolo, politely excusing myself. "I swear that I'll toast you later in the week. I'm feeling a migraine coming on, need to get some pills into my system."

A half lie, since I do have a headache.

"Doris," Paolo barks. "What's wrong with you? You're living like the Unibomber. Just one drink. Get out of your apartment."

"Any other night this week," I say. "I promise promise promise."

I'm a tad remorseful on the ride back to my apartment, but I just don't have it in me to be the odd gal out at the Office Saloon, listening to how awful Langsdale is and wishing that Zach would walk through the door. I'd rather watch Letterman and pull a Scarlett O'Hara: *tomorrow is another day.*

Tomorrow comes faster than expected. At 3:00 a.m. I'm awakened by the sound of my picture frame flying halfway across the room. I bolt upright in my bed, equal parts groggy and panicked. I look to see where the sound originated and notice, in fact, that everything in my windowsill has been knocked off, scattered across the floor. It's only then that I hear the distant wailing of the storm-alert siren. The winds are howling, and I stumble into my living room to flip on the weather station. Every channel has a small graphic at the bottom of the screen, a little funnel cloud with the words "Tornado Warning" flashing in bold letters beneath. "Tornado Watch," and I'd stay in my apartment. "Watch" means that conditions are right for a tornado, but there's no imminent danger. "Tornado Warning," is something entirely different, it means that they've seen a funnel cloud forming, or worse, one's touched down.

I hate to say it, but usually—in spite of all my paranoia—I half ignore these things. Once or twice I've crawled into my bathtub and waited it out, but tonight is different. I've never been near wind strong enough to knock things around my apartment, and outside the sky is bloodred. Bloodred at 3:00 a.m., another first, and not a good one. It's not raining hard, but the wind is still picking up speed and I can hear the siren louder now in the distance. I could sit in my second-floor apartment and wait to die, or I could get the hell out.

I have on a short nightgown, so I throw on a pair of jeans, unplug my laptop and tuck it under my nightgown, locking the door to my apartment. Downstairs, I decide, is better than upstairs, but underground, I know for sure, is ten thousand percent better than above ground. I try the door to the basement storage area of my apartment building, but it's locked and I don't have the key. I'm having visions of my entire apartment building on the evening news: matchstick debris and rubble; and me, buried: crouched in a corner with my laptop close to my chest and concrete all around. Outside, more rain. The sky is the same apocalyptic red, and for the first time in my life, I have the feeling that it's between God and fate whether I get out of this. I'm just another frightened animal looking for a place to hide. I could take my chances in my car, try driving to Ronnie's place, but I don't even know if she'll be home, and I remember that cars are a very bad place to be in the event a twister touches down.

Then I remember. Zach. Zach and his basement apartment a block and a half away. Zach who will not return my calls. I've never looked worse in my life, and I'm fully aware that my arrival on his doorstep could be perceived as psychotic, needy and highly unwelcome, but I really, really, really don't want to die. Not alone and not like this.

The lights are now out all over town, but I only have to bang on Zach's door once before he answers. He's awake, dressed, and has a few candles burning in his apartment.

"I'm so, so sorry," I apologize. "I swear I'm not trying to bother you. I just got scared, and I don't have a basement, and I thought that you'd at least let me stay here until this passes. You don't even have to talk to me if you don't want to."

Zach lets me into his apartment and closes the door.

"It's okay," he says. "I actually just gave you a call, but there wasn't any answer. The lines might even be down. I was worried about you up in that apartment."

I'm so happy to be in a dry basement that I could almost cry.

Zach's looking at me, real strange, nothing you'd confuse for lust, more like I might light up a cigar, humanzee-style. Then he starts to laugh.

"Ordinal Doris," he says. "Doris-in-the-rough."

It is only then that I fully realize how absurd I look. I have on jeans, a nightgown, a laptop bulging out like some cybernetic hysterical pregnancy, no shoes and my night-guard, a small piece of plastic that keeps me from grinding my teeth to shreds while I sleep, is still in my mouth, no doubt impairing my ability to speak clearly.

"Now I know what I'd save," I say, removing my computer from beneath my gown, conscious that I'm not wearing a bra or any other form of underwear. I try to remove my night-guard inconspicuously and rest it on the laptop.

Zach motions for me to sit down on his couch. It's difficult to see much, but I can tell that Zach's apartment is all one room. There's a kitchen off to the side, and what I'm guessing is a bathroom, but it's one big studio. We sit on his couch and he tosses me a thin, yellow blanket. I look discreetly for his bed, trying to put the whole place together in my mind.

"You're shivering," he says.

"Paolo's dance recital," I say. "I think I caught my death of cold sitting through the performance wet tonight."

I wrap the blanket around me and avoid Zach's gaze. His apartment has a nice smell, like he cooked something fresh and garlicky for dinner.

"You know Paolo," I say. "My 'stooge.'"

Zach pushes his foot against the side of my leg, playfully.

"You're not going to let me live that down, are you?"

"Mean," I say. "You were very, very, very mean to me."

He shifts his body, moving closer to me on the sofa.

"I'm sorry." He apologizes, his voice rough and low.

"I thought you were mad at me."

"I was," he says. "I was jealous, too. I'm not now."

The siren has finally quieted, and aside from our breathing, there's only the sound of rain beating against the lone window. Warmth spreads underneath my skin that has nothing to do with the blanket or the candles.

"You never called me back," I declare, finally looking directly at him. "Why not? It hurt my feelings."

Zach shrugs.

"Seemed like the right thing to do. Besides, I could see you walking back and forth in front of my apartment. It was almost like having you here."

I pull the yellow blanket over my head.

"I'm so embarrassed," I say. "I just wanted to make sure you weren't dead."

"I'm not dead."

I feel Zach's body next to mine as he pulls the blanket down from my face. His bare arms are on either side of mine, propping him back from the couch, looking straight into my eyes.

"I look terrible," I say.

"Doris, if you say one more word about how you look, I'm going to send you back into that rain and not think twice about it."

Zach kisses me, slow and soft. His skin smells like the rain itself, clean and natural, and like the rain, his touch is calm and even, rhythmic and gentle. He pushes the blanket aside, and like small-town life itself, everything from that point moves unhurried. Waking up the next morning, watching Zach sleep, one arm sprawled in front of his face, the other cupping me securely to his side, I feel something that I never thought I'd feel. For the first time since I came to Langsdale, I know for certain that people on the Coasts have nothing on me.

# Ronnie

It's my last night at Valtek. Bita's check came, and I stared at the sum: two thousand dollars. Enough to get me through the summer easily. I could eat anything I wanted, anything but ramen. I would pay my rent, go to movies, go to bars. I would finish my Othello paper, which I was already researching, read books for pleasure and for study, and sleep as long as I wanted. And I would be comfortable. What a difference a day makes.

"Well," Mona says, taking a puff of her cigarette, "I guess you made enough to make it through till school."

We're sitting on the picnic table. I stare out beyond the parking lot, at the thick trees. I take a deep breath of the moist green air and exhale. We've got a full eight minutes left to our break. My last break. "I have enough."

"Good for you," she says, flicking ashes.

We sit in silence for a while until two more workers

come out for their breaks. "Evenin'." "How y'all doin' tonight?" they ask. One lights his cigarette right away and the other takes out some tobacco and breaks off a piece. He's handsome in a rugged way, with golden skin and deep blue eyes topped off by white-blond eyelashes. He looks to be my age—or an older thirtysomething. I don't know their names.

He and the other man stand smoking and chewing and no one says anything for a while.

"It's so loud at night," I say finally. I have never been able to figure out what makes the so-called quiet country loud as hell. It's a combination of clicks, screeches and gurgle sounds, to me.

"Loud?" the blond one says to me. "Huh," he says. "I ain't never thought of that. Guess you right though." He spits into a patch of weeds. "Where you from? You don't sound like you from here."

"Larry, you talking to an L.A. woman and a California girl," Mona says, patting me on the back.

"That right?" Larry stares at me. "I ain't never been to California. Seems nice out there."

"It is," I say. "I like it."

"I bet you I'd like it, too," Larry says. He spits again.

"Well, I wouldn't," the other man says. "L.A. looks as strange as can be, from what I can tell on the TV. All them liberal types. Thank God they didn't have their way and put that Gore in the White House, with all his talk, like he's better'n anybody."

"Bush givin' us them tax cuts, too," Mona says. She checks her watch. "He knows about working folks. Bet you that Gore wouldn't of done that."

I pinch my lips together to keep from opening my predictable, liberal mouth. And I wonder. What's the difference between my brother and his buddies who talk trash about Bush, and Mona and Larry and almost any hardworking Midwesterner? Both sets of folks have the same jobs, but one can't stand Gore for being too uppity, and the other can't stand Bush because they think he's a racist rich boy grown up to take over the family business. I get lost trying to unpack it all: *race and class,* I think. My mind wanders to my paper and my desk at home, where I have Marx, Žižek, Toni Morrison and Fanon all stacked up and ready for me to come home to and open them up.

"Last election was the first time I was old enough to vote," Larry says from the side of his mouth. "But next time I'ma vote Bush again."

I look at Larry and wonder how in the world I could have added ten years on to his age.

"Well," Mona says. She yawns. "I think I would love California. I think my little girl, Tiffany, could go out to L.A. and be in something. She's a pretty little girl. Smart, too. She can sing and dance real good."

"Wow. That's cool," I say.

"We ought to go out to L.A. and get her on something."

"Sure," I say, but I hate the thought of Tiffany becoming another naked, precocious, exploited performer.

We all turn toward the door when we hear it open. Ray comes out scratching his elbows.

"We got two more minutes, Ray," Mona says. She lights another cigarette to prove her point.

"I ain't saying nothing," Ray answers. He props up one of his legs on the bench and leans into it. He looks at me. "Well, well, well, College. Your last night. I didn't b'lieve you'd last as long as you did."

"Me, neither."

He takes his foot off the bench and then adjusts his cap. "I heard you and Earl had you some lunch."

"Yes," I reply. "It was nice. I like Earl. He's a nice guy."

"Damn right he is," Ray says. He looks at me but I look away. *Ray says you think you're better than the folks at the fac-*

*tory.* "He's a nice guy," Ray says again. He glances at me and looks out into the trees. "But he's always been kinda different."

I have a feeling that whatever I'd say would be the exact wrong thing to say. So I say nothing.

"Party's over, y'all," Ray announces after a while. "Let's go build us some cars."

And we do. We build cars until the shift's over and it's time for more folks to come in and build some more cars. At the end of my shift, Mona only tells me to take it easy, and that she'll see me around. Ray tells me to hold on to my notes. "Ain't no telling when you might have to come back," he says. It sounds like a warning.

So, this is it. On my last night, as I predicted, I feel fine— more than fine. I also sense the same thing I sensed on my first day at Valtek when I realized that nobody cared about my arrival. Nobody cares about my departure.

*You are a fraud,* I type on my laptop. *Veronica Williams Lo Vecchio,* I type right after it. I leave the line about me being a fraud, and delete Veronica Williams Lo Vecchio. I wonder why I'd type such a thing in the first place. Very junior-high-school Peachy folder, and very unlikely, me and Earl, like Eva Gabor and Eddie Albert in *Green Acres.* But I sat at the bar and watched him work the other night while Doris and Paolo played pinball in the game room. He kept sliding me Jack and Cokes and we talked about anything that was on our minds. One of his old friends came into the bar, a lanky black man, and I just about fell off my stool.

Earl introduced him as Bill, and while they caught up with each other he popped the cap off a Miller Lite and gave it to him. "Who's that?" I asked after he left.

"Bill Bosely," Earl said. "Went to school with him way back."

I tried to imagine Bill going to school around here,

with a bunch of guys who looked like Earl. "What was *that* like? For him, I mean."

Earl poured some maraschino cherries into a compartment next to the olives, lemons and limes. He looked at me. I thought I saw him turn a hint of red. But it was too dark to tell for sure. "I heard and saw some things," he said, somber. "You know how ignorant folks talk." Earl wiped the counter slowly and avoided my eyes. "Billy got messed with some."

No doubt. I decided to lay it all out. "You and I, we're very different, you know."

Earl stopped wiping the counter and leaned on the bar with both hands in front of him. He looked me in the eyes. "I know it," he said. A kid who had FAKE ID written all over him came up and asked for a shot of tequila. Earl gave him a sharp look, but since he made it past the doorman, he had to tend to him.

I let my mind sweep over all the ways that Earl and I were different, and it worried me as much as his big hands, dimples and easy ways made me stay at that bar and hang around him like a groupie. But I tried to picture him on Bita and Charlie's deck, drinking Campari and soda. My head almost exploded. I could, though, picture him shooting the shit with my brother and his buddies. And not only that. Earlier that day I'd read some pages of Chinua Achebe for fun, and while I watched Earl take money for the tequila, I thought, *He doesn't know a thing in the world about Achebe or post-colonial discourse*—but neither did the Princeton graduate I dated for two minutes, proud of his Jewish heritage and flashing his class ring. "Who's Achebe?" he'd asked, and then went on and on about D. H. Lawrence. I turned all this over and over in my head—and still flirted like crazy with Earl, because truth be told, I liked that he liked me. And I liked him back.

Instead of thinking about Earl, I'm supposed to be

making brilliant connections between Morrison and Shakespeare, but I can't. I'm supposed to be thinking about poor tragic Othello and something—anything—original that hasn't been played out and that hasn't already been theorized since time immemorial. I stare at the books laid out in front of me and pull on my lip. I drink some tea and change my CD from Elvis Costello to Howlin' Wolf's *The Real Folks Blues.* I crack every one of my knuckles and twirl around in my swivel chair. I stare at the books again and get overwhelmed. How in the world do all these things go together?

To keep from writing, I drink tea and think about the factory, Mona, and Jimmy D., the other guys at the factory who love our president, my brother and his buddies who hate our president. The interesting thing, to me, is that the same guy represents two different types of a man. The down-home country boy versus the elitist oil heir, depending on one's position and point of view. Obvious enough. I get to thinking about pictures of ourselves that we hope to present to the world. What did a brochure of me playing tennis say? Especially since I'd never held a tennis racket until that damn picture. What would a picture of me working in a factory say to students of color hoping to study at Langsdale? Which picture did *I* prefer? Which one, if either, was really me? I keep thinking of pictures and politics and start to flip through Morrison's *Playing in the Dark.* I stop at the epigraph in the chapter called "Black Matters," and read a T. S. Eliot quote about fancies curled around images.

Interesting, but nothing helpful. I go to my bookshelf because I remember that I have another book edited by Morrison, a book on the Anita Hill-Clarence Thomas hearings, and "the construction of social reality." Professor Lind put the book on the suggested reading list, which meant *required*. I flip through the pages. This is it. Politics. Clarence Thomas. Othello. Both suffering under pictures other people have of them, but both trying to create a picture for themselves that they hope will make their lives easier. Bingo. I get nervous and excited and type my paper title:

A Picture Worth a Thousand Gazes
Othello the Moor of Venice, and Clarence Thomas,
the Supreme Court Justice Nominee:
Two Brothers Who Believed the Hype

I don't kid myself. I'm no Derrida, Morrison, Žižek or Lacan. But I do have ideas. I have some fun with the paper, and I write all day and all night. I don't answer my phone, I don't go out for anything. I stay underground, and I write. I open with a paragraph that's borderline cheesy but writerly, and I almost delete it when I remember what Professor Lind told me about my last paper: it sucked. I was trying to be something that I wasn't. Even that obvious observation is so suddenly relevant to my paper, and my paper is relevant—I think, I hope—to life.

In two days, I go from excited about my paper, to tired of it. I can't wait to hand it off to Professor Lind. I hope it's good, but I'm so burnt-out that it doesn't matter. It's not a Valtek kind of burnt-out, but the kind of burnt-out that won't allow me to put two words together and have it make sense. But I don't care. The paper's done. I'm done. I knock on Professor Lind's door, which is still a scary thing. I knock softly, almost hoping she's not there, so I can just put it in her mailbox.

"Come in."

It's a sharp and loud command, almost as if there's no

door between us. I turn the knob and poke my head in.
"Hi, Professor Lind."

"Veronica. Sit." She motions toward The Chair with
her glasses.

When I sit, she reaches for my paper. I give it to her
and remember that I forgot to spellcheck the damn thing,
like one of my undergrads. *I'm a fraud.*

She puts her glasses back on and lifts the first page by
the bottom corner. She reads the title aloud. "That's *interesting*," she says, peering at me over her glasses. I pick
at a hangnail while she starts reading with a raised eyebrow, and I imagine my sentences in her head as I watch
her read the first paragraph:

> *One picture. A sharecropper. I was looking at an old pho-
> tograph of a black man in overalls, sitting in a chair in a
> field. He looked like he was a sharecropper or some other
> kind of field worker, much like many pictures of black rural
> men circa 1930. That's exactly what it looked like, so that's
> what he must have been. But he wasn't. This man, my
> grandfather, a man I'd never met, worked in a rock quarry,
> nowhere near a field or a crop.*

I go on to make, I hope, salient, fascinating points
about multiple gazes and identity; "decolorizing" and
"reclassing" oneself. I cite it up the ass, too, so the paper
can be a legitimate, graduate seminar paper with all the
obligatory heavy hitters. Of course, it's probably full of
typos, which I try not to think about.

Professor Lind puts the paper down on top of a stack
of papers, probably that horrible Iris's and know-it-all
John's are already there, perfect, not a typo in sight.

"Well," she says, propping her foot up on her knee.
"Do you?"

I clear my throat. "Do I what?"

"Believe the hype."

"About what?" I'm still feeling like an idiot here, and this conversation ain't helping me out. I picture Ray staring at me and adjusting his cap.

"Continuing for a doctorate degree. Have you figured out why you're thinking of doing it?"

Not really. I don't know what I'll do. Maybe I'll take the MFA and run. Maybe I'll stay on for five more years so I can walk away with a Ph.D. I ask myself why I'm drawn toward something that I'm calling the Country Club. The answer, I guess, is that I don't want the club, the MEMBERS ONLY elitism. What I want is the stuff *in* the club. And I want the stuff in the club to be for me, and for everybody—if they want it. And I know Earl is right. You're lucky if you end up doing what you love to do. And why can't I make a life out of books? Why should I have to do what my father wants, take up something more "practical" so I can make the money that he and my mother never have been able to make? Am I supposed to hand over the academic job to people like Iris and John because they're entitled to it and I'm not? Do I find another La Varian and become a nice little professor's wife? Hang up my fishnets forever? Does everything have to be so either-or? A perfect fit? I remind myself: *Don't think binaries. A little of this, a little of that.* "I haven't figured it out," I answer.

Professor Lind gives me one of her long stares. "Fair enough," she says. "I, myself, am still trying to figure out why I do it."

I smile. Then I stand up.

"The papers will be graded by next week," she says, turning away from me and back toward her desk. "You can leave the door open on your way out."

We're all standing under a banner that says WELCOME TO THE LANGSDALE COUNTY FAIR—

149TH YEAR! The sun is vicious and it smells like hay, swampy mud, animals and corn dogs. James keeps cleaning his sunglasses and bending down to wipe the mud off his fancy running shoes, Paolo rambles on about the baby pageant at one o'clock, Doris is walking hand in hand with Zach, looking like Holly Golightly out on a date with Clark Kent, and I'm standing around in a bright green silk sarong and my dreadlocks pulled up in a loose bun. It's noon, and Earl's going to meet us in front of the baby pageant at one.

"It'll tickle me to see you at the fair, Ronnie," he'd said when we stopped by the Saloon a few nights ago. I was going to ask, What do you mean by that? But now that I look at us all standing around looking crazier than any hog wrestler—which we, of course, made fun of the whole way here—I see Earl's point.

"At one is the baby pageant," Paolo reminds us again. "And then at two-thirty is hog wrestling. We *have* to."

James looks around suspiciously. I follow his gaze and it seems like everything at this fair is covered in red, white and blue. "I don't think we should walk around too much."

"What?" Zach asks. "Why?"

"The natives look restless," he says. When Paolo tries to take his hand, he pulls it away. "Toto, we're definitely not in San Francisco anymore."

Paolo smirks. "Not standing by your man?" He sighs and looks down at the fair schedule he's been carrying. "Pictures with Pete the Pony at four," he announces. "I'm totally doing that."

"I'm getting my corn dog first," Doris says. She adjusts her big black hat and pushes her sunglasses up the bridge of her nose. Then she fluffs out her red polka-dot skirt, which looks as if it has a petticoat under it. She's beautifully and appropriately dressed for the fair— if it were 1952.

Zach looks at her, admires her, but also shakes his head. "Aren't you hot with all that on?"

"Nope," she says. "I got this skirt, *and* these shoes, on-line for a steal. Marc Jacobs," she says.

"Well," Zach says, "as long as you're comfortable." He puts his arm around her waist and pulls her close to him. Her hat pokes him on the ear, but he doesn't seem to mind. He kisses her on the cheek.

"I'm getting my fried green tomatoes," I add. "I keep seeing people walking around with big plates of greasy burnt tomatoes, and I want."

James scrunches up his face. "Gross. Have you guys heard of these things called arteries?"

"I'm in," Paolo says. "I'm going to try it all. Corn dogs, corn on the cob, tomatoes, pickles, cotton candy. But *baby pageant,*" he says. "Let's at least start walking toward it."

"Okay," James agrees, still looking around. "But remember, I was like the guy in the horror films who says, 'Let's not go into that abandoned house.'"

We weave ourselves slowly through the crowd and stop now and then at a food stand or game booth. The Langsdale fair *does* look like something out of a movie. Not a horror film, but any film set that's supposed to look like any small town in the middle of America. There are American flags everywhere, tiny plastic ones, big banners, ribbons decorating all the booths, show stages and rides. People look robust—hearty and cornfed—or they look thin and raillike, character actors with leathery faces. The kids are tall and lanky or thick and round, with golden complexions and long shiny hair or crew cuts. Every once in a while, we get what I think is a "look" from someone and then I believe James is right about us all walking together. We are an odd group of folks, like stray members of an old-fashioned freak show. Instead of the Bearded Lady, the Monkey Boy or the Giant, we've got the San Franciscans, the Anachronistic Fashion Plate, the Man Who Knits and the Lone Negro.

When we reach the pageant stage, there's a small crowd. I look for Earl but I can't find him in the crowd. He blends like any other Langsdale man here.

"It's going to start soon," Paolo says. He pulls a pink piece of fluff from his cotton candy.

"I've never seen a baby pageant—except for on TV," Doris says.

I look up at the stage, which is still empty. It's five minutes before the pageant starts. I've seen the pageants on TV, and I do think they're a little strange, the sexualizing of little girls, dressing them up like little come-hither women. But I want to see them anyway.

"Ronnie."

I turn toward the voice to see Earl grinning at me. "You found us," I say. I hug him hello and feel self-conscious about it, partly because touching Earl is still a new thing to me, and partly because I can't help but feel that the Lone Negro hugging the Biker Lawyer is a strange sight.

Everyone says hello to him and I introduce him to James, who immediately glances at Paolo. I'm mad at myself for a second, because that fool's glance actually makes me more unsure of myself, like a high school kid not sure she can be in with the in crowd.

"Show's starting," Zach says. We all turn toward the stage. A woman with a neat bun clears her throat into the microphone.

"Welcome to the 25th Annual Langsdale County Fair baby pageant!"

The crowd claps and whistles.

"In a minute, we gone start the show," she says, "but first I want to thank our sponsors—Laney's TV and Antenna, Al's Glass Service, Hurm's Pulverized Topsoil and Grandview Aluminum Products!"

More claps and whistles.

"And I just want to remind y'all that the Little Miss Langsdale County, Junior Miss Langsdale County and the Miss Langsdale County Fair Scholarship pageants are all coming up later in the day, and our sponsors have generously donated more than two thousand dollars in prize money!" She tucks the microphone under her arm so she can clap. "And now, let's start the pageant. Y'all are going to see some beautiful little angels today."

Paolo turns to look at me and Doris. He winks. Then he hunches his shoulders and claps his hands like an excited kid.

The little girls come out one by one and it *is* the cutest thing. They're so tiny and perfect, they don't seem real. The next little girl who comes out is especially beautiful, with jet-black curls and sharp green eyes. She's wearing a miniature pink chiffon gown and little pink fishnets.

"Look at that one," Paolo says. "She's *fabulous.*"

The woman with the microphone says, "Tiffany's hobbies are singing, dancing and playing with her pet frog."

The crowd laughs and claps.

Someone screams out, "That's my baby! Yay, Tiffany!"

I turn in the direction of the voice because I know it's Mona. I've never seen her looking so excited and happy. She's standing next to a tall boy who must be her son.

"There's Mona Cantrell," Earl says. He's been standing behind me the whole time and I've been leaning into him, but not too much.

"You know Mona?" I ask. "Don't tell me she's your cousin, too."

Earl laughs. "I know practically everybody, Ronnie. Mona used to go with a buddy of mine."

"Her little girl's gorgeous. I bet she wins."

"Bet you she does, too," Earl says.

At the end of the pageant, Mona's little girl takes second place and one hundred bucks. Mona would have to work two days at Valtek to earn that kind of money. I know what that hundred bucks means to Mona and her kids, so I don't think about Tiffany's objectification as much as I think about how hard it is for some folks to get ahold of one hundred dollars. And who knows? Maybe Tiffany will go to L.A. and become a big star. Make enough money to buy her hardworking mother a big house. There are worse fates.

We've seen it all: the puppet theater, the egg toss, the hog wrestling and the demolition derby. Even James liked that. The sun's going down, and all of us—except for James—look a little green from all the fair food. We're walking to the parking lot slowly, looking deflated.

"Why did you all let me eat two corn dogs?" Doris moans and rubs her belly.

"Three," Paolo corrects her.

"Ronnie?" Earl says. He stops walking. "Let me give you a ride home on my bike."

I shake my head. "No."

"You didn't even think about it before you said no," Doris says. "You should totally ride it."

"Yeah," Zach adds. "I love motorcycles. *I* would."

Doris looks at him. "You *would?*"

"Can we see it?" Zach says, and soon we're all walking over to Earl's bike. We stand around admiring it.

"This is my hog." Earl beams with pride. He runs his hand along one of the handlebars.

It is kind of neat-looking. Earl's got it shined up perfectly. It's black with a lot of chrome.

"Wow," Paolo utters.

"Come on, Ronnie. I ain't gone let nothing happen to you."

I'm thinking about it and am almost convinced, when

I notice a tall man leaning against the back of his truck. Staring. He's parked behind Earl's bike, about two feet away. His arms are crossed and his long ponytail trails down over them. When I see his dark eyes, I have to look away because they aren't nice.

Earl follows my gaze. "Evenin'," he says, and nods at the man. When the man doesn't say anything, Earl says it again. "Evenin'."

The man mutters something that none of us catch—except for Earl.

"See?" James whispers. "What'd I tell you? We're going to get strung up."

Because the man's leaning against the center of his Chevy, I can read the letters CHE to his left and LET to his right. I can see the stickers on either side of his bumper, too. MY GUN KILLED LESS PEOPLE THAN TED KENNEDY'S CAR and GUN CONTROL MEANS USING TWO HANDS.

Shit. That pain-in-the-ass James is right.

Earl stands up straight. "What'd you say?"

The man says nothing. Then he spits off to the side.

I touch Earl, and he looks down at my fingertips resting on his forearm. "Let's just go, Earl, okay?" He puts his hand on top of mine and squeezes it before he lifts it off his arm. "No, Ronnie," he says slowly. "It ain't okay." He turns toward the man. "You got a problem?"

The man narrows his dark eyes. "No," he says. "But it looks like by the company you keeping that you do."

Everybody's quiet. The rest of us all stare at one another. Zack points his thumb over his shoulder and mouths *let's go.*

"Let's go, Earl," I say.

Earl won't leave it alone, though. "Buddy," he warns, and takes a step toward the man. "I think you're tending to somebody else's business."

He and Earl hold each other's gazes for a moment, and then the man finally uncrosses his arms, stands up and walks to the driver's side of his car. It feels as if we're all holding our breaths until he drives away.

"I'm sorry, y'all," Earl tells us.

Doris shakes her head. "What are you apologizing for? That was awesome. Total Clint Eastwood."

I remember how Charlie shook hands with Pat Boone's look-alike in L.A. and I'm proud of Earl.

Earl grins. "Sometimes folks can't help being assholes. Excuse me, ladies," he says, looking at me and Doris. "I don't mean to cuss in front of you."

Paolo's eyes get big. "Oh, puhleeze," he says. "These two sailors?"

Earl laughs and then turns to me. He sounds serious. "Get on the bike, Ronnie. I ain't gone ask you again."

Maybe it was Earl's tone that sounded full of machismo and testosterone. Very Italian. But I decide to get on his bike. Earl gives me his helmet, and I have to take my hair down so I can wear it. Earl watches my hair spill around my shoulders. "Pretty," he says. He hesitates and then he says, "Give me a kiss."

I panic because I wasn't expecting that request. I look at Doris, Zach, James and Paolo all staring at us. Doris has a big grin on her face and Paolo looks charmed and misty, like he's watching a chick flick.

"No," I say. I don't even think about the words coming out of my mouth. They're automatic, because the truth is I'd like to kiss Earl.

"Why not?"

"After what just happened?"

"Forget about him," Earl says. "A woman ought to be able to kiss a man. This is America," he declares. "Ain't it?"

Exactly my point. But I look into Earl's blue eyes and lean in to kiss him anyway.

"You survived that all right," he says. He brushes my cheek with the back side of his hand and smiles at me. He pats the top of the helmet. "Put this on now, so I can introduce you proper to my hog."

I put the helmet on and give a thumbs-up sign to Doris and Paolo.

"So cool!" Paolo shouts. "Like *Grease* when they ride off together at the end!"

"Or Jane Austen—or Brontë," Doris says, adjusting her hat. "Trials, tribulations, misunderstandings and then the guy."

I try to speak, but it's hard to do with the helmet on, so I take it off again. "This is not some corny Austen knockoff or a movie," I say. "This ain't no *Pride and Racial Prejudice.*"

"Isn't it?" Zach says. "In a way? Very postmodern."

Earl folds his arms across his chest. "Post what?"

"I'll tell you later," I holler. Earl shrugs, gets on his bike. I put the helmet back on, and hold on to him tight. He revs his bike and all of it feels good: the bike, the man, the moment. I wave to everyone, and then we're on the road, scenes and images whipping past us faster than I can make them out. We pass a shed, or is it a house? And me and Earl. I wonder what kind of picture we make as we pass people on the road. Depends on who's doing the looking. They have to see a man and a woman, for starters. The rest is up to interpretation.

We've not been on the road too long before I feel the bike slowing down. We stop at an intersection.

"You okay back there?" Earl calls out. He turns his face so that I can see his profile. I can tell he's smiling because of the deep dimple in his cheek.

"I'm fine!" I yell above the roar of the bike. "Let's keep going!"

"You're the boss," Earl says, and revs up the bike. I lose

my balance when we take off again, but it doesn't scare me. I'm surprised that I'm not scared, and I know it won't be long before I'll be revving the bike, myself. It doesn't take much to go from timid to taking charge.

I, Veronica Williams, am in the process of figuring things out. I will keep envisioning pictures for myself and see what develops between the picture I envision and the picture that materializes. Earl and I are different people, but whose fault is that? The picture, then, is this: Clair Huxtable—not with Cliff, but with Erardo—sitting high on a hog, not living high on the hog. But as my mother would say about matters that turn out to be nearly the same thing, depending on your point of view: six of one, a half dozen of the other.

# *Book Club Questions*

1. One of the more challenging problems for women today is the tension between being independent, career-oriented people who are taken seriously in their places of work and by the world around them, and wanting to dress, act or be "feminine." How are Doris and Ronnie walking the line between being "girly" and being taken seriously as women? When are they most or least successful at each?

2. Often in chick lit the protagonists are white, middle- to upper-class women who don't stop to consider their race or socioeconomic status. How are Doris and Ronnie different from this stereotype? How do their own perceptions of race and class inform their behavior?

3. When Doris is teaching TROOPS, she talks to her students about advertising and commercial culture, and how it shapes identity. Claus, for instance, thinks he wouldn't wear Wrangler jeans in the same way that Doris refuses to look at Birkenstock shoes. In what way are the characters products of their environments, or shaped by their culture? Does it help Doris at all to know that she has succumbed to cultural dictates about such things as fashion and music?

4. There are many kinds of language at work in the novel: the academic discourse of Žižek and Freud, the local Indiana accents of Earl and Mona, the modified valley-speak of Doris and Ronnie, among others. How are the characters defined or judged by the way they speak? How are certain kinds of language used to include or exclude other people?

5. Throughout the novel Ronnie struggles with the idea of attaining a "higher education" versus doing "real work." What are the ways in which a higher education is real work, and real work, in the case of Valtek, a higher education?

6. In some ways Doris and Ronnie are a study in opposites: white/black, East Coast/West Coast. What qualities do they each have that have drawn them to one another as friends?

## COASTING

*(Doris and Ronnie have left Langsdale behind,
but not each other....)*

# Ronnie

My boss is fifteen years old. Now, I'm not one to complain, but if I may for a moment. It's a hard life and a cruel world when you're a thirty-year-old woman and your livelihood depends on whether or not the 15-year-old boy you're tutoring thinks you're a "total bitch" or a "complete idiot."

I've had the pleasure of hearing my boss mumble both sweet nothings while I tried to help him toward his pretty-much-solidified future of privilege. My paycheck isn't in immediate danger, but if Ian stops mumbling or just stops showing up, my fat checks—proof that rich people do throw money at problems—will be a beautiful memory. For now I've got a little time because I'm still new, Ian's here and his parents—TV writers and guilty liberals—don't want to fire the black chick right away.

"They think they'd look like racist assholes," Ian informed me the second time we met and I'd ripped him a new one for not doing what was the first and only reading I'd assigned him. He only needs help in his literature class. Short attention span or ADD or Lazy Shit-itis, he's supposed to have. "*The Bluest Eye* sucks, and you suck, but I'm stuck with you until I fuck up so much, they'll think I'm hopeless. Then they'll get rid of you with a clear conscience. So," he'd said, "I see, in your future, you being nice to me." He tipped back in his chair and pulled at the gelled tips of his spiky black hair.

Good times, I tell you. Good times.

But that was last week, and here I am again, working hard for the money. Ian and I sit out in his backyard in Beverly Hills—though "yard" is a sad, working-class way of putting it. His "yard" looks more like one of those vast museum gardens, like at the Getty. We face a long, rectangular pool and statues all around seem to mock me with demure grins or solemn, pitying stares. I imagine them placing bets with each other. "I give her two weeks," fake *David* says, while Venus gives me a bit more credit. "Ha, David, a month. At least."

Ian faces the pool, though it would be much more natural to face me at the table. We've still got Toni Morrison between us. "Ian," I say. "Give me a break here."

He sips the lemonade his housekeeper, Maricela, brought out for us.

"Why?" He puts his hands behind his head and stretches.

Because I'll strangle you and have to go to jail?

"This is a complete waste of time. If I'm not feeling it, I'm not feeling it. Everything will work out for me, even if I screw up in school."

*So* true. The statues stare at us as if they agree with Ian. Sadly, I can't argue with a fifteen-year-old. I sip my lemonade and decide to stop dealing with a kid. "Not feeling it," I say, closing *The Bluest Eye*. I slouch down in my chair. "What're you, *down* or something? Chillin' with the homies?"

"You're hardly a homie," Ian says, looking directly at me, finally.

"What's *that* supposed to mean?"

"It means that I know *way* more about music, about hip-hop, than you do, which is why I don't need any of this, which is why I'm going to be successful."

Dear God. Please, not another blacker-than-thou white boy in love with hip-hop, who has no idea where it all came from. Time to get schooled. I stand up to pack my notes and books. "Okay, Malcolm X. You know hip-hop?"

"Did I stutter?" Ian says.

"Right. Smart-ass. Who is Gil Scott-Heron?"

Ian shrugs.

"Heard any spirituals or work songs before?"

"Work songs? What are you *talking* about?"

"Ever hear James Brown—"

"No shit—"

"James Brown's *Funky Drummer,* recorded November 20, 1969 in Cincinnati, Ohio?"

Silence.

I look at Ian lounging by his pool, drinking the lemonade his housekeeper brought out to us because *his* rude, lazy ass couldn't offer to get me some himself. "You don't know shit about hip-hop." *Goodbye job.* "See you next week," I add for a touch of performative bravado and walk away. But I won't be surprised if I never see the kid again. My boss has gotten hopeless sooner than I thought.

# Doris

Something has become very clear to me in the past week. In fact, it has crystallized with all the disturbing, make-it-go-away luster of a home-shopping network zirconium ring: living alone and being alone are *not* the same thing.

Some facts about my life which should be made clear:

I now live alone in Atlanta.

I now *am* alone in Atlanta.

If you'd asked me two weeks ago before I screwed things up with my longish-term boyfriend, I might have sounded excited about this prospect. I am, after all, alone in a gorgeous loft apartment, which, as a bona-fide *professional* professor-type, as of next week, I can finally afford. I might even have waxed rhapsodic on the prospects of Zach moving with me and finishing his dissertation from my living room—a swank-kept man in true early-twenty-first-century fashion. And I might have made funny jokes about the South *having* to be better than Langsdale, Indiana; as a native New Yorker, Indiana was as far off the edge of the world as I could possibly imagine myself falling. And the South has character. After all, any region of the country that can deep-fry a cheesecake or macaroni and cheese has a *slight* edge up on a Midwestern enclave that contents itself with frying Twinkies.

"It's just going to be Langsdale with accents," Zach told me our last night out at the Office Saloon. We were with Ronnie and Earl, who had actually agreed to follow Ronnie to the West Coast for love. At that exact moment it was all I could do to get Zach to follow me back to my apartment at night.

"Nothing wrong with accents," Ronnie said, squeezing Earl playfully beneath the chin.

"You better make sure to eat up when you get there," Earl said. "Looks to me like you're wastin' away, Doris."

Earl was right. Between arguing with Zach about his latest "career change"—opening an old movie theater to show classic films in Langsdale, Indiana, *instead* of finishing his dissertation—and thinking about a new job, the move, everything, I'd been forgetting to eat. (And not to go off on Zach, but do the words *NO MARKET* mean anything to anyone? Selling vintage movies to the locals seemed to me a uniquely vexed venture. After all, you can't just walk in and sell tofu burgers to a meat-and-potato populace. Don't even get me started.)

"There's no danger of Doris starving," Zach said. "Believe me."

Hmm. Not exactly words to warm a girl's heart. Zach stood up and stretched, then headed for the men's room.

"Sooooo?" Ronnie asked. "A little trouble in paradise? What are you going to do about the move?" Earl's brow knit together with concern. Ronnie and Earl were wearing matching black T-shirts from a Tom Waits concert they'd attended in Chicago, a fashion accident, but proof that they were on the same wavelength. And a reminder of how far off Zach and I had become—his hippie sine running counter to my urban cosine. That night, Zach was wearing Birkenstocks to my Charles David, a Target T-shirt to my Betsey Johnson baby-doll dress and patchouli to my Hypnotic Poison. No, things were not going well.

Things hadn't, in fact, been going well for some time, and had only been made worse by Zach's and my recent trip to Atlanta where he helped me look for an apartment. It was definitely a functional, find-a-slightly-yuppie-but-funky-diverse-neighborhood-in-which-to-live kind of visit. Rent the apartment. Remind self that anyone can live anywhere for a year. See what's left to salvage of one's relationship of the past fourteen months.

"I like this place," Zach had said, when we were shown the ever-so-chi-chi loft, with exposed brick walls and tin roofing.

"It's a studio," I said. "I'm not sure I'm a studio-loft kinda gal. And where are you going to put your stuff?"

Zach sighed. He'd grown his hair out long, a little longer than I like it, and had it knotted in a lazy ponytail. When he went to run his hand through it, it got stuck.

"Didn't we already talk about this? I thought we talked about this."

"I think Ronnie's right," I said. "You're starting to turn into Earl, and Earl's turning into you."

He gave me a look that would have sent a lesser woman packing.

"And what's that supposed to mean?"

There are certain phrases that are never part of a healthy relationship: *We need to talk. I'd like you if…, You remind me of my mother,* and of course, *What's that supposed to mean?* (Frankly, I'd add *You'd do it if you loved me* when related to any and all less-than-kosher ideas for sexual experimentation, but that's a totally different story. I digress.)

The issue at hand is bickering. Zach and I were bickering. And once you become a bickersome couple it's a short ride to bitter and trapped.

"I meant your *hair,*" I said. "Stop being so sensitive."

And *stop being so sensitive.* Another definite no-no. We'd gone from a fun, opposites-attract academic thrill-ride of a couple, to a *Lifetime* movie-of-the-week, complete with recycled dialogue and the occasional semi-public tantrum.

What he thought I meant was the fight we'd had the week before. It started out innocently enough: I'd bought a fabulous, vintage piece of lingerie off of eBay, in which I felt very Marilyn. It was a baby-doll slip-type piece in sheer pink. Nothing kiddie-porn, but still naughty enough to be nice. And did Zach, the über-hippie of my dreams, even *notice?* The answer, unfortunately, is "Yes." He took one look at me and said, *Jesus, you trying to look like Mrs. Roper?* Then he tried to recover with *You know I just like you naked, baby.* To which I responded: *Of course you do, it requires the least amount of effort.* So much for a sexy evening. I then proceeded to turn into someone's mother, yelling things like "YOU HAVE TO FINISH YOUR DISSERTATION" in a pink nightgown and false eyelashes. I was going for a look. "YOU CAN'T QUIT AND OPEN SOME STUPID MOVIE THE-ATER." It was just plain mean of me—stomping on the dreams of another—to which I plead demonic posses-sion at that exact moment.

And our final night together wasn't repairing any of the damage.

"He's still staying here," I said to Ronnie, sloshing my watered-down Jack and Coke around in a lone cube of ice. "I think we might have technically broken up last night. But it was such a horrific conversation that I re-fuse to go back in and clarify. I think that when I get to Atlanta I'll be trading in the whole men thing for a dog. Something I can properly accessorize that leaves me alone when I'm trying to write poetry and shuts up as long as it's fed."

"You think that a dog'll do that?" Earl asked, laughing. "Poor dog!" He made a "woooo-hoooo" noise, and Ron-nie leaned toward him unconsciously. Zach returned from the bathroom and sat next to me with his legs splayed apart at a ninety-degree angle, rubbing the fine hair on his knees and putting as much distance between the two of us as possible.

"Don't know," I said, thinking that I still wanted to cross that distance between me and Zach, that even his knobby, hairy knees were making me sad tonight. "The way things are going it's worth a shot."

Later that night, Zach and I did clarify things. We broke up. At least, temporarily. Six weeks and then he says he'll visit, that we'll reevaluate, blah blah blah. Sometimes

being in a relationship feels like you're in eternal deten-
tion. You just keep getting reevaluated and hoping that
someone will either promote you or let you off the hook
once and for all. This afternoon, though, in my Atlanta
abode with ninety-five-degree heat and humidity stew-
ing outside my door, it felt more like Doris + boxes piled
all over fabulous loft apartment + only Doris to unpack
them = maybe Zach and I should have tried a little
harder. Still, I can't turn this into Sadlanta, or I won't be
putting my best foot forward at the new job, and I'll have
that horrible stink of needy and alone that new potential healthy-minded friends *and* boyfriends can smell from
miles away. I do not want to become the emotional equivalent of deershit, in which only animals with no home
training are permitted to roll.

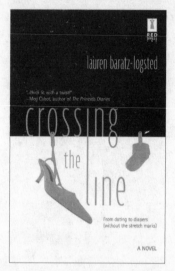

Don't miss the book that *People* magazine
called "Spring's Best Chick Lit 2004."

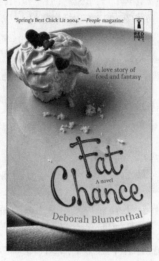

# Fat Chance

## Deborah Blumenthal

Plus-size Maggie O'Leary is America's Anti-Diet Sweetheart.
Her informed column about the pitfalls of dieting is the
one sane voice crying out against the dietocracy. She is
perfectly happy with who she is and the life she leads.
That is, until she gets the chance to spend quality time
with Hollywood's hottest star and she vows to be the
*skinniest* fat advocate ever. But is it possible for Maggie to
have her cake and eat it, too?

# Are you getting it at least twice a month?

**Here's how: Try RED DRESS INK books on for size & receive two FREE gifts!**

**Bombshell**
*by Lynda Curnyn*

**As Seen on TV**
*by Sarah Mlynowski*

# YES! Send my two FREE books.

There's no risk and no purchase required—ever!

Please send me my two FREE books and bill me just 99¢ for shipping and handling. I may keep the books and return the shipping statement marked "cancel." If I do not cancel, about a month later I will receive 2 additional books at the low price of just $11.00 each in the U.S. or $13.56 each in Canada, a savings of over 15% off the cover price (plus 50¢ shipping and handling per book*). I understand that accepting the two free books places me under no obligation ever to buy any books. I can always return a shipment and cancel at any time. Even if I never buy another book from Red Dress Ink, the free books are mine to keep forever.

160 HDN D34M   360 HDN D34N

---

Name (PLEASE PRINT)

---

Address                                                              Apt. #

---

City                        State/Prov.                        Zip/Postal Code

*Want to try another series? Call 1-800-873-8635
or order online at www.TryRDI.com/free.*

**In the U.S. mail to: 3010 Walden Ave., P.O. Box 1867, Buffalo, NY 14240-1867
In Canada mail to: P.O. Box 609, Fort Erie, ON L2A 5X3**

*Terms and prices subject to change without notice. Sales tax applicable in N.Y.
**Canadian residents will be charged applicable provincial taxes and GST.

All orders subject to approval. Offer limited to one per household.
® and ™ are trademarks owned and used by the trademark owner and/or its licensee.

© 2004 Harlequin Enterprises Ltd.

RED
DRESS
INK

RDI04-TR